Life Eternal

Heart-Glow Volume IV

Life Eternal

Heart-Glow Volume IV

SHEILAH R CRAFT

STARLIGHT BOOKS

STARLIGHT BOOKS

This novel is a work of fiction. Names, characters, places, and incidents either are products of the author's imagination or are used fictiously. Any resemblance to actual events, locales, or persons, living or dead, is entirely coincidental.

Cover photograph taken by Sheilah R Craft. The doll in the cover photograph represents Angilia in Heaven. The front piece photograph also depicts Angilia in Heaven, amongst the clouds with a unicorn. Both versions of Angilia were customized by Laurie Lenz. The dolls were manufactured by the Tonner Doll Company. The author does not have any business affiliations with Tonner Doll Company or ANGELS Doll Studio.

This novel is registered with the United States Library of Congress.

First Starlight Books edition March 2015

ISBN-13: 978-0615965086

ISBN-10: 0615965083

ACKNOWLEDGMENTS

This book completes the chronological story of Angilia and her family that began in 2012 with <u>Heart-Glow</u>. By its conclusion, this book circles back to the first, when one of 16-year-old Angilia's prophesies comes true. Getting to this point has been a journey of love, for I dearly love the DeBruce Martineau family. They truly are among the greatest gifts I will ever receive. They live in my soul, and now they live eternally in these four volumes.

Of course, this is not the absolute end. Following this volume will come two prequels that take us into the past, before the beginning of <u>Heart-Glow</u>, which is January 3, 2012. There is much more to learn about and to share with these characters. For that I am grateful, for I am admittedly reluctant to retire them.

Writing itself, as I have mentioned before, is a very solitary act. What follows is far from solitary, and I am so thankful for those who have assisted me. Foremost among them is my publisher, the proprietor of Starlight Books, Miss Lillian, as she prefers to be called. Her belief in these characters and their story has been a constant blessing. Thank you, Lillian.

Lillian is not the only person who responds to the characters. The readers who take the time to contact me, who tell me what they think and feel, make the writing process so very worthwhile. Words can never adequately impart my gratitude, but I do thank you sincerely. Even when you become upset over something that happens to one of the characters, I know that is because you do care about them. They are real and alive to you, just as they are to me. That warms my heart. Thank you.

Most of all, I thank God. He created me for a reason, and I am certain that this novel series tops the list. I have written stories since my early childhood. I always said I wanted to be a writer when I grew up. I am. The DeBruce Martineau family's story is the story I was born to write. These characters are my most intimate creations, pieces of my soul, and I treasure them as I never imagined I could feel about fictional people.

DEDICATED TO C.A.M.—

A WOMAN I NEVER MET BUT KNOW SO WELL.

YOU ENJOYED LITERATURE AS I DO, AND

I AM CERTAIN YOU ARE PARTLY RESPONSIBLE

FOR PLANTING THIS SEED IN MY DNA.

THANK YOU.

AND TO HER WAS GRANTED THAT SHE WOULD BE
ARRAYED IN FINE LINEN, CLEAN AND WHITE: FOR
THE FINE LINEN IS THE RIGHTEOUSNESS OF SAINTS.

—REVELATION 19:8

CHAPTER 1

"Welcome to the daybreak news on this Monday, November 17, 2070. I am Jason Fuller, and I thank you for joining us. Today marks a solemn anniversary. One year ago, our beloved Queen Angilia died on her father King Eric's birthdate. People still mourn Her Majesty, and thousands of people fill the mall outside the palace. Hundreds have already left flowers in Christ Church Valmondois, at Prince Patrick's grave in the church cemetery, and especially at her statue and her father's statue in King Eric Celebratory Park.

"Today is also His Majesty King Eric II's 49th birthday and Prince Eric's and Prince Patrick's 14th birthdays. The young Princes will depart for high school, as usual on a November Monday, in a couple of hours. King Eric and his sons are expected to pay their respects at the Royal Vault this afternoon.

"There has been no official word on how the Duc de Valmondois will spend this day. His Royal Highness is, for all intents and purposes, retired from public life. His Royal Highness attends weekly and holiday church services, and is seen walking to the Royal Vault every day, where he spends a few hours alone. Our thoughts are with the Royal Family today in particular as they face this somber anniversary."

Eric listened to the news as he stood on his balcony. Tears filled his eyes as he relived that afternoon one year earlier when his mother had died in his arms. "Oh, Mommy, I love you. I miss you so much." He placed a hand over his heart and felt the pendant there, under his shirt. He pulled it out and watched his grandparents and parents together in Heaven. "How I miss you, Mommy."

Eric felt an arm around his shoulders at that moment. "Hey, Eric. Your mom is just fine, you know. She and your grandparents are so very happy." Eric nodded his head as the tears slid from his eyes. "She asked me to give you a message." Patrick felt Eric's shoulders tense and saw the longing in his grandnephew's eyes as he relayed Angilia's message. "*I love you, Eric, and I am so very proud of you. I always knew that you would be an amazing king, and you are. I know how much pain you feel, my darling son, but that has not interfered with your duty. You are such a godly man, Eric, and someday we will be together until the end of time, beyond eternity. You, Daddy, and I belong to one another, and we are part of one another. We will live together forevermore. Hold onto that beautiful promise, Eric, until God calls you home to Heaven. Daddy loves you so, Eric. I love you.*"

Eric began crying uncontrollably, and he clutched the pendant so tightly that his hand turned white. Patrick pulled Eric close to him and felt his pain and heartbreak as if they were palpable. "Oh, Uncle Patrick, I feel so hopelessly empty without Mommy. I know she is happy and fine, I do, but I just can't stop this pain in my soul. I'm so sorry. I know it's wrong."

"No, it's not, Eric. Your mother felt like this after your grandfather died, and even with her knowledge and experience, nothing could ease her pain. Nothing except her death." Patrick felt Eric tense again. "Eric, when I escorted her to Heaven and she ran to her parents, their joy was so immense, I can't tell you. She finally met her mother. She reunited with her father. Oh, Eric, that's what she spent the last four years of her life waiting for."

Eric nodded his head. "I know, Uncle Patrick. How long do I have to wait?"

"I don't know that, Eric. But however long it is, you will be fine. God is with you, you know that. He has always been with you.

He will always be with you. Hey, Angilia is with you, too, you know."

"I know. I'll get through this, I will. I will, because that is what Mommy and Grandfather want. That is what will earn me a place in Heaven so that I can be with them again. I know that. I'm worried about Dad, though, Uncle Patrick. He hasn't done well at all this past year."

Patrick nodded. "Yeah, I know. I'm gonna pop in and visit the boys before school, and then go visit Matthew. I've got messages for them, too. I love you, Eric," Patrick said, hugged Eric, and went to his great-grandnephews. He called them together in Prince Eric's sitting room. "Hey, guys, your grandmother asked me to tell you both a very happy birthday. She loves you both so very much."

Tears filled the teenagers' eyes as they hugged Patrick. "We know, Uncle Patrick," Prince Eric said. "We love her a whole lot, too. Tell her that, please."

"Yeah, please tell Grandmother that we love her and miss her, but we do know how happy she is in Heaven. Is it wrong to feel that it's kinda special that she died on our birthday?" Prince Patrick asked.

"Wrong? Heck, no, it's not wrong. November 17 is such a very special date, you know," Patrick smiled.

"We know," Prince Eric replied. "Great-grandfather, Dad, Patrick, and I were all born on November 17. We all love Grandmother so much. It's only right that we're all connected on this date."

"You are both so smart and wise. I love you," Patrick smiled.

§§§§

Patrick stood in the door of Matthew's suite and watched his nephew-in-law with sorrow. Patrick knew that Matthew's routine had not varied since the day after Angilia's funeral. Matthew held

Angilia's pillow to him every night, often crying himself to sleep. He arose at the time Angilia typically had, 5:00, showered, and dressed in a black suit and tie. He wore only black suits, an outward symbol of his mourning. He rarely left the suite he had shared with Angilia, except for occasional meals and church. He did indeed walk to the church every day, where he sat beside Angilia's tomb for hours.

Patrick had witnessed the same scene every morning since November 20, 2069. Matthew sat on the floral sofa in the sitting room, a large wooden box open on his lap. Matthew lifted each of the hundreds of ribbons, one at a time, looked at them, ran his fingers over them, and even smelled them. Matthew kept the box on Angilia's side of the bed at night, never far from his reach. Matthew was mired in the deepest grief Patrick had ever beheld, and it saddened him—and Angilia.

Patrick walked to the sofa and sat beside Matthew. "Go away," Matthew said without looking up from the ribbons.

"Matthew, I. . . ."

"Go away. You're the one who took her from me. I don't want you here," Matthew interrupted with anger in his voice.

"Even if I hadn't been Angilia's Spirit Guide, that wouldn't have stopped it from happening, Matthew. She was meant to return to Heaven that day. No one could have prevented that, Matthew."

"You don't know that. I could have saved her if I had begun treatment in time. This didn't have to happen. Why didn't she tell me?" Matthew looked at Patrick with such anguish in his eyes, where his love for Angilia had once shone.

"I do know that, Matthew. God is the one who sent me to Angilia's side that afternoon. God. Angilia didn't tell anyone, because she knew it would happen, and she didn't want to put you and the boys through more pain than need be. She didn't want you to see her die. She was ready, Matthew," Patrick gently told him.

"Well, I wasn't! I never will be. My life means nothing without my Angilia. I just want her back," Matthew confessed, and began crying. "She's all I want and need."

"I know. But you'll be with her again someday. Forever."

"Forget someday. I want her now."

"I'm so sorry, but. . . ."

"Then bring her back," Matthew commanded.

"I can't, Matthew."

"You took her away. You bring her back."

"Matthew, I do have a message for you from Angilia. She asked me to give it to you," Patrick said, hoping to bring some peace to the heartbroken man.

"I don't want to hear from you. If she has something to tell me, she can do that herself. Leave. I want to be alone."

"Matthew, please. Angilia doesn't want you to suffer."

"Then tell her to come back, and I won't. She's the only one who can take my pain away. Go," Matthew insisted through clenched teeth as he clutched the wooden box close to him.

"Angilia loves you, Matthew. She's in Heaven with her family waiting for you. She doesn't want you to spend your time cocooned in sadness this way. You hold onto those ribbons as if she's somehow with them. She's not," Patrick tenderly rebuked Matthew.

"These ribbons are the last piece of her. You don't understand."

Patrick watched Matthew open the box and touch the ribbons again. Pink, red, yellow, green, blue, gold, silver, white, and purple ribbons mingled like a rainbow. Matthew had taken the silk and satin ribbons from the hundreds of floral arrangements at Angilia's funeral, and had placed them in the wooden box. They were his last tangible ties to Angilia.

"I do understand. The ribbons are the last things connected to Angilia. I get it, I do. But she doesn't want you to live in this sadness for the rest of your life, Matthew. Angilia is not dead. You know that. Her soul lives in Heaven, and she awaits you. Please don't make her sad."

"She's made me sad," Matthew softly replied. "I want to be alone now."

"All right. Just remember that we all love you. Angilia loves you, Matthew." Patrick disappeared and shortly returned to Heaven.

Matthew reached into the box, under the many ribbons, and pulled out a sheet of stationery. The last note Angilia had written and left on his side of the bed one year earlier: *I love you A*. "I love you, my Angilia. I love you, and I want you back," Matthew said as he cried and held the note to his chest.

§§§§§

At noon, Eric went to his father's suite, and his shoulders drooped. Matthew still sat on the sofa with the box of ribbons. Eric, like Patrick, had seen his father do that daily since the day after Angilia's funeral. "Dad, it's lunch time. Let's go down together."

"I'm not hungry."

"You didn't eat breakfast. You have to eat," Eric stated.

"I'm not hungry," Matthew repeated. "I want to be alone."

"I love you, Dad," Eric said as he sadly went to the dining room to eat lunch with Leigh and Yvonne. As much as Eric missed his mother, he knew that she did not want him to stop living, to ignore his duty and his family. She had not done so, despite her intense pain after his grandfather's death. Life would never again be the same as it had been before her death, but Eric knew he had to adapt. That is what God, his grandfather, his mother, his sons, and the citizens of Valdavia wanted and needed. He had to adapt for their sake, as well as for the ultimate reward of eternal life in Heaven with his precious mother and grandfather.

§§§§§

Instead of eating lunch, Matthew got the key to the Royal Vault and left the palace. Those gathered on the mall greeted him, but as usual, he ignored them and walked slowly but determinedly to the church. A crowd was gathered at the Vault door, praying and leaving flowers. As Matthew stepped to the door, some of the people put their hands on his arms.

"Duc Matthew, we love and miss Angilia," one woman said.

"Yes, we do, Your Royal Highness. We know how you feel," a young man added.

"No, you don't. No one knows how I feel," Matthew said as he unlocked the Vault door, went in, and locked it behind him.

"Poor Matthew. His grief for Angilia is so intense. It's been this way for the past year. I hope he finds peace and closure," another woman said as she made the sign of the cross and left. The other people finished their prayers and left, giving Matthew total solitude.

Inside the Vault, Matthew stood at the foot of Angilia's tomb, leaned over it, bowed his head, and cried. "Oh, Angilia, I do love you, and I just want you back. Please come back to me. Nothing matters without you. I need you."

Matthew stood for many minutes, crying, before he sat in the wooden chair that had been placed for him beside Angilia's tomb on November 19, 2069, the day of her funeral. Matthew had sat in the Vault until after midnight that day. It was as close to his wife as he could physically get—or so he thought. "I just want you back, Angilia. Please. Please come back to me."

Matthew leaned close to Angilia's tomb and stretched his right arm over the plaque on the top. While he cried, he ran his hand over the plaque and suddenly felt something. Paper. Who had gotten into the Vault to leave a note on Angilia's tomb? Matthew wondered as he stood and looked at the paper. His heart raced, his breathing stopped, and he stared at the envelope in amazement. His name was written on it, in Angilia's very familiar slanted cursive handwriting.

"Angilia?" Matthew whispered. "Where are you, my darling?" Matthew looked around the Vault, searching for his wife. Then he remembered Angilia telling him about the letters from her father that Patrick had brought to her after Eric's death. This was the message that Patrick had tried to give him that morning. Patrick must have left it at Angilia's tomb, knowing that Matthew would go there that day.

Matthew slowly and reverently picked up the envelope and sat again. "This is from you, my darling Angilia. Oh, darling, thank you," he said through his tears as he held the envelope to his heart. Matthew stared at his name written on the front for several minutes. "The last time you wrote me a note was one year ago. One very long year, Angilia. We were so incredibly happy for 53 years of marriage. I never wanted to live here without you. Never. I always knew it would feel so wretched, meaningless, and lost without you here. Oh, Angilia, I know how much you longed to return to Eric. I do. But now I am the one who is utterly heartbroken without you. Why? Why did you leave me? Why?"

Matthew cried for many minutes as he held Angilia's letter to him. Finally, he sat straight and very carefully opened the wax seal on the flap, a seal that had a dove. Despite his pain, Matthew did smile when he saw the Christian symbol of love and peace. Those were what Angilia sent to Matthew with the letter, he understood that. He just as carefully removed the parchment sheet and unfolded it, his hands shaking as he looked at his wife's handwriting.

17 November 2070

My Dearest Soulmate Matthew,

Oh, my dear, I love you so. I do hope you know and believe that. My love for you is as vibrant and passionate as ever, if not more so. My love for you did not end with my physical death, my dear. Our love is too potent for that, Matthew. Our love has existed and survived for centuries, and will continue for all eternity and beyond. Our love is sanctioned by God, who allowed Michael to show us our eternal happiness together. Our miracle son Eric now wears the pendant from Michael. Look at it and remember how the sight of you, me, Daddy, and Mommy together soothed our souls. Let it soothe and comfort you once again, darling.

I never wanted to leave you, Eric, and the boys, but God called me home to Heaven. My earthly work was done, and it was time for me to return to Heaven. Oh, Matthew my love, I await you, our son, and our grandsons. Heaven is the most wondrous, perfect place in existence, it truly is. You will see that for yourself someday when God calls for you. I will be the first person to greet you when you arrive. Your parents look forward to your reunion, too, Matthew, and they asked me to tell you how very proud they are of you. Dr. Taylor and Katherine love you tremendously—you know that, my love. Daddy sends his love, as well.

Matthew, oh dear Matthew, how my soul has ached for you over this past year. Yes, it has been one year since I left earth, Patrick told me. I feel such complete sadness watching you suffer so. Oh, Matthew, darling, please, please do not stop living because I am not physically there—I am still with you. I will always be with you. Please believe that, my love—please. Your life is not over yet. God is not ready for your return to Heaven yet.

God and I want you to feel the love and joy that surround you, Matthew. You have not painted in one year. The last painting you did was one week before I returned to Heaven. Painting is your passion, what you called your life's blood. Please do not abandon your talent, your gift from God, on my account, Matthew. Please. I want Uncle Patrick to tell me about your art and your work, not about your grief. I want to watch you create your art. Please. I pray for you to resume living, Matthew, truly living.

Darling, I don't like that I caused you such pain. I don't. When I look down at you, I want to see those sparkling eyes and that happy smile. I do not want to see you crying yourself to sleep or weeping over that box of ribbons. I want to see my Matthew, the man who enjoys life and loves people.

I pray that you do find comfort and peace, my love, my Matthew. I do love you for all time. I am here, with you, even if you do not see me. I am with you, my love—always and forever with you. I love you, Matthew.

Eternally Your

Angilia

Matthew reread Angilia's letter, cherishing this gift from her while simultaneously struggling to subsume her request. She wanted him to live as he had before her death. How could he? How? Matthew sat for many moments as he sought the answer to that question. "I don't know how I can do what you want me to, Angilia. I don't. Life can never be the same without you here, physically here, with me. How can it be? How can I go on as if nothing changed? Everything did change, my Angilia, it did."

Matthew leaned his head on her tomb and cried as if his heart was breaking. His heart was broken. Angilia and Patrick watched Matthew from Heaven, and she looked at her uncle with such pain in her eyes. "I need to go to him, Uncle Patrick. Matthew needs me."

"But you're not an envoy angel, Angilia. You don't have God's permission to go to earth," Patrick reminded her.

"Then I'll ask for God's permission," she stated, stood, and ran to God's throne. The Seraphim parted and let her pass, bowing their heads as she did. Angilia bowed her head and knelt before God's throne, her hands clasped in front of her.

"I know why you are here, Angilia. I know that you seek my permission to visit Matthew on earth. Tell me what you think seeing you will do for Matthew that his faith and convictions have not," God commanded.

"Thank you for allowing me to write the letter to Matthew. In it, I requested that he resume living, not merely existing, and that he once again use his artistic talent. I reminded him of the miraculous pendant that you permitted Michael to give me on my wedding day, and to let it bring him some comfort. I watched Matthew read my letter, and even though it brought him some joy, he is more wretched than ever, God.

"Matthew does not possess the inner fortitude to do as I asked. He does not want to disappoint me or you, but he is lost. If he sees and hears me, he will truly know that I am alive and waiting for him in Heaven. When my mother was Abuelo's Spirit Guide, her spiritual manifestation reinforced my father's and my faith. My visit will do the same for Matthew, and provide him with the strength he needs in order to live the remainder of his life as you desire."

"Arise," God commanded. Angilia stood, her head still bowed in reverence. "Matthew's pain causes you pain, just as your father's pain caused you pain when Patrick died. Even here, as an angel, you are attuned to other peoples' feelings."

"I apologize if I displease and disappoint you. Rebuke me and teach me how I can change to be as you prefer me to be," Angilia replied.

"On the contrary, Angilia. You have never displeased or disappointed me. Come," God said, surprising her. Angilia glanced up and saw God's hand motion her closer to his throne. Still not looking at his face, Angilia stepped to his throne. She felt his hand on her chin, lifting her head so she would look at him. "Your entire life, mortal and immortal, is built upon your unwavering belief and trust in me and upon your helping other people. You still do that, praying on behalf of those who pray to you. You have always placed other people before yourself.

"Now you long to ease Matthew's suffering and grief. You may go to him this once, Angilia, and reaffirm the promise of eternal life for him. Go, my dear child."

Angilia looked into God's eyes for the first time, her own eyes filled with tears of gratitude. She kissed his hand, and said, "Thank you, dear God. Thank you." Angilia curtseyed and returned to Uncle Patrick. Eric, Marisol, and Michael were with him. Angilia hugged the four of them, and smiled up at her uncle. "God has permitted me one visit with Matthew. Please pray that this eases his deep-seated grief."

"Sure thing, Little One," Patrick told her, kissed her cheek, and smiled.

"Oh, Angilia, my beautiful daughter, I have no doubt that this is just what Matthew needs," Eric said and smiled at Marisol. "I know what a blessing such a divine visit is," he softly said and kissed his wife.

"Go, my Angel, and comfort your husband," Marisol told her daughter and kissed her.

"Go to him, Angilia. God would not have permitted this if he did not know that this would ease Matthew's suffering," Michael stated.

Angilia smiled, kissed them, and went to the Royal Vault, where Matthew still sat crying and lamenting over her tomb. "Why can't you come back to me, Angilia? Why? I just want you back," Matthew wept just as Angilia appeared.

"Matthew," she very softly said at that moment, and she saw Matthew tense.

"Angilia? Darling?" he asked in a quivering voice, not yet moving, afraid to move lest the sound of her voice be proven a hallucination.

"Yes, my love. I am here."

Matthew felt her hand on his, and he inhaled sharply and looked up at her. "Angilia, oh my darling, you came back," Matthew said as he began crying again, and he reached for her. She gently tugged his hand, and he stood, stepped around her tomb, and pulled her into the hug for which he had longed so desperately for one year. "You came back to me. Oh, I love you, Angilia. I love you."

Angilia put her arms around him, kissed his cheek, and felt him tremble in her embrace. "God allowed me to return for a little while, Matthew. I love you, my white knight."

"A little while? You aren't staying?" Matthew asked and looked into his wife's hypnotic turquoise eyes.

"I can't stay, darling. But I am here now, to show you that I am still me. I am still Angilia. I am still your wife. I still love you. Nothing has changed except where I live, just like Uncle Patrick all of these years. That is the only difference, Matthew. I am always with you, my love, always. My love lives inside of you, as it always has. My soul is around often, even though you do not see me. You can feel me."

Matthew looked at her with such torment in his amber eyes, and said, "That isn't the same. That isn't enough. How can it be?"

Angilia put a hand over his cheek, and he sighed, buried his face in her palm, and kissed her hand. "This is what I want and need, Angilia. I want to feel you, I want to see you, I want to talk with you, just as I always did."

"I know, darling, and this is what we will have for eternity when you join me in Heaven. Before I came to visit you, Daddy said how he knew my visit would help you. When Mommy was Abuelo's Spirit Guide, she appeared to Daddy, and she kissed him. That verified what he knew—that she was alive and waiting for him in Heaven. Oh, Matthew, Daddy lived on earth without her for 70 years. Seventy years. That was a very long time, but that does not matter now. That is forgotten now. They are together, and their love truly is epic and eternal. So is ours, Matthew. So is ours."

Matthew took a deep breath and held Angilia's arms. "I know, my love. I do know. I am not as strong as Eric. I've always known that. I'm going to sound like Darlene now. I'm 84. I know I won't live nearly as long as Eric did, so my life will end soon. Then I will be with you. That is all I want and need, Angilia, to be with you."

Angilia smiled, her head tilted in that oh-so-charming way she had. "Wrong. Your life won't end. You'll just move to Heaven. You will live forever. That's the big lesson here, Matthew. You didn't lose me. I'm not dead. I'm still Angilia." Matthew caressed her shoulder with one hand and ran his other hand through her iconic long blonde hair. "I look the same. I sound the same. I feel the same to your touch. I am the same."

"Yes, you are," Matthew murmured and kissed her mouth. He softly moaned when Angilia put her arms around him. After their kiss, he stared at her for several moments. "When I die, I know what I'm doing first when I get to Heaven."

Angilia laughed in that engaging way he had not heard in one year, and said, "So do I, Matthew." She saw the question on his face. "We saw that on our wedding night. Michael's gift?"

"Of course. I will run to you and pull you to me, my darling," Matthew said, and did just that, drawing his wife into a jubilant embrace.

Angilia laughed when he waltzed her into a dip and kissed her again. "I love you, Matthew."

§§§§

Matthew emerged from the Vault three hours later, and those who had come to pray or to leave flowers expected the melancholy Matthew they had seen every day for the past year. Imagine their shock when he turned, after locking the Vault door, with gleaming eyes and a smile. He nodded to them, and walked home to the palace with a lilt in his step. No one could know what had caused such a change in the Duc, but they thanked God.

So, too, did those gathered on the mall, who were accustomed to Matthew's intense grief. His smile surprised them, albeit pleasantly, and he greeted them with a nod and a wave before he entered the palace. Matthew took the elevator to his suite, where he changed into a navy blue suit and a red and white tie that Angilia had given him. He sat at her desk and wrote about the life-altering day in his diary.

17 November 2070

Oh dear God, what a glorious day you have turned this into. What began as such a devastating anniversary filled with despair and heartbreak became a miraculous dream come true. I have missed Angilia so very much for this one year. I have longed for her return. Every moment of the past year, I dreamed of holding her, kissing her, talking with her. One very long year.

You allowed that to happen. You allowed her to come to me this afternoon. My Angilia came back to me! Every day, I have prayed for her return, and suddenly today, she did return. To see her, to hear her, to hold her, to kiss her! Do you truly know what that means to me? My Angilia came back!

She explained that this was a one-time visit, and while that utterly disappoints me, I am grateful that you allowed her to visit me. I do remember what Patrick told Darlene four years ago today when she asked why Eric didn't visit us— Patrick is authorized as an envoy angel. Eric is not. Angilia told me that she is not.

I understand why she isn't an envoy angel like Patrick. I see people pray to Angilia in the church, and I know they also leave their prayers at her statue. I

14

have been told that many of these prayers have been answered. I didn't care about that too much before today. I was too caught up in my grief to care.

But I do see how Angilia, my angel and your angel, is still doing your will and work, but from Heaven. People have been cured and helped in response to their prayers to Angilia, which I know she transmits to you as she has always done. She is still their link to you.

Her visit today is the answer to my year-long desire and prayer. We enjoyed the entire afternoon alone together in the Royal Vault. After our magical kiss, we sat leaning against Eric's tomb. We held each other, much as we did at the Turnberry Castle ruins on our honeymoon! For hours, we held one another while we talked—and, yes, laughed! Oh, how thrilling to hear my Angilia's laugh again after so very long!

Angilia wore the long while dress we had seen on her in the blessed pendant. She told me that it was the same dress she had worn in the Unborn Children Sphere and the Angels Choir prior to her physical birth. Her long blonde hair cascaded around her shoulders and down her back, more lustrous than ever. Those remarkable turquoise eyes of hers sparkled as never before. Angilia's beauty has always lit my veins, but never more than today. My Angilia is even more beautiful than ever, if that is possible. How can that be possible? How can the most beautiful woman to ever exist be even more beautiful after her death? Oh, I know, God—she is an angel, a Supreme Angel blessed by you! Angilia's physical beauty reflects and radiates her soul's beauty and purity. Of course she is heart-poundingly stunning!

Angilia told me so very much more about what Patrick calls regular Heaven. She told me about that day one year ago when Patrick escorted her to Heaven, to the field of exquisite flowers we had seen in the pendant. She told how she saw her parents there, and how her being had filled with incomparable joy. She ran to them, and her life-long dream of hugging her mother Marisol came true. The look of pure happiness in her eyes when she described meeting her precious mother for the very first time made me so happy for Angilia. How could I ever want to deny her that? How? More amazing is how her eyes seemed lit from within as she described her reunion with Eric. Oh, how she had longed for that, I know. My darling spent her last four years on earth longing, waiting for that moment. The exultation that emitted from her as she told me in vivid detail about that reunion with her father made my heart soar.

It also made me feel ashamed. When Darlene did say four years ago that she wished Eric had lived forever, Angilia stunned us by saying she did not. She explained how selfish that was, and that it would only keep Eric from his love Marisol, the woman he lived without for 70 very long years. God forgive me. This one year without Angilia has felt so incredibly long, but is nothing compared to what Eric endured. I know he is far stronger than I will ever be. Still, I do understand better what Angilia meant.

To keep her here, with me, would deny her a home in Heaven. It would deny her the company of her parents and the rest of her family and friends. Oh, yes, Angilia is surrounded by many hundreds of ancestors and friends. She told me about meeting her grandfather Gerard, Eric's father, for the first time, and how much they enjoy talking about their family history together! She told me about seeing her grandmother Matilda again, the grandmother who died when Angilia was five. She said they have lovely visits in Matilda's gazebo!

Angilia also told me about meeting her 18th great-grandfather Robert the Bruce. When she saw him, she ran to him and hugged him—without saying anything first. He knew who she was, and said he had watched us pay homage to him on our honeymoon in Scotland. Her love for him touched him deeply, and they are great friends. I remember when we were at Turnberry Castle and Angilia wondered if Robert had sensed his future while he grew up there. I told her she could ask him someday. Today, she told me that the first time she and Robert talked, she did ask him if he had known or felt what the future held in store for him and his place in history. Robert told her that when he was a boy, he knew that he was descended from two great and powerful lines from both of his parents, and that he was the heir to titles and wealth. At that time, he could never have anticipated all that did happen and the destiny in store for him. He trusted that he would always do his utmost to do right, and although he admitted to many mistakes and misdeeds, he knew in the end that he did stand more on the side of right than on the side of wrong. Angilia told me that she had smiled at Robert and reminded him that he would not live in Heaven if his life had gone against God. To think that she and I discussed this in 2016, 54 years ago!

Angilia also told me about Mom and Dad and what they do in Heaven. I can just see them as she described them! They have a lovely cottage where Mom finally has the flower garden she always wanted but never got around to planting. She was always too busy for that here on earth, so she really enjoys that. Her father, the RAF soldier whom Angilia saw at the accident that day, is also there, and he visits the cottage often. He remembered Angilia, and they spent a long time catching up when she met him! How neat is that? Dad sits with

Mom and Grandpa on the cottage porch often—when he isn't doing what he enjoys—playing golf!! Of course! (As Angilia reminded me, doctors aren't needed in Heaven, so Dad has all of eternity to enjoy his golf. I'm not surprised really.) This fills me with such contentment to know, as if everything is perfect.

Everything is perfect! I will see that for myself sooner rather than later. Like I told Angilia earlier today, I am 84 years old, so my earthly life is nearing its end. When it does, I will go to Heaven. I will then run into my Angilia's arms, and we will live happily ever after!

Thank you, God.

§§§§

At 7:00, Matthew went to the dining room, took his usual seat, and greeted his son with a smile. "Happy birthday, Eric," he said for the first time that day, just as his grandsons entered the room. "Happy birthday, Patrick and Eric."

The three men were stunned. "Thank you, Grandfather," Prince Eric managed to say as he hugged Matthew.

"Yeah, thanks, Grandfather," Prince Patrick said, and put both of his arms around Matthew's shoulders.

The twins took their seats while Eric stared at his father, the same man who had dwelled in angst and isolation for the past year. "Thank you, Dad. The boys and I are going to the Vault after dinner. We didn't want to disturb you earlier."

Matthew smiled, winked, and replied, "We appreciate that. I want to go to the music room this evening and listen to some of Angilia's music," he added, as Leigh and Yvonne entered, their eyes and mouths wide. Matthew had refused to listen to Angilia's music at all since her death. Suddenly, on the first anniversary of her death, he was smiling and wanting to hear her. What had happened?

The five of them were flabbergasted by the change in Matthew. Eric was especially shocked. His father had refused to eat breakfast or lunch, preferring to sit with that box of ribbons all morning. Matthew had worn black clothes for one year, and now he wore a navy suit. What exactly had happened? Why was he smiling? Why were his eyes gleaming?

When dinner was served, Matthew stunned them further by saying grace. "Dear God, thank you for your abundant gifts and blessings. You give us far more than we deserve, but we are so very grateful for all that you do for and give to us. Amen."

"Are you all right, Grandfather?" Prince Eric hesitantly asked.

Matthew placed some potatoes on his plate and smiled at Prince Eric. "I'm fine, Eric. I haven't felt this fine in a long time. In fact, today has been one of the most fabulous days of my earthly life."

"I'm happy to hear that, Grandfather. It's nice to see you smiling and happy again," Prince Eric said, unsure of what had happened, but silently thanking God for whatever it was.

"So am I, Dad. So am I. I don't know what happened while you were alone in the Vault, but whatever it was, I'm thankful for it," Eric proclaimed with a smile of his own. His father was back.

"I am, too, son. I am too. More than you can ever know," Matthew said as he took a bite of roast beef.

§§§§§

After dinner, Eric and his sons walked to the church, which was typically filled with people praying and leaving flowers or lighting candles outside the Royal Vault. "God bless you, Your Majesty and Your Royal Highnesses. You are so strong, just like Angilia was. I just want you to know how much I love her and miss her, but I know what I feel can't compare to what you feel," a woman said to them.

"Thank you, ma'am, Prince Eric replied. "Our grandmother is still the most amazing woman."

"Yeah, thank you," Prince Patrick added. "I'll never know another woman anywhere, anytime as fabulous as Grandmother. Never."

Eric smiled and put his hands on his sons' shoulders. "Neither will I, Patrick. Thank you for remembering her," he told the woman.

"People will always remember Queen Angilia. She was far more than a princess and a queen. She was one of God's angels living among us on earth. Now she continues her divine work from Heaven," a young man stated with tears in his eyes. "We see it all around us. She still causes prayers to be answered and miracles to be performed."

"Thank you," Eric said, knowing that his mother was never comfortable taking the credit for any answered prayers. She always gave the credit to God.

The three men entered the Royal Vault, where they bowed their heads in prayer. "Dear God, We know that our precious Mommy and Grandmother is alive and happy in Heaven. We do love her so very much, and we miss her every moment. She taught us many important lessons, the most valuable being the truth and beauty of eternal life. Our comfort lies in that truth. That truth makes life without her more tolerable, because we know that we will be with her forever someday. We know we will be, because she also taught us to love and obey you, God, and to live godly lives. We pray that you continue to walk alongside us as we fulfill the earthly lives you predestined for each of us. We thank you most of all for blessing our lives with our beloved Mommy and Grandmother. Amen," Eric prayed.

The twins echoed the Amen, and then Prince Patrick said, "Yes, we do, God. She is the best Grandmother, the best teacher, and the most incredible woman you ever created. Thank you for her."

Prince Eric hugged his brother and cried. "She sure is. I love you, Grandmother."

§§§§

When the three men returned home after 10:00 that night, they began walking up the marble staircase to their third-floor suites. On the landing of the second floor, they heard Angilia's music softly wafting through the hallway.

"Grandfather's still listening to Grandmother," Prince Eric said.

"Yeah. How strange. I mean, he hasn't wanted to listen to any of her music for a whole year. I wonder why he does now, today of all days," Prince Patrick added.

"I'm not sure, boys, but I'm just grateful that he made it through his dark tunnel. He's been so isolated and closed off for a year, and it's nice to have him back with us, among the living," Eric said with a smile.

"It sure is, Dad. I missed Grandfather," Prince Eric smiled up at his father as the three of them continued to the third floor. Their small love-filled family was whole once more.

§§§§

After breakfast, Matthew walked to the church, wearing Angilia's favorite burgundy suit and tie and clutching one dozen long-stemmed red roses. Those gathered on the mall had left flowers at the gate in honor of the 75th anniversary of Angilia's birth. They rejoiced seeing Duc Matthew every day since his intense grief had ended six weeks earlier. He greeted them with a smile and a wave, as he did to those inside the church.

Matthew entered the Royal Vault and stood at the foot of his wife's tomb for several moments while he read the plaque:

Angilia Erica Charity DeBruce Martineau Taylor

3 January 1996

17 November 2069

We love him, because he first loved us.

--1 John 4:19

"I love you, my Angilia. Happy birthday, my love," he said, and kissed her name on the plaque. Matthew placed the red roses above the plaque and smiled down at her tomb.

"Oh, Angilia, I do love you. You know that. You feel that. I feel your love, too, my darling. You opened my heart and soul to that. Thank you for that. What a miraculous gift you gave to me six weeks ago. I relive that day in my dreams every night. You literally revived me, brought me back to life. You saved me. You saved me from grief and darkness. Life is not the same without you here. It never can be. But I am able to survive that now thanks to you. Your love saved me."

As Matthew stood next to his wife's tomb, a sheet of parchment appeared beside the roses. Matthew inhaled sharply. "Angilia?" he whispered. Matthew's hand shook as he picked up the parchment. *I love you, my white knight. Your Angilia* "It is you, my darling. Oh, how I love you, Angilia." Matthew began sobbing, and then suddenly felt a hand on his shoulder. It was not Angilia's. "Patrick. You brought her note to me."

"Yeah. We've been watching you, Matthew. Angilia wrote this just a moment ago and handed it to me. As an envoy angel, I can deliver messages to and from earth," Patrick explained.

"From earth?" Matthew asked.

"Yeah, sure. Angilia wrote a letter to Eric on her birthday one year after his death, that she planned to leave on his tomb that day. I came to her early that morning with a birthday letter from Eric to Angilia. She asked if I could take her letter to Eric, and I did. You should have seen his face when I handed it to him and he recognized her handwriting. It really made my soul happy to see," Patrick smiled.

"So. . . .Does that mean. . .? Could I. . .? Can you. . .?" Matthew struggled to ask Patrick a question.

"Sure. You can write her a letter, and I can take it to her," Patrick answered, knowing what Matthew wanted to ask.

"Really?"

"Sure. You write a letter to your wife, and let me know when you're done. I'll pop in, pick it up, and deliver it to Angilia. She'll get a real kick out of that."

Matthew's eyes sparkled in that familiar way that Patrick had seen for nearly six decades. Patrick smiled at the sight, and his smile grew larger when Matthew said, "I'm going home to write her a letter now." He turned to face his wife's tomb. "I love you, my Angilia," he gushed as he quickly left the Vault and locked the door.

The people on the streets and the mall were surprised to see Matthew briskly walking to the palace gates and across the courtyard. Inside the palace, Price Eric was just as surprised to see his grandfather run to the elevator. "Grandfather? Is everything all right?"

"Everything is just perfect, Eric. I have a very important letter to write immediately," Matthew answered just before the elevator door closed.

When the elevator door opened on the third floor, Matthew all but ran to his and Angilia's suite and breathlessly sat at her desk. He glanced around, and remembered where she had kept her stationery and pens. He removed several sheets of notepaper, an envelope, and a pen. Her favorite pen, one Eric had given her when she had earned her DPhil at the age of 11. Matthew smiled when he recalled her showing it to him in 2012 and telling him when and how she had received the pen. He had come by her suite to check on her one morning, to find her writing at her desk. He had commented on her pink agate pen, and she had beamed when she described her father giving her the box after her degree ceremony.

Now Matthew used that treasured pen to write his treasured wife a letter:

3 January 2071

My Dearest Darling Angilia—

How I love you! You are my one and only love, my eternal love. You consume my heart. You have filled my whole being with pure, true love and happiness for

59 years, from the very first moment I saw you. I knew. I felt my love for you from that moment, and I knew.

I knew you were meant for me. You were! What a glorious truth that is, my Angilia. For all time, from the beginning of time, we were destined to share life. Do you have any idea what a blessing that is? Of course you do! You know that more than anyone does!

I thought my life ended when you left earth. I thought nothing else mattered. I felt alone and lost without you here. I was wrong. You left earth, but you did not leave me. You are still with me. I know that. I feel that. That has brought back my happiness, darling. You know that. You see that. You saved me from despair and sin. You saved me so that we can live together in Heaven for all eternity!

What a beautiful reality that is! We will be together forever, never to part. How I long for that, my love. I know you understand that.

Oh, my Angilia, I love you! I love you!

Yours Eternally,

Matthew

Matthew ran his finger over the letter before he folded it and placed it in the envelope. He wrote *Angilia* on the front and then kissed the letter. "I'm finished, Patrick."

Within seconds, Patrick manifested before Matthew and smiled at him. "Cool. I didn't tell her about your letter, so she'll get a real surprise when I hand it to her, a pleasant surprise."

"I hope so. That's what her note this morning was for me. Thank you for this, Patrick."

"Yeah, sure. It's no big deal."

"Oh, yes it is. You have no idea how big a deal this is. This is the difference between peace and turmoil, hope and despair, lightness and darkness. This is everything to me, Patrick," Matthew stated, stood, and hugged his uncle-in-law.

"Hey, I know, Matthew. Eric's letters to Angilia soothed her soul, too. I just meant it's not a problem to do this for you and Angilia. It makes me happy to do this for you both."

Matthew nodded, clasped Patrick's hand, and said, "It makes me happy, too."

Patrick soon left, returned to Heaven, and found Angilia sitting and talking with Abraham Lincoln. Abraham stood and extended his hand when Patrick approached. Angilia smiled, stood as well, and introduced the men. "Uncle Patrick, please meet Abraham Lincoln. Abraham, this is Patrick DeBruce Martineau."

Patrick smiled, shook the man's hand, and said, "Yeah, I know. Everyone knows who Mr. Lincoln is. It's a pleasure to meet you, Sir."

"Thank you. That is very kind of you. It is my honor to meet you. Angilia has told me about you. Angilia and I were just discussing the positive effects and benefits of aggregative democracy."

Patrick could not help but giggle. "I'm sorry. It's just that Angilia has always been into these deep, abstract, complex ideals, even in the Angels Choir. It's all above my head, though, I'm afraid. I wouldn't have been a very good king at all. There's a reason Eric was born first."

"That's not entirely true, Uncle Patrick. Yes, God ordained Daddy as the King de Valdavia. We know that. But you are far more intelligent than you realize. You wouldn't have been asked to teach that literature class otherwise."

Patrick appeared completely shocked. "What? What literature class?"

"In July of 1977 at King Philippe High School," Angilia reminded her uncle.

"Huh? Oh, that. Yeah, but I never got to do that. I came here before it started," Patrick replied nonchalantly.

"You were supposed to teach the class, Patrick. You had been asked to do so because of your innate intelligence and insight. You were thought highly enough of that you were entrusted to impart ideas and information to those seeking knowledge," Abraham inserted.

"Heck, it was just a four-week class where we talked about poems, plays, and stories. Students were supposed to write short papers every week. That's all," Patrick explained.

"The point is, my boy, that the administrators thought highly enough of your intelligence and ability to entrust you with this huge responsibility," Abraham added.

"Gosh, you make me sound more important than I am," Patrick countered with the hint of a blush.

"You are important, Uncle Patrick," Angilia firmly said. "What's even more impressive is that neither you nor Daddy ever mentioned this. Neither of you possesses an ounce of narcissism."

"I enjoy literature immensely. Which works were you planning to teach, Patrick?" Abraham asked.

"Oh, just stuff like <u>Hamlet</u>, poems by Byron, Arnold, Whitman, Spenser, Gray, and Dickinson, stories by Faulkner, Porter, Wolfe, O'Connor, Styron, and Fitzgerald."

"Gray is my favorite poet. I would enjoy discussing his work with you, young man," Abraham enthused.

"Yeah, sure. Hey, but, I have a letter for you, Angilia," Patrick said and handed her the envelope from her husband.

Her eyes lit from within, she softly said, "It's from Matthew."

"What a most wonderful gift, my dear. Why don't you go and read your beloved's letter while your uncle and I have our poetic discourse?"

Angilia nodded and kissed both men before she found a quiet, secluded spot under a tree. There, she read Matthew's letter and held it to her heart when she finished. "Thank you, dear God. My Matthew is truly back."

§§§§

"Hey, Grandfather, can you please come to the sitting room? I need you," Prince Patrick requested of Matthew by phone after school on Wednesday, September 30, 2071.

"Of course, Patrick. I'll be there in a few minutes," Matthew answered, hung up his phone, and took the elevator to the second floor.

"He's on his way. Everybody hide," Prince Patrick quickly told those gathered in the sitting room. They dutifully ducked behind furniture and curtains, waiting until Matthew arrived. Prince Patrick stood at a bookcase, watching the door.

Moments later, Matthew entered the room, and Prince Patrick said, "Thanks for coming, Grandfather."

That was the signal. Everyone jumped out and yelled, "Happy birthday!"

Matthew laughed and shook his head. He had never suspected a surprise party, although after 59 years of them he should have. He looked at his son, grandsons, and friends, his heart bursting with love and happiness.

"Eric, I can't believe you managed to pull this off on a Wednesday afternoon," Matthew told his son and hugged him. "Leigh. Yvonne. Scott. Darlene. Shannon. Nicole. William. Billy. Thank you all for coming. Eric, I love you. I love you, too, Patrick." Matthew hugged each of his friends and family members.

"We all love you, Grandfather. Well, what's a birthday party without cake and presents?" Prince Eric asked with a huge smile.

Matthew laughed again when he was encouraged to blow out the candle. "Thank goodness there's only one candle and not 85," Matthew joked. Everyone cheered, and then Yvonne served the cake.

After everyone enjoyed the cake, it was time for Matthew to open his presents. "Happy birthday, Matty!"

"Patrick. It's good to see you," Matthew said and hugged the eternal teenager.

"I couldn't miss this. It's your birthday. Here. I have a gift for you," Patrick said, and handed Matthew a box wrapped in pink paper. "Open that one later, when you're alone," Patrick whispered to Matthew. Patrick felt Matthew's heartbeat race, felt him tremble, and Patrick knew what the gift meant to Matthew.

"Thank you," Matthew said through the tears that choked him.

"How's Angilia?" Nicole asked Patrick. "What a stupid question," she immediately said. "She's in Heaven with God and her family. Of course she's fine. Tell her I said hello and that I love her."

Patrick smiled as he sat on the arm of the sofa near Matthew. "Sure thing. Angilia is fine, really. She's truly in her element. I mean, you all know how important history is to her, right? Well, now she gets to discuss all of that with the people who lived through it. It's a blast for her." Patrick told them about her conversation regarding democracy with Abraham Lincoln on her birthday earlier that year, and how he had gotten pulled into a literature discussion with the President. "Now that was trippy, I tell you. Can you picture me analyzing Gray's poetry with *the* Abraham Lincoln? Talk about a fish out of water."

Shannon smiled, recalling the story of Patrick's and Eric's summer literature class that the elderly gentleman had told Angilia and her five years earlier. "No, you aren't, Patrick, not really. No one believes this whole dunce image you cultivated, you know."

"No, they don't. People who knew you never bought it for a minute," Scott added. "That whole devil-may-care bad boy image might have flown in 1973 or so, but not once you started your patronages and work. People saw how much you deeply cared and how intelligent you were."

"They sure did, Uncle Patrick. We learned about your work in government and history classes. You did so much good work," Prince Eric stated.

"Yeah. We even read and talked about your speeches and essays. You were cool, yeah, but you were so smart, Uncle Patrick. I really like your speech to the United Nations in 1974 when you were 16. Now that was super cool and powerful," Prince Patrick shared.

"You gave a speech at the UN? I never knew that, Patrick. What about?" Matthew asked.

"Oh, that. I spoke about quality physical fitness as a way to bring people, countries, and cultures together and to ease a lot of problems. Sports bring people together, like in the Olympics or the World Cup. I knew that phys ed in school is a great way to improve behavior problems, as well as social and motor skills, but I also saw how it helps with health and academics. It helps the whole person. So in underdeveloped countries, where fewer children have a chance to attend school, we needed to supplement physical education with other programs and venues. The more actively engaged people are, the more likely they are to lead healthy, productive, collaborative lives. The goal wasn't to create a generation of athletes, but a generation of healthy, focused, successful people. I was living proof of sports' benefits," Patrick explained.

"Wow. You were ahead of most everyone else, it seems. UNOSDP and UNESCO created more outreach programs to target global physical fitness education in the late 1970s, Patrick. I'm very impressed," Matthew said.

"So am I," Darlene gushed. "Yes, I can quite clearly see the benefits of physical fitness."

Yvonne and Eric grinned, but stifled their giggles. At 78, Darlene was as besotted as ever. Scott, Nicole, William, and Shannon yet again sighed, realizing that some things would never change.

§§§§

That evening, after dinner, Matthew closed his suite door and sat on the sofa in his sitting room. He held the pink-wrapped gift Patrick had given him, his trembling lips smiling. He knew the gift was from Angilia.

He relished holding the package for several moments, feeling the sentiments flow from within. Finally, he breathed deeply, untied the ribbon, and pulled away the pink paper. His hand shaking, he lifted the box lid to find a note—from Angilia.

30 September 2071

Happy Birthday, my dear Matthew!

Camillus, one of the angels I long ago met in the Angels Choir, is a wonderfully gifted artist. He learned from Patrick that today is your 85th birthday. He created this for you, my love. I hope you like it. I asked Uncle Patrick to wrap it and give it to you today.

I love you!

Always Your Angilia xoxo

Matthew smiled and softly said, "I love you, my darling Angilia." He closed his eyes and silently thanked God for such a wondrous blessing.

Finally, Matthew parted the soft cotton that cocooned the gift. He audibly gasped when he saw what was nestled there. Encased in an ornate pure gold frame was the most faithful portrait of Angilia, painted on an oval of white marble. Matthew had never seen such a lifelike portrait. Angilia's white gown skimmed her slender curves, her long blonde hair gracefully flitted in the gentle breeze, her smile was sincere and vibrant, and those remarkable turquoise eyes glowed with love and happiness. Camillus captured Angel Angilia as only he could. As striking as Matthew's 2020 portrait of Angilia as an angel, it had been painted from Matthew's imagination. Camillus knew Angilia as a fellow angel who lived in Heaven. He had painted her as she appeared there.

In the portrait, Angilia stood in a field of colorful flowers as light emanated from her, creating a halo. How often Matthew had seen that ethereal effect! She was his wife, his Angilia, but she was also a Supreme Angel of God, and Camillus captured that as only an artist in Heaven could.

"Oh, my Angilia, how very beautiful you are. I will forever remember every detail of your visit with me last November 17. You know what that visit means to me and what that did for me. That's why you asked God's permission to visit me. You knew it would save me. I am so grateful that God understood that, too. I also understand why you cannot visit me anymore. I do. Of course I wish you could. I would love to see you often. That's why Camillus' portrait of you means so much to me, my darling. You are so beautiful, and I can see how happy you are. Your happiness shines in your eyes. Thank you, my love."

Matthew suddenly bounded to Angilia's desk and wrote a heartfelt thank you letter to Camillus. He sealed it in an envelope, wrote the angel's name on the front, and got the key to the Royal Vault. With a huge smile, Matthew walked to the church at twilight. People who saw him smiled at the Duc's happiness.

Inside the Vault, Matthew prayed at Angilia's tomb, kissed her name on the plaque—as he often did when he visited—and laid the letter atop Angilia's tomb. He knew Patrick would deliver it for him. Matthew smiled, placed his hand over his heart, and returned home for a contented night. He drifted asleep as he held in his hand Camillus' portrait of Angilia.

§§§§

Matthew did continue his daily visits to the Royal Vault, and the sight of his happiness when he did spread like contagion. People relished seeing his utter happiness, in sharp contrast to the intense grief they had once witnessed. No one enjoyed Matthew's joy more than his son Eric. Whatever miracle had caused his father's happiness, he did not know, but he did thank God for that.

As usual after the twins left for high school, Matthew walked to the church for his daily visit in the Royal Vault. He talked to Angilia for a while, telling her about his latest painting. "I think you'd like it, darling. I painted a scene of a forest in springtime, with trees and wildflowers in full bloom. Grazing under the trees are two young deer, with sunlight streaming down on them through the canopy of leaves. I felt very peaceful when I began the painting, and that scene is what sprang from my imagination. I know how much you love animals, and I know how much you wanted me to resume my painting. I just wanted to tell you. I love you so very much, my beautiful wife. Oh, I long to hold you in my arms again."

Tears filled Matthew's eyes as he recalled her visit and how they had hugged and kissed. As much as he did miss Angilia, he also knew how very blessed he was. He bowed his head and said a prayer of thanksgiving to God for his gifts and blessings.

Soon, Matthew walked home and wrote in his diary before lunch:

22 October 2071

I had a nice enough visit to the Vault this morning. I told Angilia about my latest painting. I knew that would make her happy, because she wanted me to paint again. I have been. I admit that I had missed art in my daily life. I didn't realize just how much.

I know Angilia hears me. Patrick often tells me that she watches me, and somehow that comforts me. It lets me know she is nearby. It reassures me that she is with me.

Still, I can't deny how very much I long for her. I want to hold my wife. I want to kiss my wife. I want to talk with—not just to—my wife. I want my wife. I want my Angilia.

I have no idea what else you have for me to do here on earth, God, but forgive me for admitting that I am ready to come to Heaven. It's not that I want to leave Eric and the boys. I love them, and I love being here with them. But I want to be with my Angilia. I do. I am ready for that, God, whenever you are ready for me.

§§§§§

After lunch with Eric, Leigh, and Yvonne, Matthew returned to his suite. He felt more tired than usual for an early afternoon, so he got the large wooden box and sat propped up in bed with it beside him. He opened the box and removed the cards, notes, and letters from Angilia that spanned the past 55 years.

He smiled as he reread them, from notes she had taped to the bathroom mirror as he had showered—which simply had *XOXO A* or *I love you, Angilia* written on them—to the note she had left on his side of the bed the day she died, to the letters and notes Patrick had delivered since her death.

Matthew then picked up the Camillus portrait of Angilia from his bedside table and held it to his chest as he reclined into the soft pillows. He felt so tired, and he had difficulty breathing. He closed his eyes for a while, hearing the faint sounds trickling up the stairs and from outside on the mall.

At 2:00, Eric checked on his father, surprised to see him lying on the bed. "Dad? Are you all right?" Eric walked to Matthew, and noticed the box of ribbons, the letters still on Matthew's lap, and a picture clutched in his hand. "Dad?"

Matthew opened his eyes and smiled at his son, a weak smile. "Eric, I love you, I hope you know that. Tell Eric and Patrick how much I love them. Please."

"Dad?"

Matthew nodded in answer to his son's unasked question. "This is what I've been waiting for, Eric. I finally get to be with my Angilia again. I am so very happy, son."

Tears filled Eric's eyes as he sat on the edge of the bed and held his father's hand. "I know, Dad. I'm happy for you. I'm going to miss you, you know that, but I couldn't deny you this happiness. I wouldn't want to. Oh, Dad, you are the best father God could give to me. I love you so much."

Matthew grasped Eric's hand tightly and said, "I love you, son, more than you know. I can never tell you what an honor it is to be your father. You really are a remarkable man, Eric."

Matthew's grasp weakened, and his eyes closed. Eric held his father's hand for more than half an hour, knowing that his father was dying. At 2:48, Eric saw someone appear beside the bed, near them. He looked up and inhaled sharply. "Grandpa. Oh, Grandpa, I love you."

Mitchell smiled, nodded, and placed his hands on his grandson's shoulders. Mitchell pulled Eric into a hug, a hug which sent such joy through Eric's being. He had last seen his grandpa 38 years earlier when he found Mitchell dead.

A minute later, Eric felt another hand on his shoulder, and he looked over to see his father's manifested soul standing beside Mitchell's. His father and his grandpa, together again. Eric hugged Matthew and said, "I love you, Dad." He hugged Mitchell again. "I love you, Grandpa. I love you both so much."

Both men smiled and soon disappeared, off to Heaven. "This is what you've waited for, Dad," Eric softly said. He pulled the pendant from under his suit, and looked at the miraculous scene of his grandparents and parents in Heaven. "The four of you are together now, and you are finally with Mommy. I know what this first hug and kiss in Heaven mean to you, Dad. I am happy for you, even if I am heartbroken. I love you all so incredibly much."

§§§§

Mitchell escorted Matthew into Heaven, and led him to the outskirts of a field of wildflowers. Mitchell smiled at his son, hugged him, and said, "Go on, Matthew. Your wife is up ahead. Mom and I will see you later."

Matthew hugged his father tight, said, "I love you, Dad," and then walked down a golden road. He saw her! Eric, Marisol, and Angilia were strolling, their arms linked. Suddenly, Angilia looked ahead, saw Matthew, smiled, and held open her arms for him. Matthew felt happiness as he had never felt before, and he ran to his Angilia. Matthew and Angilia embraced for many moments, their joy boundless, while Eric and Marisol smiled.

"I love you, Matthew," Angilia softly said and kissed her husband.

"I love you, Angilia, my love," Matthew said in a voice filled with emotions.

Matthew smiled at his father-in-law, hugged Eric, and said, "It's wonderful to see you again, Eric."

"Matthew, meet my mother," Angilia then said with a beaming smile.

Matthew smiled, as well, and turned to his mother-in-law. The two hugged, finally meeting each other. "Oh, it's so wonderful to meet you, Marisol. I've known you so well for so long, but nothing compares to meeting the woman who owns Eric's heart."

"Thank you, Matthew. And I finally get to meet the man who has owned mi hija Angilia's heart since the beginning of time," Marisol smiled.

The four of them put their arms around one another and strolled along the golden road for a while as they talked and laughed. Finally, they sat together in the lush green grass, merely enjoying being together. The pain, heartbreak, and sadness of Marisol's and Angilia's deaths were forgotten eternally, replaced by the pleasure, joy, and ecstasy of eternity in Heaven. Eric and Matthew felt elation and peace forevermore.

§§§§

Eric picked up the letters, cards, and notes, intending to put them back in the wooden box, when he recognized they were in his mother's handwriting. He smiled, realizing that his father must have kept them for years. As he picked one up, though, he noticed the date—30 September 2071, less than one month earlier. What?

Eric read Angilia's note about the Camillus portrait, and he could not breathe. His mother had been in contact with his father? Since her death? He read the other letters she had written since her death, and he finally realized what had eased his father's deep grief. She had! "Oh, Mommy, how you love Dad. You turned him around. You saved him from himself. You brought the happiness back into his heart. Your love for him saved Dad. Thank you,

Mommy. I love you so very much." Eric cried what she had always called happy tears as he held the letters, cards, and notes.

Eric lovingly placed his mother's letters, cards, and notes in the wooden box, intending to keep the box with him. That box did contain Matthew's ties to his Angilia, and Eric wanted to preserve this family relic for all time. He knew what his mother's missives to his father really represented and meant. His mother's work as an angel was as ceaseless as ever, in this case for the person who needed her most. "I really am happy for you, Dad. Now I do understand the miracle that saved you," Eric said with a smile as he placed his hand over his father's hand.

Eric felt the portrait still in Matthew's grasp, and he gently unfurled his father's fingers from around it, lifted it, and once more gasped. "Oh, Mommy!" Through his tears, Eric saw the small signature at the lower right curve of the marble—*Camillus.* "This is your birthday gift to Dad. Oh, Mommy, how he treasured this, I know that for certain. Now I will treasure this and keep you with me for the rest of my life. When I do die, I will give it to Patrick, and the holy pendant to Eric, as you requested.

"Mommy, oh Mommy, how astoundingly beautiful you are! I always thought so, and I've long known that you are an angel. This is the most beautiful depiction of you I have ever seen. You seem alive, as if you will move any moment. This is breathtaking! This is a miracle, it really is. Oh, how very happy you made Dad in this last year, you must know that. Thank you for that, Mommy." Eric held the portrait to his heart, bowed his head, closed his eyes, and prayed his gratitude to God.

§§§§

Eric heard the twins come upstairs after school, and as they neared their grandparents' suite, he called to them. He motioned them to the sofa, where he had waited for them, and put his arms around them when they sat on either side of him. "What's wrong, Dad?" Prince Patrick asked, seeing the tears in his father's eyes.

"I have something to tell you, boys. You know how happy Grandfather has been since the first anniversary of Grandmother's death, right?" They both nodded. "Grandfather is even happier now, Eric and Patrick.   He is so happy, because he is with Grandmother again."

The teenagers were silent for several moments as their father's words registered in their brains.   "Grandfather is dead?" Prince Eric asked with tears in his eyes.

"Yes, Eric and Patrick.   He died just before 3:00 this afternoon, not too long ago.   He smiled and told me how happy he felt that he would be with Grandmother again.   I saw the happiness in his eyes, sons, and I want you to know he was ready to go to Heaven.   He wanted to be with Grandmother more than anything else."

"We know, Dad.   Maybe last November he finally accepted that she was waiting for him in Heaven.   Maybe that's what made him so happy.   That truth finally became real to him," Prince Patrick said.

"You're right, Patrick.   I love Dad, and I miss him, but like I told him, I couldn't deny him the happiness of living with his wife for eternity.   I wouldn't want to do that to him.   That would have caused him far too much pain and agony," Eric said with a smile.

"Neither would we.   I mean, we know we'll be with Grandfather and Grandmother again when we die.   Grandmother and Uncle Patrick taught us that there is no death, not really.   That's what helps me through the sadness, Dad, it does.   Without that truth to comfort me, I would not make it through all the sadness," Prince Patrick said.

"I wouldn't, either.   I'm happy for Grandfather, because I know how happy he is now.   That makes the pain less.   Is that wrong, Dad?" Prince Eric asked.

"Of course it isn't, Eric.   You are both so wise and mature. I am so proud of you," Eric said and hugged them.   "I love you both."

Moments later, Prince Eric asked, "Is Grandfather still here?"   Eric nodded.   "I'd like to tell him something before they have to take him."

"Of course, Eric. He's still on his bed." Eric gently patted his son's back, and the boy walked into the bedroom.

There, Prince Eric said, "Grandfather, I love you and miss you, but I am very happy for you. I know you and Grandmother are together again, and how much you wanted that. I know you are happier than you have ever been. You are in the best place there is, with Grandmother, and that is happy. I love you." Prince Eric bent and kissed his grandfather's cheek, and then returned to his father and his brother.

Prince Patrick hugged Prince Eric and went into his grandfather's bedroom. "Hey, Grandfather, I just want to tell you how much I love you. I know what you're feeling now that you are in Heaven, because you finally got what you've wanted for a long time. You got Grandmother again. Enjoy Heaven until I see you again." Prince Patrick kissed his grandfather, too, and returned to his family.

"We really are a small love-filled family now. It's the three of us, and we will take care of each other and love each other forever," Prince Patrick said and embraced his father and his brother.

§§§§

22 October 2071

With a mixture of sadness and happiness, I tell you that my father, Matthew, Duc de Valmondois, died this afternoon at 2:50. I was by his side for the final hour of his earthly life, and I can assure you that my father did not suffer in the least. In fact, quite the contrary, he was ready to begin his eternal life.

He told me with a smile how happy he was knowing that he would soon be with my mother again. That is what he longed for, and now he is with his beloved wife for eternity. As much as I miss my father, and always will, I love him far too much to be too sad upon his death. My father is in Heaven, the most glorious place, with the love of his life, my mother Angilia.

Let that knowledge bring you comfort and, yes, happiness. Share my father's joy on this blessed occasion, as my sons and I do. While we do love and miss him, we rejoice in his immense exultation.

§§§§§

Matthew's state funeral occurred on Saturday, October 24, 2071. King Eric, Prince Patrick, and Prince Eric followed the gun carriage as the church bells tolled. Several hundred people fell in step behind the Royal Family, forming the funeral cortege. At Christ Church Valmondois, the military pallbearers carried Matthew's casket to the altar, where they placed it on the bier.

King Eric and his sons greeted people, including dignitaries, heads of state, and especially their friends. Shannon, Nicole, Scott, and Darlene had known Matthew since 2012, for 59 years. They had participated in Angilia's and Matthew's wedding in 2016. They had rejoiced with them at the birth of their son Eric, and shared their joy when Eric married Julianne. They had grieved when Julianne had died during childbirth, but had celebrated Matthew's and Angilia's two grandsons. They had mourned Angilia nearly two years earlier, especially when Matthew had spiraled into the deepest, darkest grief.

Now Matthew was dead, and they shared the family's sadness. More than that, however, they glorified Matthew's reunion with his Angilia, as he had called her. Darlene felt that especially, telling Eric as she cried and hugged him, "Oh, I just keep thinking about how very happy Matthew is now, Eric. He is with Angilia, and I know how happy they are."

"Thank you, Darlene. That's what Dad looked forward to most just before he died. His smile, his glowing eyes, his happiness, keep the sadness away. I can't really be sad when I know that they are together again."

Eric and his sons greeted Reverend Olson for what would be his last act as head of the church. After decades of dedicated service, he was retiring; his assistant, John Emerson, would assume the title of Reverend the following day. Reverend Olson wanted to officiate at Matthew's funeral, having known the Duc for nearly six decades. He wanted to do that for his friend.

Reverend Olson stood at the pulpit. "Today, we honor the life of His Royal Highness Matthew, Duc de Valmondois. The Duc became a citizen of Valmondois in 2012, when he came here as the personal physician to Princess Angilia, Duchesse de Valmondois. We watched as their friendship blossomed into true, abiding love and culminated in their romantic wedding. We shared their immense joy when their son Eric was born in 2021, as well as when their grandsons Eric and Patrick were born in 2056.

"Angilia and Matthew shared life and love. Despite the sadness and the perilous times, their lives were dominated by joy and love. Their marriage was founded on love, and it remained grounded in love. Two years ago, when Her Majesty died, we all witnessed Matthew's grief. We felt his pain. In spite of the lessons imparted by Angilia and Patrick over the years, the promise of eternal life did little to ease Matthew's grief—until the first anniversary of Angilia's death.

"Soon after that, Matthew came to me and told me that God had shown him the truth of eternal life. God had let Matthew see that his beloved wife awaited him in Heaven. God's miracle brought the happiness back to Matthew, and I know how we all rejoiced when we witnessed that.

"Let us rejoice today, knowing that Matthew has joined his Angilia in Heaven. If ever there is a fairy-tale happily-ever-after, this is it—Angilia and Matthew live together for all eternity in the most incredible place to ever exist. Let us thank God for that blessing and that truth. Let us praise God for the promise of eternal life he offers to each of us. Someday, we will once more witness the eternal love of Angilia and Matthew."

Prince Eric stood, walked to the pulpit, and bowed his head for a moment. "My grandfather liked Shakespeare's Sonnet 18. He often read it to Grandmother in the evenings, which made her smile. This sonnet is about a love that transcends time and seasons and dwells in the heavenly realm. That is where Grandfather's and Grandmother's love began, and that is where it now resides for all time.

Shall I compare thee to a summer's day?

Thou art more lovely and more temperate:

Rough winds do shake the darling buds of May,

And summer's lease hath all too short a date:

Sometime too hot the eye of heaven shines,

And often is his gold complexion dimm'd;

And every fair from fair sometime declines,

By chance or nature's changing course untrimm'd;

But thy eternal summer shall not fade

Nor lose possession of that fair thou owest;

Nor shall Death brag thou wander'st in his shade,

When in eternal lines to time thou growest:

So long as men can breathe or eyes can see,

So long lives this and this gives life to thee.

I love you, Grandfather and Grandmother."

Prince Eric returned to the pew, where Prince Patrick hugged him before he stepped forward. At the pulpit, he likewise bowed his head for a moment before he spoke. "My grandparents' love is eternal. We know that. When I get to Heaven, I will indeed see that love again, and my soul will rejoice. Solomon 8:7. '*Many waters cannot quench love, neither can the floods drown it: if a man would give all the substance of his house for love, it would utterly be contemned.*' I love you so much, Grandfather and Grandmother."

Prince Patrick returned to his seat in the pew, and Prince Eric hugged him. Eric smiled at his sons as Scott approached the pulpit for his eulogy.

"I first met Matthew in 2012, after Angilia became the sponsor of our high school's branch of Christ on Campus. I was the only guy in COC for its first months, not because other guys didn't want to join. They didn't want to deal with the bullying and teasing we got. COC wasn't seen as cool for guys. That began to change when Matthew attended a meeting in late 2012.

"He spoke about faith and purity from a man's perspective. We'd never heard that before. That meeting was attended by nearly every high school student. They all wanted to hear Matthew and what he had to say. We knew him as Angilia's cardiologist, nothing more than that. Here was this 26-year-old doctor. Many people perceived him as a playboy, this rich guy who could have his pick of women. But he told us that he had never had a girlfriend. He'd gone on dates, but nothing serious. He told us he was waiting for his one and only true love. He told us that there was nothing wrong in that, and in fact that it was the right and honorable thing to do. Lots of guys joined COC after that.

"None of us knew the truth that day, but we found out on Angilia's 17th birthday, which was in early January 2013. That day, Matthew gave Angilia a promise ring. He was the first man I knew who did that. That ring was special, too, because it was actually a purity ring that said *True Love*. Matthew met his one-and-only, or rather—as we later learned—he met her again.

"Angilia and Matthew had met in the Unborn Children Sphere, as the world learned from her autobiography. Their love really had been formed at the beginning of time. They were destined to be together forever, and they are. They are blissfully together for all eternity, soul mates in the truest sense. I learned what real, true love is just by watching Matthew and Angilia. It was such an honor to know them and to see their love. I really could see it. It was—it is—a force of its own. Their love will be remembered for as long as people inhabit this planet. Their love is eternal."

Scott hugged Eric and the twins before he took his seat. Another speaker went to the podium for his eulogy. "I am Charlie Britt, and I met Matthew through his wife, Queen Angilia, after her prayers cured me of cancer. Before I got sick, I wanted to grow up and become a doctor. When I was cured, and I knew that was a definite possibility, Angilia told me that her husband would be happy to help me when I applied to medical school.

"Quite frankly, I practically forgot her saying that until King Eric's 60th Jubilee in 2052. Matthew befriended me at the Garden Party, and he not only helped me with my medical school application, but he wrote me a glowing recommendation letter to Cambridge. Matthew and I maintained our contact over the past 19 years, and he became a wonderful friend and mentor.

"He went far above and beyond what most people would either do or expect. Matthew knew how important becoming a doctor was to me. He understood how much I wanted to help people. He championed me, and he encouraged me. He and Angilia attended my graduation from Cambridge. Matthew also helped me to get an internship at the hospital where he had worked, and where he had saved Angilia's life, John Radcliff Hospital. I owe him so very much.

"More than his professional advice and assistance, though, I am so honored to call Matthew my friend. He was the man I aspired to be, full of compassion and love. I know how very happy his life with Angilia was. And is. As Scott said, people could feel and almost literally see their love. Matthew's and Angilia's love is timeless and eternal. I know for a fact how happy Matthew is now that he is with his Angilia forever. As much as I will miss him, I cannot be sad when I think of Matthew's exultation.

"Matthew and Angilia do live and love eternally happy, surrounded by their family, friends, beauty, peace, and God. They enriched my life, and I send them my gratitude and love." Charlie stepped down, hugged Eric, the twins, and Scott, and resumed his seat.

At that moment, Christ Church Valmondois reverberated with Angilia's angelic voice as a recording of Matthew's favorite hymn filled the church. Everyone felt the emotion, truth, and power of "Where No One Stands Alone," as it played for Matthew. Many people sobbed, including Darlene, Shannon, Nicole, and Yvonne. Eric felt himself fighting emotional tears as the song played, and he felt his son Patrick's hand on his in reassurance. He smiled at his son as the song ended, and he stood.

At the pulpit, he cleared his throat and spoke from his heart. "I do love my father, and I will miss his physical presence every moment for the rest of my life. I really cannot feel sad, though, because my father's elation at his impending death was truly remarkable for me to share. He smiled and told me he was ready to join my mother in Heaven. I know what that means to him. I understand how he felt incomplete without her here on earth. I know how whole and happy he is—they are—now that they are side by side forevermore. Those of us who knew my parents know how true that is. There really can't be any sadness when we picture their contentment. My parents are proof of the divine gifts of both eternal love and eternal life."

Eric returned to the pew, and the congregation stood. The military pallbearers carried Matthew's casket into the Royal Vault, followed by the King, Princes, Reverend Olson, and the invited friends. The rest of the world watched the entombment by live feed.

As the family and friends gathered around Matthew's tomb, the pallbearers lowered Matthew's casket into the tomb. The guests placed white carnations—Angilia's birth month flower—atop his casket. Prince Eric and Prince Patrick placed white asters—Matthew's birth month flower—there, and Eric laid a sealed envelope addressed to *Dad* there. Then the pallbearers lifted the heavy lid atop the tomb and stood reverently at attention as Reverend Olson prayed.

"Dear God, We thank you for the gift of Matthew Aaron Taylor. His kindness, love, and friendship are gifts we will treasure for all time. We rejoice in Matthew's eternal life, for we do know how incredibly wondrous that life is. We rejoice that he is in your loving embrace and in the company of his beloved Angilia for eternity. Let that truth comfort those who mourn Matthew. In your loving name, Amen."

Matthew Aaron Taylor

30 September 1986

22 October 2071

Therefore shall a man leave his father and his mother,

and shall cleave unto his wife:

and they shall be one flesh.

--Genesis 2:24

CHAPTER 2

"Greetings, and welcome to the 60th annual Eric DeBruce Martineau Scholarship for Musical Excellence. I am Andrew Minor, Provost of Oriel College at the University of Oxford, and I am honored to host today's ceremony. Please join me in welcoming our special guest, His Majesty King Eric II de Valdavia."

Eric received a standing ovation as he walked across the stage and shook Andrew's hand. He bowed to the audience, thanked them, and took his seat. "Thank you for having me. This scholarship is so very important to my mother, and I know how much she enjoyed attending the annual ceremonies."

"It's our honor to have you, Your Majesty. What made the ceremonies so special for your mother, Queen Angilia?" Andrew asked.

Eric's dimpled smile shone, and he immediately answered, "My mother's fondness for these ceremonies was always two-fold. Of course, she really did enjoy awarding the scholarship to a music student every year. That is the primary function of the scholarship, after all, and she took this very seriously. She enjoyed the delight and happiness of each recipient, she truly did.

"Secondly, my mother savored seeing and hearing her adored father's performances every year. She is his most ardent fan and supporter. My grandfather never considered himself much of a singer. He never heard himself as others do. He never really noticed the fame and admiration he received. She did. She heard his remarkable baritone and his skill before her birth. She always knew. These ceremonies were a chance for people to see and to hear that in person, given that my grandfather's public performances were sporadic. My mother treasured these ceremonies."

"Neither your mother nor your grandfather ever saw themselves as others see them. Neither of them considered themselves extraordinary, but they considered one another extraordinary. Each saw the other as the incredibly gifted performer the world does, but never themselves. That lack of ego seemed to permeate all aspects of their lives. Did it?" Andrew asked Eric.

"It did. Both of them credited God and each other as the forces behind them. They performed music because it was a part of them, not because they felt they did it better than anyone else. Music was intrinsic within them, not a chance to show off.

"I was born hearing what the world heard—beautiful music. My earliest memory is being held by my mother while she sang a lullaby she had written for me. The older I got, the more I appreciated the beauty of her voice, but as a baby I just knew it made me feel safe, warm, and happy. I felt complete, whole. There is no other feeling to compare," Eric smiled.

§§§§

Matthew walked upon Angilia as she sat playing a piano in a field of flowers. He froze. Michael approached and smiled at the sight. How very often he had witnessed a similar scene so very long before.

"It is quite a lovely piece, is it not, Matthew?"

Matthew forced himself to acknowledge the Archangel, as if woken from a trance. "Yes," Matthew sighed. "Angilia fills my being."

"She always has. She had the same effect on you in the Unborn Children Sphere. She often played piano in the tower there while you painted. Most of your work depicted Angilia," Michael revealed.

"It did? I'm not surprised by that at all. But I have no memory of that. I wish I did. Our lives there were so magical, I know that."

"I knew the future lives on earth the two of you would share. The bond you and Angilia forged in the Unborn Children Sphere remained ingrained in both of you, and that shaped your choices on earth, Matthew, even if you have no memory of the Unborn Children Sphere," Michael explained.

"I'm grateful for that," Matthew smiled.

"Enjoy Angilia's music. I shall return shortly," Michael promised.

Matthew smiled as he watched Angilia. She looked up, saw him, and smiled. She motioned him to her, and he sat beside her on the piano bench. "This is exquisite, my darling. As are you," Matthew softly said and kissed her cheek. "I love you," he said, at the exact moment she said the same to Matthew. They giggled and kissed.

Angilia saw the Archangel appear behind Matthew. "Michael! What a lovely surprise visit!"

"Matthew and I were just talking about your time together in the Unborn Children Sphere as we listened to you play. I just returned from the Unborn Children Sphere, where I retrieved something from very long ago," Michael told them. He handed a book to Matthew, who looked puzzled—until he opened it.

Matthew flipped through the book, his mouth open in surprise. "Is this. . . ? It is. This is my sketchbook! When did I do this?"

Angilia smiled. "You filled quite a few of those, Matthew. You painted and drew most of the time. I've always remembered these books. In fact, those sketchbooks were the first image in my mind when you ran to me on March 7, 2012. I wondered that day how my artist was a doctor. Then it all became clear."

"Michael told me that I drew you frequently. I certainly did," Matthew mumbled as he looked through the sketchbook he never remembered. "I really am not surprised by that. You are so very beautiful, my Angilia. I know for a definitive fact that I loved you then. It shows in my drawings of you."

Angilia smiled, thanked Michael, and said, "I loved and trusted you then, too, my white knight. We really were destined to meet and to marry on earth." Angilia tenderly kissed Matthew as Michael smiled, knowing more than they how true that was.

§§§§

"Welcome to our Christmas 2072 midnight service," Reverend Emerson greeted the congregation. "Christmas is not about the brightly-wrapped presents, but what those presents symbolize. The true Christmas gift is the Son of God whose birth we commemorate on this day. Jesus was born to save us from sin and death. God loves us so much that he sent his only son to live and to die so that we may live forever. There is no greater gift."

Reverend Emerson bowed, and Eric walked to the pulpit. For the third year, he recited the Christmas story from Luke Chapter 2. Every Christmas since he was six weeks old, he had listened to his grandfather and then his mother recite that story. Eric smiled as he told that story, feeling so much love fill his being. When he finished, Eric looked at his family, friends, and neighbors.

"I am so very grateful for the birth, life, and death of Jesus. His sacrifice means that I will spend eternity with my family, which is such an amazing truth. I will meet ancestors I have only read about. More importantly, I will be with my grandfather, my mother, and my wife. How I look forward to that. I do love my life here, and all of you, especially my miracle sons Eric and Patrick. I know that they will join me in Heaven someday, too, which is such an electrifying reality," Eric stated as he placed a hand over his heart, covering the pendant that was hidden under his shirt.

"Christmas fulfilled the prophecy of Jesus' birth and Crucifixion, and the torment he endured for me actually overwhelms me. I don't deserve this gift, but I am grateful for this wondrous gift every moment. Without the gift of eternal life, there would be no point or purpose for this life."

§§§§§

Angilia went to God's throne, where the Seraphim parted to let her pass, as they always did. Angilia approached God with her head bent in prayer, and knelt before his throne. "I know why you have come, Angilia," God stated.

"If it please you, I have prayers to place before you."

"It does please me. You may proceed."

"Dear God, Gwen Jordan, her husband Joseph, and their children Beth and Jacob have prayed to me for more than two weeks nonstop. Gwen is dying of cancer, and their prayer is that you in your loving mercy heal her. I bring their prayers to you, dear God, and ask that you consider granting their prayers. I understand that you may have other plans for Gwen and her family. If you do, I pray that you ease their suffering and pain. If your will is that Gwen is not healed, I pray that you surround her and her family with your warmth and love," Angilia relayed the family's prayer requests, as well as her prayers for the family.

"Your soul is pure and compassionate, as always, Angilia. I have heard Gwen's, her family's, and your prayers, and I shall do what is right for them. You may rise."

"Thank you, dear God," Angilia said with her head still bowed in reverence.

§§§§§

King Eric, Prince Eric, and Prince Patrick maintained the family tradition of greeting parishioners at the church entrance as they arrived for that day's Mother's Day service. King Eric, at 51, looked more like his grandfather as his dimpled smile welcomed his friends and neighbors. The 16-year-old twins always charmed and

49

delighted people. The young men reminded people of King Eric I and Uncle Patrick with their handsome looks, compassion, and distinctive personalities. Just like the original Eric and Patrick, they were brothers who possessed similarities, differences, and an abundance of love and faith.

After the parishioners were seated, the Royal Family walked up the aisle and sat in their pew. Reverend Emerson nodded in acknowledgment, and welcomed his congregation. "We gather on this lovely June 25, 2073 to celebrate Mother's Day. Today is in fact the 61st Mother's Day, a holiday begun in 2012 at the instigation of Princess Angilia, Duchesse de Valmondois. This day is set aside to publicly thank and honor our mothers, which we should do every day according to God's Ten Commandments.

"Let us pray," Reverend Emerson commanded. The congregation dutifully stood and bowed their heads. "Dear God, Our beloved and merciful heavenly Father, we thank you for our mothers. Besides giving us physical life, they give us love, instruction, security, reassurance, and wisdom. We love our mothers, and we love you for gifting us to them. We ask that you let our mothers know how very much they mean to us even when we do not say it or show it. We always feel it, and we pray that you let them feel our love. In this your holy name we humbly ask. Amen."

The congregation repeated the Amen and resumed their seats. Reverend Emerson bowed, and Prince Eric walked to the pulpit. "Sixteen and a half years ago, my brother Patrick and I were born on our father's 35th birthday. He has always told us that that day is the happiest day of his life. That doesn't sound unusual for a father to tell his children, until you remember that his wife, his true love, died giving us life.

"Our mother Julianne, Princess de Valdavia, enjoyed every moment of her pregnancy. She looked forward to our births with glee, constantly telling people how much she wanted to hold Patrick and me. She had tried to get pregnant since she and our father married, and she called her pregnancy a blessing. She called Patrick and me her most beloved gifts. People saw, heard, and felt her joy as she carried out her official duties during her pregnancy. People still tell me and Patrick about meeting our mother and how she gushed and raved about us. They all tell us how happy she appeared.

"Our mother was very happy. She wanted us, and she loved us. She was never happier than on November 17, 2056, when she went into labor. She knew that by the end of the day, she would be holding Patrick and me in her arms. Before he died, her obstetrician, Dr. Henry Morgan, told me that as soon as I was about to be delivered, my mother said through the pain, '*I want to hold my Eric*'.

"She never got to. Just seconds after I was born, she died. Patrick was delivered by emergency C-section. Our mother never even saw us. Her dream of holding us never came true. But we know how much she loves us. We feel her love. We always have. Our family made sure we know her. We love her.

"We love her not just because she gave birth to us. We love her, because she is a wonderful human being. Our mother loved art, history, and life. She loved her family. She loved people, and she enjoyed meeting people and helping people. Her title enabled her to do what she enjoyed most, and she willingly did so up until her eighth month of pregnancy.

"During the last weeks as she eagerly awaited our births, she made sure our nursery was ready. She created the ideal space for two young boys to grow, learn, play, and love. That nursery remains untouched, waiting for our children, who will inherit the love and joy of our mother."

Prince Eric returned to his seat, and Eric put an arm around him. Prince Patrick stood, walked to the pulpit, and smiled. "My brother is correct. Our mother's love for us is strong. She loved us from the first moment she learned about us, and that love still exists. We feel it. I feel it every day. Her love surrounds me like a blanket. I don't have to see my mother to feel her. I don't have to see her to love her. I do love her.

"I love her a whole lot. Our mother was a happy person. Every picture of her shows her with a smile, even her baby pictures. She was also a very optimistic person, someone who always saw the best in everyone and everything. My brother and I inherited that from her. It's also how we view the world.

"I also know for a fact that our mother is alive, and that we will meet her in Heaven when we die. Then, her dream of holding us will finally come true. That is the beautiful truth that makes me not miss her as much as I could. I mean, I do miss her, and I wish she were alive here on earth. But I know she's alive forever. She is just fine. She's happier than ever, because she is in the only real Utopia that exists, Heaven.

"Our mother loves us, and even though she died giving birth to us, we do know her. She is real to us. Someday, when we die, Eric and I will meet her and fulfill her dream. That's a very beautiful thought, not a sad thought."

§§§§§

"Oh, Angilia, I do love being here," Julianne enthused. "Everything you shared with me about Heaven became so real for me when I died. When my dad brought me here, I was instantly filled with the utmost happiness."

Angilia smiled and linked her arm with Julianne's as they leisurely strolled over a lush hilltop. "I know, Julianne. Heaven is pure perfection. Light, love, peace, harmony, beauty—Heaven is all of that and so much more. I didn't necessarily want to leave Matthew, Eric, and the boys, because I truly love them and I loved my life on earth with them. But when Uncle Patrick came for me as my Spirit Guide, I knew how much I would gain here."

"I died so quickly that I didn't have any time at all to think about it. I didn't have time for regrets or fear. My soul left my dead body and came here. I love Eric and our sons so very much, but there are no regrets. There is no sadness," Julianne said.

"There couldn't be, not here," Angilia said as they stopped.

"No, there couldn't, mi hija," Marisol suddenly said and hugged her daughter.

"All of the sadness of life on earth is gone, erased forever. All I am left with is love, peace, joy, and happiness like I've never known," Eric added as he smiled at his wife, his daughter, and his granddaughter-in-law.

"That's so true. I remember the day Eric and I became friends, the day he proposed, our wedding, learning I was pregnant, everything beautiful and happy. I don't remember the rest of it, any sadness, tears, or broken hearts. All of that is gone. It's like Heaven causes this sort of magic amnesia that erases everything sad, bad, and painful and leaves everything happy, wonderful, and ecstatic," Julianne said and smiled at her family.

CHAPTER 3

After the twins left for school, Eric and Leigh had their morning brief as usual. "I know I have the meeting with the Energy Council this morning, but is there anything else that's been added to my calendar for today?" Eric asked his friend and assistant.

Leigh opened Eric's calendar for Monday, April 16, 2074. "There is an appointment for 1:00 here at your office. A group calling themselves the Queen Angilia Guild requested a meeting with you."

"The Queen Angilia Guild? I've never heard of them. Did they say why they want to meet with me?"

"When I asked, I was told it was a very important meeting. Father Fisher, who called to make the appointment, said the Guild was working on something very important, and needed to speak with you. They need vital information and access to documents only you can provide," Leigh explained the limited information he had been given.

"Documents? What documents?" Leigh shrugged his shoulders in answer. "You said his title is Father? Then he must be with the Church. I wonder what this is about. Well, I suppose I'll find out at 1:00. Let's get the files ready for the Energy Council meeting," Eric said.

After lunch, Eric was working on a speech for the following evening when Leigh informed him that the Queen Angilia Guild had arrived for their appointment. He escorted the men into Eric's office, and both men noticed that the Guild members stared at Angilia's desk for several moments. Her desk had remained largely untouched since her death, and the nameplate and pink accessories that her father had placed there in 2012 still gleamed.

Eric looked at Leigh, more confused than ever, beginning to wonder if the Guild were in fact a cult. Leigh cleared his throat and said, "Your Majesty, these gentlemen are the members of the Queen Angilia Guild."

The five men then turned to Eric and bowed. "We are honored to meet with you, Your Majesty. We have been formed to investigate and to further Queen Angilia's canonization process. I am Father Fisher, and these gentlemen are esteemed members of the Roman Catholic Church." The four men bowed again and introduced themselves: Stephen Giddings, Nicholas Sumter, Wade Jessup, and Thomas Campbell. Eric stood, shook the five men's hands, and motioned them to chairs across from his desk. Leigh took his usual seat next to Eric's desk, prepared to take notes during the meeting.

"Did I understand you correctly, Father Fisher? My mother's canonization process? Isn't that declaring someone a Saint?" Eric asked, his mind swirling.

"Yes, Sir, it is," Father Fisher confirmed. "We arrived in Valmondois last summer to begin the first stage in this process. Over the past several months, we have interviewed hundreds of witnesses to your mother's miracles, including those who were the beneficiaries of those miracles. Many of those people permitted us access to their medical files and doctors so that we could verify the miracles. We also researched news accounts of her miracles, and watched the video footage of many of those that occurred in public."

"My mother never took credit for any miracles. She always gave the credit to God, for whom she worked," Eric explained, knowing full well how she would react to hearing this.

"We know, Your Majesty. A true Servant of God never takes the glory and honor," Mr. Campbell said.

"Precisely. In every instance, Queen Angilia praised God for any healing or answered prayer that occurred. We are certain that, with a bit more investigation, Queen Angilia will be formally declared a Servant of God," Mr. Giddings added.

Father Fisher recognized the confusion on Eric's face. "There are four stages in the canonization process: Servant of God, Venerable, Blessed, and Saint. After Queen Angilia is declared a Servant of God, the second stage will begin. We need your assistance so that Her Majesty can be declared a Servant of God."

"We have read and watched Queen Angilia's public speeches, comments, and interviews. In every one, she gives credit to God. Now we would like permission to read her private writings, as well, to determine if that acknowledgment was consistent and truly within her heart. We need to confirm that her acknowledgment of God was genuine and not just for public consumption," Mr. Sumter clarified.

"You want to read her diaries and letters?" Eric asked, unsure how to feel. Of course his mother's feelings were sincere, but to open her diaries to strangers was somewhat disconcerting.

"She did use some of her diaries in her memoir, Sir, and we have studied that book thoroughly. However, we do request access to her diaries and letters so that we can prepare the most accurate report for the Congregation for the Causes of Saints," Father Fisher said. "If possible we would read and take notes from Queen Angilia's diaries and letters here at the palace. There would be no danger to these valuable documents in any way."

Eric glanced at Leigh, who nodded once, and then he bowed his head in prayer. After several moments, he looked at Father Fisher, and said, "All of this would make my mother very uncomfortable."

"We understand that, Your Majesty. Her humility and obedience to God are at the heart of this process. Her entire life was in service of and obedience to God, and through her, God performed many miracles. Declaring someone a Saint is more an acknowledgment of God and how he works through that person," Father Fisher stated.

Eric sighed deeply, and then said, "You may use the office next to Leigh's across the hall beginning tomorrow. I will bring my mother's diaries and letters there. I hope you don't mind my having a guard there, as well, gentlemen."

"Not at all, Your Majesty," Father Fisher assured Eric. "In fact, we will wear white museum gloves while we handle these documents, and we will treat them with the utmost care and respect."

"Thank you. You may arrive at 9:00 tomorrow morning. Leigh will see you to the office, and make sure you are comfortable while you are here." Eric stood, signaling the end to the meeting, and shook the Guild members' hands. Leigh stood as well, and then escorted the five men to the courtyard.

When he returned to Eric's office, he saw his friend holding a stained-glass cross that Angilia had kept on her desk. "She wouldn't like this at all, Leigh. She never wanted any of this to be about her. I pray I'm doing the right thing."

Leigh put a hand on Eric's shoulder. "I know, Eric. But people do already treat her like a Saint. They pray at her statue and outside the Royal Vault. They still send their prayer requests through her to God, and it still causes miracles. She still causes miracles. In all but title only, your mother is a Saint, Eric."

Eric placed the cross on the desk and smiled. "You're right, of course, Leigh. Her whole life was about helping others, so it's no surprise she's still doing that from Heaven."

§§§§

The Guild spent two weeks in Shannon's former office examining Angilia's diaries and letters and making copious notes from and copies of them. As promised, they were careful with the documents, but always under the watchful eye of a guard. When they finished on a Friday afternoon, Father Fisher approached Leigh.

"Mr. Graham, we would like to schedule an appointment with His Majesty. There is one more request we must make before we can make our recommendation to the Congregation for the Causes of Saints."

"King Eric has a guest in his office for the next 45 minutes. If you don't mind waiting, I will ask him if he could meet with you then." Father Fisher thanked Leigh, and the Guild members sat in the other office discussing the purpose for their next meeting with Eric.

"I fear King Eric will refuse our request," Wade Jessup said. "It was one thing to request her diaries, but this is more than we can expect him to allow."

"I fear the same. This is quite a lot to ask of her son," Thomas Campbell said.

"I understand that, I do, but if we approach this respectfully, we can convince him of the importance of this. Let me broach the subject with King Eric," Father Fisher commanded.

The four men agreed. "I just pray he at least hears us out before he has us escorted from the palace," Stephen Giddings replied. The guard wondered what the Guild had in mind, and he was immediately on high alert. In fact, he surreptitiously signaled another guard to the fourth floor just as a precaution.

When Leigh noticed that Eric's guest left, he stepped into Eric's office. "Do you have time for a meeting with the Guild? They have finished with your mother's diaries and letters, but said they have one more request before they can complete this stage."

Eric sighed, visibly perturbed. "Did they say what it is? What more could they need? My mother's life was so public, and there's nothing else private they can get from me," he said as he placed his hands over the pendant about which only he knew.

"No, they didn't, Eric. They're waiting in the office." Eric glanced at his watch. 3:00. He told Leigh to bring them in, and motioned for the six men to sit.

"What more can I help you with, gentlemen?"

"We have one remaining task in this stage of the canonization process, Your Majesty. This is the last task before we can finalize our recommendation to the Congregation for the Causes of Saints. Everyone who has been canonized has gone through this process, and we are quite cognizant of the emotional aspects of this request. We would not make this request were it not necessary," Father Fisher calmly said. The two guards stood just outside the open office door, more diligent than ever.

"What request?" Eric asked, feeling his heart pound in his chest.

"As I said, this is common in every candidate's case. There is nothing untoward or unusual in our request, Your Majesty," Father Fisher continued, hoping to soften the emotional blow.

"What request?" Eric repeated, becoming more frustrated and fearful. What did they want?

"Sir, we would like your permission to have Queen Angilia's tomb opened and her body examined," Father Fisher stated, sounding far calmer than he felt.

The office grew silent except for the ticking of the clock that had hung on the wall for more than 150 years. The guards looked aghast, and Leigh looked horrified. Eric sat motionless, devoid of expression or emotion until tears filled his eyes. The Guild members appeared devastated, knowing they had lost his support.

Everyone remained silent, waiting for Eric. After 15 very long minutes, he put his hand over the pendant again and looked into Father Fisher's eyes. "I know for an indisputable fact that my mother's soul left her body the moment she died. I was with her when she died. I was holding her close to me when she died. She died in my arms. I saw her manifested soul at that moment of her death. She kissed my cheek, and then she went to Heaven with Uncle Patrick. She lives in Heaven."

Eric shared his mother's death for the first time, stunning Leigh and the Guild members. After several moments of silence, Eric asked, "When do you want to do this?"

The Guild members were even more stunned. He had not resisted or refused their request. "We would like to complete this final step at your earliest convenience, Sir," Father Fisher answered.

"What is my schedule for Monday, Leigh?" Leigh looked at Eric's calendar on his handheld computer, and informed Eric that he had an appointment in his office for 10:00 that morning and a meeting at 2:00 that afternoon. "Reschedule the morning appointment, Leigh, for later next week. Father Fisher, we will do this at 9:00 Monday morning. I will arrange for Reverend Emerson, military soldiers, and security guards to be present. No one else is allowed in the Royal Vault. Is that understood?"

"Yes, Sir, it is. We shall be at Christ Church Valmondois at 9:00 Monday," Father Fisher said, his pleasure well under control.

"Fine. The soldiers will remove the lid from my mother's tomb, and I will open her coffin. You will have one hour, no more, and her tomb will then be resealed, to never again be opened." Eric told the Guild his conditions, not giving them any options.

"We understand, Your Majesty, and we deeply appreciate your kindness," Father Fisher replied.

Eric nodded, signaling an end to the meeting. Leigh quickly stood and escorted the Guild members to the courtyard. Eric looked up at the two guards. "You will both accompany me and Leigh to the Royal Vault on Monday." The guards bowed, still dazed by the Guild's request, but devoted to their King.

When he was alone in his office, Eric softly said, "I pray I'm doing the right thing, Mommy. I love you so much."

"Hey, Eric, what's going on?" Patrick suddenly asked when he manifested.

"Oh, Uncle Patrick, they want to proclaim Mommy a Saint. It's all so unnerving. I just want to do what's right," Eric said, sounding as emotional as he felt for the first time that day.

"You mean the Church is doing this? Little One will be named Saint Angilia?"

"That's the plan. There are four stages, and they're on the first stage now. It's almost over, but the hardest part of this stage is on Monday. I need the strength to get through that."

Patrick looked at his grandnephew in concern. "Why? What happens Monday?"

"They open Mommy's tomb," Eric stated, and could not keep the tears from his eyes. "I know she's not there, but this is still so hard. I wish you could be there, too, Uncle Patrick."

"I can be, Eric. I will be. If you need me, I'll be there. Angilia would want that," Patrick promised Eric. "I can't say this whole thing surprises me. I mean, Little One has always been a Saint by God's standards." Eric smiled, stood, and hugged Uncle Patrick. He had his answer. He was doing the right thing.

ʃʃʃʃ

May 7, 2074

Today will be the most emotional day since Mommy's death. Her tomb will be opened so that the Guild can examine her body. I know that <u>she</u> is not there. I do. I saw her soul after she died, and I know she is alive. But this will still be incredibly difficult for me. I need God's strength to get me through today, or otherwise I will fall apart completely.

Thank God that Uncle Patrick will be there with me. I need him there. He sees Mommy all the time, and his strength will help to keep me strong. Uncle Patrick is the one who eased my concerns about this whole process on Friday when he said that Mommy has always been a Saint by God's standards. That would ease her mind, as well, and that's what really matters to me—God and Mommy, and how they feel about this.

ʃʃʃʃ

Before he called Leigh, the guards, and the soldiers, Eric called for his Uncle Patrick, who manifested in Eric's office. "Thank you for coming with me, Uncle Patrick. I can't tell you what this means to me. I need you there. I need your strength to help me stay strong. I have no idea how this will affect me, but I know it will. I haven't seen her since the day she died, and now this. I never imagined having to do this, Uncle Patrick."

"I know, Eric. You don't have to do this. I can do it in your place," Patrick offered.

Eric smiled as tears of gratitude filled his eyes. "Thank you, but I do have to do this, Uncle Patrick. I have to do this for Mommy." He cleared his throat. "I best gather everyone," he said, and made two quick telephone calls. Then he and Patrick went across the hall to Leigh's office.

The three men joined the two guards and walked to the church, where they were greeted by Reverend Emerson. The soldiers stood at attention outside the Royal Vault. Eric stopped before the altar to pray, and the other men bowed their heads as well. When Eric finished, Uncle Patrick put his arm around Eric and smiled at him. Eric breathed deeply, unlocked the Royal Vault, and walked in with Patrick. The others followed.

Eric stood beside his mother's tomb, and he suddenly felt warm air encircle him. He inhaled sharply, and looked at his granduncle. Patrick smiled, nodded, and whispered, "She's here."

At that moment, the five Guild members arrived, and were greeted by Reverend Emerson. The Guild had met with him months earlier, so had been prepared for that day's events. Father Fisher shook Eric's hand, and pleasantly surprised him by asking, "Is it all right if I lead us in prayer before we begin?"

"My mother will appreciate that. Thank you."

Father Fisher smiled, bowed his head, and prayed, "Heavenly Father, we ask that you bless us today, and that you especially embrace His Majesty during this very difficult and emotional event. We thank you for the inspirational life of Queen Angilia, and for allowing her light to remain unextinguished. Our prayer is that within her canonization people will see you working through her for centuries to come. That was always her intention. She always gave the glory to you, God, and we know that if she could do so at this moment, she would tell us that you are responsible for the miracles performed. In declaring Queen Angilia as Saint Angilia, our goal is to acknowledge her as one of your Supreme Angels. You created her as such, and as such will she forever be known. Amen."

Everyone repeated the Amen, and Patrick smiled at his grandnephew. Eric nodded to the soldiers, and the eight men stood around Angilia's tomb. They lifted the heavy lid and leaned it against the wall. Angilia's white coffin—one just like her mother's and her father's—appeared for the first time in over four years. Eric squeezed Patrick's hand and stepped to his mother's tomb. "I love you, Mommy," he said, placed his hands on her coffin, and raised the lid.

"Mommy!" Reverend Emerson, Father Fisher, and the Guild members made the sign of the cross. The soldiers could not help but stare in wonder. Patrick stood behind Eric, his hands on his grandnephew's shoulders. "Oh, Mommy, you are just as beautiful as always."

Angilia's body had not decayed. Her body looked as it had at the birthday party the afternoon she had died. No one moved or spoke, too stunned to do so. Several men audibly gasped when Eric reached down and put his hand over his mother's cheek. He sobbed, and Reverend Emerson was on the verge of putting a halt to the proceedings when Eric said, "Even physical death cannot destroy your body, Mommy. You are just as beautiful and perfect as I always remember. When I was a child, before I knew the truth about you, I always said you look like an angel. This is proof of your divinity. Oh, Mommy, how I love you."

Patrick put his arm around Eric. "She is as beautiful as that day 97 years ago, when she was my Spirit Guide. This is how she still looks in Heaven. She's never changed, not even in death." Patrick gently lifted Angilia's hand. "Her body even feels soft," he marveled.

Reverend Emerson asked Eric, "May I?" Eric nodded, and Reverend Emerson placed his hand over Angilia's hand. Then, as if doubting his senses, he gently caressed her cheek. "This is remarkable," he whispered.

Father Fisher also asked Eric's permission to touch Queen Angilia's body. He carefully lifted her hand, finding it soft and supple in his hand. Next he pressed her cheek with a finger, and her still-elastic skin resumed its shape immediately. "Remarkable indeed," he said and looked at Reverend Emerson.

The other Guild members likewise touched Angilia's dead body, amazed that after over four years it felt human and alive. "She looks as if she will awake at any moment, like Snow White before the prince's kiss," Mr. Jessup marveled.

After longer than the one hour Eric had promised, the men still stood around Angilia's open tomb. "This is a miracle," Father Fisher declared. "May I take photographs of Queen Angilia's body for our report?"

Eric looked at Patrick and then at Reverend Emerson, who nodded his approval. "I suppose," he said, more overcome by the experience than he had ever expected.

Leigh had stood in stunned silence since Angilia's coffin had been opened. "This is a miracle, Eric. Your mother looks just like she did when I met her the first time 30 years ago."

"Leigh, cancel my meeting for this afternoon," Eric requested of his friend. "I'm staying here for a while." Leigh nodded and reluctantly returned to the palace. Suddenly Eric turned to face Father Fisher and asked, "What is the next step in my mother's canonization process? What do we do next?"

"Well, Sir, we prepare our written report for the Congregation for the Causes of Saints, who sends the cause to a Realtor, and if he votes in the affirmative, the cause is then presented to the Cardinal, Archbishop and Bishop members of the Congregation. Upon their affirmative vote, the recommendation of a Decree of Holy Virtues is sent to the Holy Father for his vote. His affirmative vote would officially make your mother known as

Servant of God of Queen Angilia. From there, the process moves to the second stage, Venerable," Father Fisher explained.

"Is there anything I can do to help this process?" Eric asked. "Would it help if I write my account of what I see today?"

"While the votes are based primarily upon our report, we do have written statements included from some of those who experienced or witnessed your mother's miracles. Such statements can only bolster the validity of our report, Your Majesty."

"Fine. All of us here today will write an account of what we see here. Reverend Emerson, could you get some paper and pens for us, please?" While the minister quickly got the items from his office, Eric called Leigh and told him to return to the Royal Vault.

"Sir, may I make one more request? Would it be possible to take pictures of you next to your mother's tomb, with her body?"

Eric quickly wrote that day's date on a sheet of paper and held it while he stood next to his mother, his hand over hers. He motioned Uncle Patrick next to him for some pictures, and then asked that Reverend Emerson join them. "Thank you for agreeing to this. These photographs are proof of what we claim we witnessed today. Throughout the Church's history, cases of well-preserved dead bodies are seen as evidence of the person's sanctity. These photographs will do much in support of our cause," Father Fisher told Eric.

"Prince Patrick, you are dead," Thomas Campbell matter-of-factly stated, to which Patrick nodded. "Your niece wrote about being your Spirit Guide in 1977 and being in the Angels Choir with you. Your manifestations became common after the publication of her memoir. Manifestations of dead bodies are quite uncommon. Why, how, do you manifest?"

"Not all angels do manifest. Most don't. I'm an envoy angel, someone God sends to earth on his behalf. I asked Michael why God approved of all this, and he told me that since I'd been kinda well-known when I was alive that people would recognize me. My death was pretty public, so the whole world knows I died on July 19, 1977. Then when people see me, they literally see the truth of eternal life. Well, after they get over the shock of seeing me," Patrick said with a giggle.

"Of course," Mr. Campbell said. "When His Majesty opened his mother's coffin, you said Queen Angilia looks like this in Heaven," he said and waved his hand over Angilia's tomb. "You see your niece constantly in Heaven. She is the same?"

"Yeah, sure. Little One, Angilia, is the same as always. I met her almost 100 years ago, and she never changed. Her looks didn't change, except when she was a baby and a young girl. It was kinda strange to visit her when she was a newborn, so tiny and all. But even then, I knew, I saw, that she was the same. Her soul was the same. Her soul, her essence, never changed at all. She never did and never will."

"Queen Angilia never manifests?" Wade Jessup asked.

"Angilia isn't an envoy angel," Patrick truthfully replied.

Eric looked his granduncle in the eyes. "No, but she did manifest once. You know that, Uncle Patrick."

Patrick looked stunned. So did everyone else. "How do you know about that?" Patrick asked.

"Dad kept her letters, and he wrote about her visit in his diary," Eric admitted.

"Yeah. That was a special one-time thing just for Matthew. He came here on the first anniversary of her death, and he was a wretched mess. Angilia and I watched him from Heaven, and his grief broke her heart. She can't come to earth like I can, so she ran and asked God's permission. He allowed her to make one visit, and that is what saved your father. She saved him."

"Are you saying that the Duc saw his dead wife?" Stephen Giddings asked.

"Yes," Eric answered. "When my father died, he had letters from my mother on his lap. I didn't realize some of them were written after her death until I read them. Then I read Dad's diary.

His entry for November 17, 2070 describes her visit here in the Vault."

"Sir, may we see these letters and your father's diary?" Father Fisher asked. "Please."

"Of course. If you all don't mind, I'd like to be alone for a little while," Eric said.

"Of course, Eric. We'll wait out here," Leigh said and squeezed his friend's shoulder. The men quietly left and waited in front of the altar.

"Oh, Mommy, I so dreaded today, but what a miracle this is. You are just as always, and even though this is your dead body, that is very comforting to me. There is no longer a pain in my soul. It's gone now, occupied once more by you. I know more than ever that you are as always. You are my beautiful, loving, compassionate, godly Mommy. You are in Heaven, waiting for me to join you someday. I love you, Mommy. I love you." Eric bent and kissed his mother's soft cheek. He stood, tears in his eyes, removed a crucifix he always carried in his pocket, and placed it in her hand. "I love you, Mommy," he said once more and closed her coffin.

Eric opened the Vault and told the soldiers to replace the lid on her tomb once more. When they finished, they saluted Queen Angilia. Eric thanked them, and locked the Vault behind them. Reverend Emerson accompanied them to the palace, where Eric asked Leigh to take Reverend Emerson and the Guild members to the sitting room. He went to the third floor, where he got his father's 2070 diary and the wooden box from his suite, where he kept them. He carried the items to the sitting room.

Eric closed the sitting room doors behind him and motioned everyone to the large table. He opened his father's diary to the November 17 entry and handed it and his mother's posthumous letters to Reverend Emerson. After he read them, he smiled. "Your father told me and Reverend Olson that he received a miracle that day that completely changed him. He never told me exactly what miracle, but of course I saw an immediate change in him. We all did.   He went from the deepest, darkest grief to joy in mere moments. It was indeed a miracle."

Reverend Emerson handed the diary and letters to Father Fisher, who read the entry twice before he passed the documents to Mr. Giddings.   Once the Guild members finished, Leigh read Matthew's diary entry and looked at his friend with a huge smile. "Now it all makes sense. Matthew changed so suddenly, and no one ever figured out just what caused that. It was the only thing, the only person, who could change him. His wife."

"That's why God permitted Angilia's visit," Patrick said. "God knew that seeing her, touching her, would save Matthew. It did. I'm the one who delivered her letters to him. You should have seen him each time," Patrick smiled.

"So you knew about everything, Uncle Patrick?"

"Yeah, sure. It tore Angilia apart to see Matthew in so much pain and distress. She had to save her husband. She had to so they could be together now. They're so happy, Eric, they are. Matthew still looks at her with those puppy dog eyes. Like when she and Gabriel played a concerto for us, it was splendid. Matthew just sat there staring at her with that look in his eyes. You know the one."

Eric smiled. "I do. Everyone who ever saw Dad saw that look. Nothing has changed."

"Nope.   In fact, it's been going on since the Unborn Children Sphere according to Michael," Patrick revealed.

"I don't doubt that, Uncle Patrick. This has been one incredible morning," Eric said.

"It certainly has, Sir. May we have copies of the letters your mother wrote after her death and of your father's diary entry?" Father Fisher asked. "With these documents added to support our cause, I feel certain we will obtain affirmative votes."

"Of course. Leigh, would you mind making the copies?" Leigh nodded and took the documents to his office, where he made copies of them for the Guild.

Father Fisher then asked the question that Eric had dreaded. "What was the painting that Camillus made and your mother gave as your father's birthday present?"

"Oh, just a painting of something beautiful in Heaven," Patrick answered truthfully, but without revealing the exact subject. "I'm the one who brought it to Matthew at his party that day," he said, and patted his grandnephew's arm. Eric smiled in gratitude.

Eric pulled a vial from the wooden box at that moment, and looked at it. "Dad saved this all these years. This bullet brought him and Mommy together. It should have killed her, but it didn't. He kept it. I don't think anyone else knew he did."

The Guild members stared at the vial in wonder. "Is that the bullet that he removed from her aorta in 2012?" Wade Jessup asked. Eric nodded, still looking at the bullet.

"Sir, there must be a reason that your father saved that bullet and that you removed it from the box just now. You found this with these other items after your father's death?" Father Fisher asked.

"Yes. Dad never mentioned the bullet, but he did keep it."

"Sir, that bullet represents Queen Angilia's miraculous survival of the assassination attempt. It is standard that we have a relic for each Saint. Would it be too much to ask that this bullet become the relic of Queen Angilia?" Father Fisher asked.

Eric looked at the bullet for a moment, and then handed the vial to Father Fisher. He had the pendant and the Camillus portrait, neither of which would ever leave him or the family. Those were too important to the family. Eric knew why his dad had kept the bullet, but he also understood its metaphysical significance. He did not need the bullet in order to keep that meaning in his heart.

"Thank you, Sir, thank you. This is indeed a wondrous day," Father Fisher stated.

Eric then pulled another vial from the box and, after looking at it for several minutes, handed it to Father Fisher. Father Fisher looked at the vial in stunned pleasure, and then looked at Eric. "Is this a bone fragment from your mother's body?"

"Yes. My father kept that after my mother's surgery in 2012. It's a small fragment from her sternum when he performed the thoracotomy. I know the Church has a relic that came from the person, like John the Baptist's bones, so I want you to have these two items," Eric explained.

Before the members of the Guild could reply, Leigh returned with the copies. He handed them to Father Fisher, who thanked him. Father Fisher then held Eric's hand in both of his and kissed it in gratitude. "I and the other Guild members thank you tremendously for all of your assistance and for the gift of these two relics." He and the other four men stood and thanked everyone.

"I will be in touch once we submit our report, and to let you know the progress throughout the process. I can never thank you enough for your assistance in our cause," Father Fisher said as he shook Eric's hand.

"Thank you. Let me know if there is anything else I can do to help," Eric said before Leigh escorted the Guild members to the courtyard.

When Eric was alone with Patrick and Reverend Emerson, he said, "Thank you both for being with me today. I had my doubts about this in the beginning, but not anymore."

"Little One may not like all this fuss, but she understands it's about more than just her. Michael talked to her when I told her about this. That's why we felt her soul near us in the Vault this morning, Eric. That was her way of giving you her blessing."

Eric smiled, hugged Patrick, and silently thanked God for his amazing mother.

§§§§

May 7, 2075

One year ago this hour, I opened Mommy's coffin at the request of the Guild. The thought of that initially sickened me, but I soon realized that she is not in her coffin. Her dead body is, but she is not. What I saw that day remains vivid—my beautiful mother's body, perfectly preserved.

How that affected me, God knows. Yes, it is her body, but it is proof of her divinity. I know that. To me, her pristine body is a symbol of her eternal life, as well as of her angelic status. Mommy is an angel, an Angel of God. She is a Servant of God. She has been since he created her. Her entire life has been dedicated to his service. Titles aside, I know in my heart that Mommy is at the forefront of God's Army.

I am so honored to have known her and to call her Mommy. I love her so very much. Thank you for creating me her son, God.

§§§§

Later that morning, after Eric finished a meeting, his office telephone rang. "Father Fisher, it's nice to hear from you. What can I help you with?"

"Sir, I am calling to let you know that the Holy Father has given an affirmative vote. Your mother is officially Servant of God Queen Angilia. The official statement is to be made shortly."

"This is wonderful news, Father Fisher! Thank you for letting me know. I want to get my sons from school before this news reaches them. Thank you for everything."

Eric quickly told Leigh and Yvonne, who were equally dazed by the news. He drove to the high school and entered the office, surprising the staff. He requested that his sons be called to the office immediately, and within minutes both teenagers arrived from their classrooms. Eric noticed their concerned expressions.

"Everything's all right, but I have some very important news to share with you." Eric thanked the staff, and motioned his sons to follow him. He told them he would explain everything when they got home.

At the palace, he led them to the sitting room, where he told them to sit. "What's going on, Dad? It has to be important for you to pull us out of school like this," Prince Eric said.

He sat between his sons, and said, "It is important. The day after Easter last year, I was contacted by a group of five men who call themselves the Queen Angilia Guild." Eric explained the two weeks he had been involved in the process, culminating exactly one year earlier with the opening of Angilia's tomb and her new status.

"You saw Grandmother again?" Prince Eric asked. "She looked exactly the same? Her body hadn't. . .you know?"

"No, her body had not decayed. In fact, she felt as soft as ever."

"I want to see her," Prince Patrick said.

Eric sat silent for several seconds until Prince Eric said, "I do, too. Please, Dad."

Eric finally relented, and called Reverend Emerson and the local Army troops to arrange for eight soldiers. One hour later, as the news of Angilia's Servant of God status spread and people gathered at her statue, the church, and the mall, the Royal Family entered Christ Church Valmondois. They spent several moments speaking with those there to pray, and even accepted flowers to place at Angilia's tomb.

Eric unlocked the Royal Vault, and the soldiers, Reverend Emerson, the Princes, and Eric entered. Eric locked the door from inside. He put his arms around his sons, and stepped to Angilia's tomb with them. Eric asked Reverend Emerson to pray before the soldiers removed the heavy lid.

"Dear God, We thank you for the eternal life of Servant of God Queen Angilia. Her life is a model for all who seek to do your will and to follow your Commandments. As the world rejoices in this honor bestowed upon Angilia, we ask that you keep the focus upon you, as Angilia always did. We also ask that you embrace Angilia's family and friends, who love her and you, as they are thrust into this global fervor. Protect and guide them as they go through this emotional process. In your holy name, this we ask. Amen."

The others repeated the Amen, and Eric nodded to the soldiers. They carefully lifted the lid and leaned it against the wall. They stood at attention as Eric asked his sons if they were ready. One year later, would Angilia's body still be preserved? The twins nodded, never even considering that their grandmother's body would have decayed.

Eric placed his hands on his mother's coffin, said, "I love you, Mommy," and raised the lid.

Prince Eric gasped deeply, and said, "Grandmother," while Prince Patrick began crying.

Finally, Prince Patrick said, "That's how she looked at our birthday party when she kissed us and went upstairs to die."

"I know, Patrick. I know. That's what hit me one year ago," Eric gently said.

"She looks alive," Prince Eric whispered. "She is as beautiful as always. I always thought she looked like an angel, and now I know for certain that she is one."

"Oh, Eric, that's what I said one year ago. I knew Mommy is an angel, but this proves that God preordained her. He created her as this wondrous, special woman, as one of his Supreme Angels."

Prince Patrick still cried, and reached to take his grandmother's hand in his. Her soft, silky, skin made him cry more. "I love you, Grandmother," he said as he leaned down and kissed her cheek.

"I love you, too, Grandmother," Prince Eric said through his tears. He looked at his father, and Eric nodded. Prince Eric leaned down and kissed his grandmother's cheek as well.

"A Saint is someone recognized by the Church as perfect in holiness. That's Grandmother," Prince Patrick said.

Eric kissed his sons' heads and said, "Yes, it is." Several moments later, he closed his mother's coffin, and the soldiers replaced the lid on her tomb. As they had one year before, the soldiers saluted their Queen.

Eric and his sons placed the flowers people had given them on Angilia's tomb before they left and locked the Royal Vault. They were once more engulfed in a sea of people there to offer prayers to God and to Angilia. The Royal Family and Reverend Emerson spent more than two hours speaking with those who had made the pilgrimage.

Eric and his sons were likewise surrounded on the walk home, which ended up taking another two hours. Now that Angilia's road to sainthood was public, it seemed like everyone had a story about her to share. "Thank you very much," Prince Patrick said to a group of pilgrims who stopped him. "Our grandmother has always been touched by God, and she spends her eternal life helping people still. We love her tremendously."

Eric smiled and put a hand on his son's shoulder. "Yes, we do. She loves all of us. She loves all people, which is but one of her godly qualities."

"She is perfect," Prince Eric said as tears began to choke him.

"God bless Servant of God Queen Angilia!" dozens of people chanted.

§§§§

Five weeks later, on June 15, the mall and streets were once more filled with Royal fans. That day, the twin Princes graduated from high school, and like their great-grandfather and father before them, they were the most famous graduates in the world. When their security officers Travis and Colin drove them to King Philippe High School, they were relentlessly cheered and even followed.

Eric, Leigh, and Yvonne watched from the courtyard. "How can your sons be 18 already? It seems like yesterday that they were born. In fact, it doesn't seem that long ago that we graduated together," Yvonne told her friend.

Eric beamed. "I know, Yvonne. They are incredible young men. They are the reason I was born. I love them so much."

Leigh put his arm around his best friend's shoulders and smiled. "They know that, Eric. And they love you with all their hearts. Everyone can see it. They're your sons. They were destined to be wonderful men with your example and guidance."

"Yes, they were," Yvonne agreed as they entered the palace to prepare for the graduation ceremony. When they arrived one hour later, King Eric was cheered. Just as his grandfather had, Eric downplayed the reaction. He greeted his neighbors and those who had come to Valmondois to see the young Princes on their graduation day.

Finally, Eric and his party were escorted to their seats, from which they shortly stood for the singing of the national anthem. Principal Devon Adams welcomed everyone and then explained that the first degree would be awarded to the valedictorian. "The Class of 2075's valedictorian has not only a perfect 4.0 grade point average, but a quite busy schedule. Not only has he consistently taken an overload of credit hours, but he was a member of the History Club, the French Club, and the Shakespeare Club, becoming its president during his junior year. In addition to his academic career, he is a member of Valdavia's Royal Family, and undertakes duties on his father King Eric's behalf. Please join me in congratulating Eric DeBruce Martineau Taylor."

Eric had listened in stunned silence to Principal Adams' introduction, realizing that his son Eric was the valedictorian. Eric wondered why his son had not said anything, until he caught sight of Yvonne's smile. He then remembered that he had not told his family that he had been the 2040 valedictorian. He had not wanted to brag in any way about his achievement, and he understood the same was true for Prince Eric.

Prince Eric walked to the podium, received his diploma and medal from Principal Adams, and blushed at the standing ovation he received. When everyone stopped, he heaved a sigh of relief and began his speech. "Thank you, Principal Adams. My classmates and I owe you and all of our teachers a debt of gratitude. That is a debt which we can repay by using the knowledge you have helped us gain to make this world a better place for ourselves and for future generations. We are the stewards who will lead the future.

"How we do that is our destiny and our legacy. I learned about destiny from my grandmother, Queen Angilia. Destiny is that which God predetermined for each of us. God has a plan and a purpose for each of us—our destiny. Free will means we can choose to disregard God's chosen path for us, but that would be doing ourselves the most heinous wrong. If we are created from God's love and in his image, then it is our duty to obey our Father. It is our duty and indeed our privilege to fulfill his purpose for us.

"My grandmother did that her entire life. She never questioned or doubted her destiny one minute. She willingly and happily fulfilled God's purpose for her. She still does, as you all now know. My grandmother is my inspiration.

"She was born heir to the throne of Valdavia, a duty she took very seriously. How easy it would have been for her to do as she pleased and to use her wealth for her own desires. That was never an option for her. She used her title, position, and wealth to help people and to do God's work. She learned that not only from God, but from her father King Eric I, my great-grandfather.

"I have learned from both of them and from my father. I am the first-born twin, and as such I am the heir to the throne. That is my destiny. Like my great-grandfather, grandmother, and father, I take this very seriously. I want to do what is best for God, for my family, for the majority of people, and for the world. Becoming King de Valdavia is my birthright, yes, but it is a privilege and an honor to do what God destined for me.

"I challenge my friends and classmates in the Class of 2075 to fulfill your destinies. Doing so will not only guarantee that you do what is best for this world as we near the 22nd century, but that you nourish your souls. My grandmother told Patrick and me, many times, that she felt her best when she helped people and knew she was doing what God wanted her to do. That is how I want to feel, and I hope you do, as well."

Prince Eric thanked everyone and took his seat. Principal Adams returned to the podium. "Our next degree is awarded to our salutatorian. This young man achieved a near-perfect grade point average of 3.9, and is also a member of the History Club, as well as of the Future Educators Club. He, too, maintained an overload of credit hours, and is a member of Valdavia's Royal Family who performs several public duties each year. Please welcome Patrick DeBruce Martineau Taylor."

Prince Eric smiled as he watched their father. Eric stood, his mouth agape in surprise, and applauded his son. Patrick accepted his diploma and medal, and then launched into his speech. "Destiny. Yeah, that unseen force that guides our lives. Destiny isn't about titles and awards. It's about doing what you're meant to do, and doing your best at it. I learned that from my grandmother. I know at some point I'll get a title, but that is the least important thing in my life. I've known in my heart for a long time what I'm meant to do, and you better believe that's what I'm going to do.

"That's why I joined the Future Educators. I am following my fabulous grandmother into education. As perfect as Valdavia is, there is one thing we lack. A university. I'm going to change that. I'm going to my grandmother's alma mater in the fall with a major in education, specifically education administration. After that I will get my Masters and DPhil. Then I'll open Valdavia's first university. I will.

"I told only one person this—my grandmother. I want to do this, sure, but more than that, I have to do this. This idea has been in my heart since I was seven years old. This is my destiny, and I am on the path to doing what my brother said, fulfilling my destiny. When I return from Oxford, you will all see me make this a reality, I guarantee you that."

Everyone cheered as Patrick sat beside his brother. The twins hugged, and knew in their souls that their grandmother was pleased.

§§§§

"Oh, Daddy and Mommy, I love Eric and Patrick so very much. They are both such strong, wise young men," Angilia said as the family watched the twins' graduation from Heaven.

"Yes, they are, Angel. Valdavia is very blessed to have them both," Eric said and kissed the top of his daughter's head.

"Yes, indeed, mi nieta. I may not have lived to meet them, but I love them very much," Juanita said while Alejandro and Eduardo hugged her.

"My babies are men now, fine, godly men. Oh, they are indeed destined for great things. I am so happy," Julianne gushed, and hugged everyone, including her parents.

"Their love for you is so vibrant and beautiful, Julianne. It always has been. You are as alive and real to them as Mommy always was to me," Angilia said and kissed her beloved mother. "There is no love to compare to a mother's love."

"No, there isn't," Eduardo whispered and kissed his mother's cheek.

§§§§

"Good morning. I am Stacy Williamson, and I welcome you to Valdavian News on this glorious Friday morning, January 3, 2076. Today marks two important milestones. Servant of God Queen Angilia was born 80 years ago today. The world has very good cause to celebrate Her Majesty's life, as she is on the path to sainthood. Thousands of pilgrims are in Valmondois, many of them already praying at Queen Angilia's statue in King Eric Celebratory Park. In fact, one man has been at the statue all week, fasting and praying to Queen Angilia. He would not cease his prayers to speak with us, but his friend, who made the pilgrimage with him, did tell us that the man is praying for his daughter, who is suffering from one of the most fatal types of childhood cancer, diffuse intrinsic pontine glioma, a brainstem tumor. The friend informed us that surgical intervention is futile, which is why this father made the pilgrimage to

Valmondois. We certainly extend our thoughts to him and his daughter.

"In lighter news, today sees the release of The Angilia DeBruce Martineau Collection, a comprehensive collection of Angilia's recorded work. This collection includes every song Angilia recorded, from the very first at the age of six to the last, not long before her death. This is the most extensive collection of Angilia's music ever produced. This includes her instrumentals, her solo performances, and those with Tom Greenfield, as well as her recordings with her father King Eric, her uncle Prince Patrick, and her husband Matthew, Duc de Valmondois. As a bonus, also included are King Eric's and Prince Patrick's solo recordings.

"This collection was a labor of love, first proposed by the music faculty at Angilia's alma mater and home of the Eric DeBruce Martineau Scholarship for Musical Excellence, the University of Oxford. This beautiful collection also contains an essay written by Her Majesty's son, King Eric II, and a photograph album spanning her career. What a wonderful tribute to this amazing woman, as well as a reminder of her remarkable talent."

§§§§

"Eric, turn on the news!" Yvonne screamed as she rushed into his office not long after lunch that day. Leigh ran from his office into Eric's, wondering what was wrong.

Eric looked visibly worried as he turned on the news. "We're just getting the official statement," Valdavian News Network anchor Beverly Willis announced. "The Pope has issued a Decree of a Miracle, which makes Queen Angilia henceforth the Venerable Servant of God Queen Angilia. This means one true miracle has been credited to Queen Angilia since her death.

"In March 2070, Gwen Jordan's breast cancer metastasized, and her oncologists believed she had mere months of life left. From her hospital bed, Gwen prayed without ceasing to Queen Angilia, asking to be cured. Gwen's husband and two teenaged children likewise prayed to Queen Angilia. Not long after, the oncologists found that Gwen's tumors, which had spread to her liver, lymph nodes, bones, and brain, had shrunk. Within a week, Gwen was declared cancer free.

"Gwen's case has been thoroughly examined and verified by both the Scientific Commission, which concluded that Gwen's healing was not due to medical treatments, and the Theological Commission, which determined that this miracle resulted from Queen Angilia's intercession.

"Ladies and gentlemen, the Holy Father's approval of this Decree of a Miracle means that the Venerable Servant of God Queen Angilia will be beatified. She will, at that point, become Blessed Queen Angilia. That is the final stage before she is canonized as Saint Angilia.

"What a glorious announcement on the 80th anniversary of Angilia's birth. We will of course keep you informed as new details are made available."

Eric sat rigid in his desk chair, while Yvonne and Leigh stared at the screen. Suddenly, the twins ran up the stairs shouting for their father. Eric regained his senses as they breathlessly rushed into his office.

"Dad, did you hear? About Grandmother?" Prince Eric panted.

"Yeah, she's one step closer to being Saint Angilia!" Prince Patrick exclaimed.

"Yes, Eric and Patrick. We just saw the news," Eric replied as his, Yvonne's and Leigh's phones began ringing. As the three of them were in the throes of the deluge, Billy arrived.

The twins had known him all of their lives. They warmly greeted him, and then excitedly explained about their grandmother. "I know. That's why I'm here. I knew this onslaught would happen, so I came to help out. Excuse me." Billy took the phone in Leigh's office, and sent Leigh to handle the calls in Eric's office.

Eric was grateful, as he and his sons were overwhelmed by the announcement. They had little time to gather their thoughts before Shannon, Nicole, William, Darlene, and Scott arrived. The lifelong friends were understandably excited, so Eric and the twins went to the second floor sitting room with them.

Before anyone could say or do anything, a sobbing Darlene grabbed Eric in a hug. "Oh, Eric, I am so happy. My friend is practically a Saint. Well, she is a Saint, but I mean in the eyes of the Church."

"Thank you, Darlene. This has been a whirlwind experience. I expected the entire process to take years," Eric replied.

"It often does, but in cases like Angilia's, the facts are pretty easy to verify. Her life was so public that an extensive investigation wasn't needed. The Guild spoke with all of us months before they approached you. Shannon and Nicole witnessed at least three of Angilia's miracles, so they provided eyewitness testimony," Scott explained.

"We were happy to do anything to help. We were thrilled when the Guild contacted us," Shannon added.

"Yes, we were. I never doubted that Angilia's cause would be approved. This is just public confirmation of what we've known since 2012," Nicole beamed.

"This never really surprised me, I've got to tell you. It is exciting to know that our friend will be publicly acknowledged this way for all time," William said.

"I know. This is awesome. If ever there was a true Saint, it's our grandmother," Prince Patrick said.

"I just hope I live long enough to see her Rite of Canonization. I'm 82, and I know I won't live nearly as long as King Eric did." Darlene dreamily sighed. "Gosh, I do miss him. But every day that passes, I'm one day closer to seeing him again!" she gleefully said and hugged Scott. "And Angilia, too."

CHAPTER 4

"Oh, Daddy, isn't this just glorious?"

Eric smiled at his beaming daughter as they rode Midnight and Starlight over the lushest, greenest meadow. "Yes, it is, my beautiful daughter Angilia. We should have asked someone to come with us so Rocket could enjoy the ride, too."

"Hey, Eric. Hey, Little One," Patrick greeted them as he and Rocket caught up.

"Uncle Patrick! You brought Rocket!" Angilia smiled and reached over to rub Rocket's head. "Daddy just said we should have asked someone to ride Rocket with us, and here you are!"

Patrick giggled. "Yeah, I've ridden him a lot since he came here. I know Eric misses him, but he knows Rocket is here waiting for him."

Angilia smiled at her uncle and her father. "I love you both so very much. Do you know how utterly wonderful it is to be here with you both?"

Eric smiled and softly said, "Yes, I do, Angel. Since you came here, I have felt more peaceful than ever."

Patrick smiled that charming slanted smile, and said, "Yeah, sure, I do. My niece and my brother. What more could I want?"

"Your friends?"

"Roger! Daniel! Hey, buddies, how's stuff?" Patrick greeted their friends.

"Stuff's fine," Roger giggled. "We just wanted to see you all, and Marisol told us you'd gone horseback riding. We finally found you."

"Why don't we join you for a walk? We can let these handsome fellows run and play," Angilia suggested. She, Eric, and Patrick dismounted, and she kissed Starlight before the horses trotted away.

"I know I've told you this before, but dying and coming here was not as frightening as I feared," Roger said. "I was absolutely terrified of death, you know that," he said and looked at Angilia. "That day in the hallway, when I knew I was dying, I was so scared. But then I saw my dad, and I knew I'd be okay.

"See, my dad died at the age of 58 of a fatal heart attack. When I had that first heart attack, I thought the same thing was happening to me. It terrified me. I didn't want to die. I didn't. But when I had the second heart attack, I knew I was dying. I didn't want to, but I knew there was nothing I could do to stop it. Then Dad appeared, and I knew everything would be all right. I knew. And it has been all right. You were right, Patrick. The fear just went away, like that."

"Oh, Roger, when I saw your father appear that day, I knew you would be fine. I knew he would bring you to Heaven, and that you would see how absolutely glorious everything here is. The amazing thing about Heaven is that it instantly erases fear, doubt, and worry. Heaven really is the only perfect place to ever exist," Angilia proclaimed with a smile.

"It sure is," Daniel agreed. "I was asleep when I died, so I wasn't aware of it until it happened. Suddenly, my grandfather was beside me, and we came to Heaven together. It's not that I wanted to die and leave my friends and life on earth, but I have to say that being here is a total blast."

Patrick giggled. "It most definitely is. I wouldn't want to be anywhere else but here."

"Neither would I," Eric said with a smile and hugged his friends.

§§§§

Yvonne tapped on Eric's office door, and when he looked up at her, he became worried when he saw the tears in her eyes. He immediately stood, walked to her, and asked, "What's wrong, Yvonne?"

"Mom just called me. Dad died a little while ago."

Eric held his best friend close to him while she cried. He had known Nicole and William his entire life, and they were loyal friends. He knew his words would do little to comfort Yvonne, but he said, "I know how much you love him, and how much you will miss him. Come on, let me drive you home."

Eric and Yvonne arrived at her parents' home moments after the hearse left with William's body. Yvonne ran to her mother, and grabbed her in a tearful hug. "I don't know how I'll learn to live without him. I barely remember what life was like before I met him. I feel so lost right now," Nicole cried.

"I know, Mom," Yvonne cried. "Dad was always here for me, and I don't know what I'll do without him. I just hope he knew how much I love him."

Eric stood beside Nicole and Yvonne, and put his arms around them. "He did. He does, Yvonne. He always did, and he always will. He will always be with you, surrounding you with his love."

The next day, Eric and Leigh escorted Nicole and Yvonne to the crematorium where they picked up the urn containing William's ashes. Eric and Leigh stayed with them throughout the day as the four friends reminisced, shared laughter and tears, and ended the day with a heartfelt prayer said by Nicole.

"Dear God, Thank you for bringing William into my life so many years ago. Thank you for the unconditional love, friendship, and happiness that filled our lives. Thank you for the gift of our magnificent daughter, Yvonne, in whom I see so much of her father. I pray that you ease our pain as we learn to live without William. We know that his soul lives eternally with you in Heaven, and I pray that this truth carries Yvonne and me for the rest of our lives, until we reunite with William. Thank you for our wonderful, loving friends who fill our lives with hope and truth. We love you, and we anticipate our eternal lives in Heaven with you and our families. Amen."

William Christian Alexander

28 April 1991

3 June 2077

That whosoever believeth in him should not perish, but have eternal life.

--John 3:15

§§§§

Valmondois was filled with revelers whose screams, chants, and music filled the churchyard, the park, the streets, and the mall. The sounds awoke Eric, Leigh, Yvonne, and the twins who were home from university during summer vacation. Prince Patrick got dressed, went outside to the courtyard, and was instantly greeted with screams.

"What's going on?" he asked everyone.

"We want to see Patrick!" a woman in the crowd yelled.

"Oh, please ask your uncle to come!" another young woman pleaded.

"Huh? Isn't it awful early? What's with all the excitement today?" Prince Patrick asked.

"Because it's July 19th," yet another woman answered.

"Oh, okay, but it is very early. Everyone's still asleep. Just wait a little while, and I'll see what I can do. I promise."

Prince Patrick stumbled back upstairs, flung himself across his bed, and fell back asleep. A few hours later, his father listened to the morning news as he shaved.

"Today is July 19, 2077, the 100th anniversary of Prince Patrick's death. Hundreds of Patrick's fans have filled Valmondois to celebrate this anniversary. They began gathering at midnight at his grave in the Christ Church Valmondois Cemetery, the statues of his brother and his niece in King Eric Celebratory Park, and the mall outside the palace. We spoke with some of them before daybreak, and their desire is to see Prince Patrick manifest today. Given his track record, we have every confidence that Patrick will not disappoint his fans."

Eric smiled as he finished, well aware of his granduncle's popularity. Patrick was forever 19, handsome, charming, talented, and godly—what was there not to like? Eric realized that the noises he had heard earlier that morning came from Patrick's fans. Eric finished dressing, and stepped onto his sitting room balcony.

He could not help but see the hundreds of fans crowding the mall. He giggled, and decided to surprise them. He knocked on Prince Eric's suite door, which was opened by his dressed son. He then knocked on Prince Patrick's door, and roused the drowsy young man. "What are you doing sleeping in your clothes?" Eric asked his son.

"I didn't mean to, but I threw these clothes on to see what was going on a few hours ago. There's a bunch of Uncle Patrick's groupies out there. They want to see him," Prince Patrick explained.

"I know," Eric said. "Today is not just July 19th; it's the 100th anniversary of Uncle Patrick's death. His fans are celebrating, not mourning. I say we give them what they want. Let's call Uncle Patrick."

"Yeah, I promised them I'd do that after everyone woke up. This will be a hoot," Prince Patrick said.

Prince Eric laughed at how similar his brother was to their great-granduncle. "It sure will," he said.

"Uncle Patrick, can you come to the palace for a little while?" Eric asked out loud.

Less than one minute later, as he manifested, they heard Patrick say, "Sure. What's up?"

"You're the most wanted man today, Uncle Patrick," Prince Eric said.

"I am?"

"Absolutely. Hundreds of your fans are gathered outside, waiting to see you today. We thought it would be a nice treat if you visited with them. What do you say?" Eric asked.

"Yeah, sure, I always like doing that. What's the big deal about today, though?"

"Well, it's July 19, 2077 today," Prince Patrick said.

"Huh?" Patrick asked, confused. Suddenly he realized what the big deal was. "Oh, I get it. Let's go."

Within minutes, the four Royal men opened the front door and stepped onto the courtyard. At that moment, several hundred people erupted in screams. All of them were screaming for Patrick. Eric and his sons smiled as they watched Patrick greet and mingle with the hundreds of well-wishers who had come to commemorate him on this once-in-a-lifetime milestone.

As word spread of Patrick's manifestation, people ran to the mall from the park and the cemetery to see him. Patrick spent most of the day with his adoring fans. All of them were very aware of the phenomenon they experienced that day. How often did people get to see and to speak with someone 100 years after his death?

"I love you, Patrick. My grandmother loved you. How amazing is it that both of us saw you and met you? Having you here today is like the most awesome miracle," one young lady said to Patrick.

"It really is," another woman said. "Seeing you here today, 100 years to the day after your death, is proof of eternal life. You are the coolest angel ever."

§§§§

People had a very good reason to gather on the mall on November 17, which was Eric's 56th birthday and the twins' 21st birthdays. Sure enough, as they expected, Eric drove Prince Patrick and Leigh drove Prince Eric where most people went on their 21st birthdays—the Valmondois Bureau de Permis de Conduire. Everyone cheered them on their way, anxious to see the handsome young men driving the cars home after their driving tests.

As they had on Angilia's 21st birthday and on Eric's 21st birthday, crowds also awaited the Princes at the Bureau. The twins waved as they entered, never perturbed by peoples' interest in them. Both of them understood that the attention they received was due in large part to the love and respect people had for their family. Prince Eric and Prince Patrick were both aware of the privilege and the responsibility that came with their birthrights, and more importantly, they understood how important it was for them to help their fellow Valdavians.

Prince Eric and Prince Patrick registered for the written and eye examinations, and both waited until their numbers were called rather than cut line. Prince Patrick completed his examinations first, and he scored perfectly on both. Soon, he drove Leigh's car for his driving test. Several minutes later, Prince Eric finished his examinations and drove his father's car for his driving test. Eric and Leigh sat and waited in the Bureau lobby.

Eric smiled at Leigh when they heard the screams from outside nearly one hour later, and he knew that Prince Patrick had finished. Moments later, Prince Patrick and the driving instructor entered the Bureau, where the instructor congratulated Prince Patrick. A clerk took Prince Patrick's official picture, and prepared his driving license. While Patrick waited, everyone in the Bureau heard the eruption of screams outside, and knew that Prince Eric had just returned from his driving test.

Prince Eric and his instructor entered the Bureau, where Prince Eric was similarly congratulated. After he had his official picture taken, his driving license was also prepared. After both young men's' licenses were stamped and signed, the clerks handed the licenses to the Princes. Everyone inside applauded, which made them both blush. That only charmed and delighted people, especially the ladies present. The twins were asked to pose for a few pictures with their licenses, and they unquestioningly did so.

Moments later they, their proud father, and Leigh left the Bureau, only to face more applause and requests for pictures. The Royal Family happily obliged before Prince Patrick climbed into the driver's seat of his father's car. Prince Eric got into the driver's seat of Leigh's car. As they drove, they were saluted and cheered. They were besieged by more picture requests when they pulled into the palace courtyard, and the twins once more posed for their admirers.

Several minutes later, Prince Eric and Prince Patrick thanked everyone for their support and birthday wishes. The young men drove the cars into the garage, and entered the palace with their arms around their father. "Hey, Dad, Eric and I want to take you to dinner tonight. Just the three of us," Prince Patrick said.

"You've done so much for us, this is the least we can do for you. We made reservations at your favorite restaurant for 8:00," Prince Eric added. "Patrick will drive us there, and I'll drive us home. You don't have to do anything except enjoy the evening."

Eric turned, faced his sons, and hugged them. "How did I get so blessed? You guys are amazing. I love you both."

§§§§§

Father Fisher surprised Eric, the Princes, and Reverend Emerson by attending the Christmas 2077 midnight service. After the parishioners had left following the service, Father Fisher requested a meeting with the four men. Reverend Emerson invited them into his office, where Father Fisher told them why he had come. He had very special news to share with them on the holiest of days.

"The Venerable Servant of God Queen Angilia's Beatification Mass is scheduled to take place on Holy Saturday, April 2, 2078. The Beatification Mass typically occurs where the subject lived, which means that Venerable Servant of God Queen Angilia's Beatification Mass will take place here, at Christ Church Valmondois."

Prince Patrick began crying, and Eric put his hand on his son's back. He understood how emotional this process was for both of his sons. It was very emotional for him, as well. Suddenly, Prince Patrick pulled something from his jacket pocket and held it reverently. "I asked Grandfather for something of Grandmother's the day after her funeral. He gave me this. He had kept this since the day of Grandmother's shooting. He had a special wooden box where he kept his personal treasures, and this was among them. I carry it with me at all times, in my pocket."

Eric was stunned. He had never mentioned the wooden box and what it held. He had no idea that his son Patrick knew about that box. What had his father given Patrick? "What is it, son?"

"It's a piece of the white satin blouse that Grandmother was wearing when she was shot. Grandfather kept it as a tangible reminder of the miracle that brought him and Grandmother back together. He gave it to me, so that I could have a piece of her with me at all times," Prince Patrick revealed.

Prince Patrick handed the piece of cloth to his father, and Eric gently held it in his hand. Blood was visible on the cloth—his mother's blood. Tears filled his eyes, but he smiled at his son. "That is such a beautiful sentiment, Patrick. Thank you for sharing this special treasure with us on Christmas."

"Dad, Grandfather gave me something of Grandmother's, too," Prince Eric shared. He also removed something from his jacket pocket. "He gave me Grandmother's favorite pink hair ribbon." Prince Eric handed the ribbon to his father.

The twins looked at one another and nodded. "Dad, we know that Grandmother will be declared Saint Angilia, and we know that a Saint has relics. We want to give these as Grandmother's relics," Prince Patrick said.

"Yes, we do," Prince Eric said. "We are surrounded by Grandmother's possessions. She belongs to us, to the family, but in larger ways, she belongs to the world. We want these to be her relics."

Eric smiled and kissed both of his sons. "This is the most beautiful, selfless act anyone could do. I am indeed honored and blessed that you are my sons. These are perfect relics for your grandmother." Eric looked at Father Fisher, and handed the relics to him. "Thank you for supporting my mother's cause. Thank you for publicly acknowledging what mattered most to her."

"There could be no greater symbol of your grandmother's sanctity than these relics, especially today. Christmas 2077 marks 83 years since Venerable Servant of God Queen Angilia's soul entered her father's heart," Father Fisher said with tears in his own eyes.

§§§§

People began arriving in Valmondois in mid-March, more than two weeks before the Beatification Mass. By March 30, every hotel room in Valmondois and the surrounding cities was booked. Leigh and Yvonne worked overtime in coordination with Reverend Emerson and Archbishop Murphy from Rome, who had been sent ahead to prepare everything for the Mass. Prince Eric and Prince Patrick had been excused from classes during the week leading up to the Mass.

Eric and his sons met with the Archbishop on the morning of Thursday, March 31. "The Beatification Mass begins at 10:00 on Saturday morning. The Holy Father will arrive in Valmondois this afternoon, and he will preside at the Venerable Servant of God Queen Angilia's Beatification Mass.   The Holy Father does not preside at every Beatification Mass, but he wanted to preside over this Mass.

"A vigil usually takes place the night prior to the Mass. The vigil for the Venerable Servant of God Queen Angilia will be the night of Good Friday at Gateway Arena. I will be there to lead the faithful in prayer. You are not required to attend, but you are very welcome to attend," Archbishop Murphy explained.

"We want to be there, at least part of the night," Prince Patrick stated. His brother reaffirmed this, and Eric added his sentiments. "We have to be there for Grandmother."

"Venerable Servant of God Queen Angilia's coffin will be placed upon the Christ Church Valmondois altar at sunset tonight in a private ceremony. You will be there, as will Reverend Emerson, the Queen Angilia Guild, and military pallbearers. I will be there, along with the Holy Father.

"The coffin will be returned to its tomb before Easter Sunday services on April 3rd. The four relics of Venerable Servant of God Queen Angilia have been placed in three reliquaries that will be displayed for veneration during the Mass. We typically ask someone close to the Venerable person to carry the reliquary to and from the altar. Since there are three reliquaries, it is preferable to have three persons carry them. Do you have any preferences, Sir?" Archbishop Murphy asked Eric.

Eric looked at his sons and smiled. "I do. Since Patrick and Eric donated two of the relics, and were very close to their Grandmother, I think it would be most than appropriate if they carried the reliquaries containing the relics they donated. Do you want to do that?" Eric asked his sons.

Both young men had tears in their eyes. "I would be honored to do that for Grandmother," Prince Eric said.

"Yeah, so would I, Dad," Prince Patrick agreed.

Archbishop Murphy nodded his approval. "What about the third reliquary? Would you like to carry that one, Sir?"

"Actually, I know someone who deserves to do that more than I do. My Uncle Patrick," Eric said. "He has known Mommy for over 100 years. He's the only one who should do this."

"Did someone mention me?" Uncle Patrick asked with his charming slanted smile as he suddenly manifested.

"Yes, I did. During the Mass, Eric and Patrick are carrying the relics they donated. I would like for you to carry the third reliquary, Uncle Patrick. I can't think of anyone else who should do that."

"Really? Thank you! I'd be so honored to do that for Little One," Uncle Patrick said and hugged his grandnephew and great-grandnephews.

§§§§§

Eric and his sons went to the palace chapel late Thursday afternoon. They wanted to be alone and pray before the private ceremony began. Angilia's coffin would be placed for public veneration before, during, and after the Beatification Mass. Pilgrims would be allowed to file past her coffin and pray during the several hours leading up to the Mass. As much as Eric and the twins understood the great honor bestowed upon Angilia and the reverence people felt for her, the process itself was emotionally draining and overwhelming for them.

The three men bowed their heads in prayer as they stood in front of the small altar. Prince Patrick was especially emotional throughout his grandmother's canonization process, and he could not stop the tears from trickling down his cheeks as he prayed. Eric instinctively placed his hands on his sons' backs as they prayed.

"Grandmother!" Prince Patrick whispered suddenly. All three men felt warm air swirl around them—the same warm air that Eric had felt when he had first opened his mother's tomb. "She's here!"

"Yes, she is, Patrick and Eric. This is her way of giving us her blessing. This is her way of telling us that she's okay with what we're doing," Eric softly said.

"This is like a hug from Grandmother," Prince Eric smiled.

"Yeah, it is.   The safest place I've ever been is Grandmother's embrace. This feels just like that," Prince Patrick said as tears once more trickled from the corners of his eyes.

"I know, Patrick. Mommy's hug was the warmest, most loving one thing I have ever felt. Feeling her warm soul embrace us is no less loving. We know that she is with us forever and always, and that she is okay with everything that's happening," Eric said.

"I'm glad she let us feel her soul before the ceremony tonight. I do thank God that she is our grandmother," Prince Eric said as he smiled at his father and his brother.

§§§§

Shortly before sunset that evening, Eric, Prince Patrick, Prince Eric, and Uncle Patrick walked to the church. Hundreds of people were gathered along the streets and applauded the Royal Family when they arrived. The four men spent a few moments thanking those had come to pay respects to Angilia, and then entered the church for the private ceremony. Guards closed the church doors, and Reverend Emerson greeted them. Eric and his family warmly greeted the Guild members, Archbishop Murphy, and His Holiness.

Reverend Emerson blessed the proceedings with a prayer of thanksgiving for the life of Venerable Servant of God Queen Angilia.   After everyone repeated the Amen, Eric unlocked the Royal Vault, and the military pallbearers entered. Several moments later, they carried Angilia's white coffin to the altar, where they placed it on a bier bedecked with white and yellow roses. They saluted their Queen, and stood at attention. The Guild members, Reverend Emerson, and Archbishop Murphy bowed in reverence.

So, too, did His Holiness, who then spoke a prayer to Saint Mary, the "Hail Mary." When he finished, he made the sign of the cross and bowed once more. Before he left, His Holiness clasped Eric's hand in both of his and kissed it as a token of his blessing.

Eric, his sons, and his granduncle stood before Angilia's coffin and bowed their heads. They not only sent a prayer of thanksgiving to God, but sent their love to this remarkable woman who bound them together. When they finished, Reverend Emerson also gave them his blessings and bid them good night. The soldiers remained on guard in the church, which would stay unlocked so that pilgrims could pay their respects at Angilia's coffin. The church would remain open to the faithful until Saturday morning, a few hours before the Beatification Mass began.

When they left, the Royal Family was surrounded by dozens who were already waiting to pay homage to Angilia. People kissed their hands and cried, overcome with emotions as Angilia's beatification drew near. The four men spent more than two hours talking with people before they returned to the palace. The vigil began in 24 hours, and the Beatification Mass in 36 hours. They needed time to process their emotions throughout the very holy weekend.

§§§§

On Good Friday, Eric and his sons, accompanied by Leigh and two security officers, walked through Valmondois, beginning on the mall. They spent a couple of hours talking with people there before they moved on. Along the streets, people stopped them, offering their prayers and stories of Angilia. The three men smiled broadly, their hearts filled by the immense love and respect people had for Angilia.

They went to King Eric Celebratory Park, where they knew people were congregated at the statues of Angilia and Eric I. Eric and the Princes were immediately engulfed by dozens of people gathered in preparation for that night's vigil and for Saturday's Beatification Mass. Most of them were in the park to leave their prayer requests at Angilia's statue, and just as many shared stories of prayers they had previously left that had been answered.

"Thank you for loving Grandmother. She is such an amazing woman, and even though she is easy to love, so many people do love her for her benevolence. She means so much to me. I'll never know anyone like her," Prince Patrick said as a group of pilgrims told him how much they loved Angilia.

Eric spoke with another group, who likewise shared their admiration of Angilia. "Thank you. My mother lived such an amazing life here on earth, and she still lives that life in Heaven. I know how much she means to all of you, and that really does fill my heart with joy. I am so grateful that she is my mother, but just as grateful that she is an angel of God. She is the most remarkable person I will ever know," he said with his charming dimpled smile that was so similar to that of his revered grandfather who was depicted in the statue.

"God bless you, King Eric. You are your mother's son. We see so much of her character in you," a woman told him as she clutched his hand.

"Yes, and I also see her influence in these two young men," a man in the crowd said as he grabbed the Princes' arms.

"Thank you, sir. Our grandmother taught us so much, and we can only aspire to be half as godly as she," Prince Eric said. Prince Patrick nodded in agreement as tears filled his eyes.

The Royal party slowly walked through the park and the streets of downtown Valmondois. They were constantly surrounded by groups of people, all of them sharing their exhilaration about the impending Beatification Mass. A few hours later, the Royal party arrived at Christ Church Valmondois, which had a very long line of pilgrims waiting to file past Angilia's coffin.

As they made their way up the church stairs and into the nave, Eric, Prince Patrick, and Prince Eric greeted those who stood in line. They continued to shake each person's hand as they strode up the aisle toward the altar. Eric put his arms around his sons' shoulders, and they stepped upon the altar to face Angilia's coffin. The three men bowed their heads and prayed as pilgrims continued to walk slowly past Angilia's coffin. They were all there for the same reason—to honor her.

When the Royal party arrived back at the palace, they were once more enthusiastically greeted by hundreds of well-wishers. It was now early evening, and the vigil started in a few hours, but they spent more than an hour with those who had come for Angilia. Finally, they entered the palace so they could eat and write their reflections in their diaries. Each of them felt an overabundance of emotions, such as they had never felt before. They needed time to process their feelings as they lived through one of the most intense weeks of their lives.

§§§§

Eric had always been cognizant of the historical significance of his diaries, apart from the personal significance they held for him. He was, therefore, acutely aware of the importance of his insights, experiences, and feelings during his mother's canonization process. He knew that his descendants and historians would read and learn from his diaries.

April 1, 2078

This has been quite a whirlwind experience. Everything has happened so quickly. Father Fisher told me and the boys that the process leading up to Mommy's beatification is the shortest in modern history. The boys and I have barely had time to subsume everything that has happened so far and everything that is happening this weekend.

She has always been Mommy to me. She has always been the one person above all people who made me feel love and faith. She made me feel important. Since I was a child, I have felt a special bond with her that is difficult to explain. She has always seemed to be part of me, part of my soul, in a far deeper way than anyone else. There is a part of me that has felt empty since her death, and no one else can fill that hole. That hole will remain unfilled until I die and join her in Heaven.

She is Mommy, yes, but since early childhood I have understood that she is far more than that. When I was a very young child, she, Grandfather, and Dad started explaining that she would become the Queen de Valdavia. They explained what that meant, and that she would work on behalf of the country and its people, doing what is best for both. When she was coronated, I was eight years old, and I understood that she really was more than my mother—she belonged to the world, as well.

In many ways, she has belonged to the world since her birth. She was an internationally-famous songwriter and performer, a best-selling author, and a professor. Through her multiple roles, Mommy touched so very many people. She helped people as a teacher, as a performer, as the Queen, and as intercessor for God. Her entire life has been spent as a global citizen, someone whose reach extends far beyond the walls of our house or the borders of our country. She truly belongs to the world.

Mommy's canonization process continues this. Tomorrow she becomes Blessed Queen Angilia. Yes, this process acknowledges her godliness, but more than that, it symbolizes the fact that she belongs to everyone, everywhere. She is forever my mother, but she is an Angel of God, and as such she does belong to the world as long as people exist.

§§§§§

Prince Eric also understood the historical importance of his diaries, and like his father, he was astutely aware of the fortunate perspective he had during Angilia's canonization process. Since he was destined to be the future King de Valdavia, he knew that his diaries would be studied long after his death. Although his grandmother's beatification was a personal event, it was also a global event, and his diary reflected that.

1 April 2078

Tomorrow, Grandmother becomes Blessed Queen Angilia. This means that the Catholic Church believes that she is in Heaven and intercedes on behalf of those who pray to her. This is public acknowledgment of what I have known since the day she died. Grandmother's life as an Angel of God is well known, and her beatification is actually no surprise to me.

I was born knowing her as Grandmother, not Queen Angilia or a famous performer. She is still Grandmother to me—she always will be. She is the one who held me, who fed me bottles, who bathed me, who played with me, who read to me, who sang lullabies to me, who taught me, who loved me. I never knew her as anyone other than Grandmother until I was nine years old.

Still, that never changed our relationship or how I felt for her. Actually, the older I got and the more I realized everything she did, I did grow to admire her and love her even more. She did so very much for so very many people for her entire life. To me, that is what tomorrow is all about.

I love her, and I am so thankful and blessed to know her. Having her honored in this way tells me that the world sees and feels her good works. This is

99

just public acknowledgment of what we, her family and friends, have always known—Grandmother is a Saint.

§§§§

Prince Patrick was also quite aware of the historical importance of the Royal Family's diaries. Nonetheless, he was too sensitive to focus on the historic perspective of his grandmother's beatification. His entry on Good Friday evening was written entirely from his heart, capturing for all time the emotions of Angilia's now-adult youngest grandson.

1 April 2078

Grandmother, oh how I love you! I always have, and I always will. You are the most incredible person I will ever know. My earliest memory is about you. I don't remember much from before the age of four, but I do have one memory from when I was a baby. You were holding me. You fed me my bottle, and then you held me for a long time. You gently rocked me in your arms, trying to soothe me to sleep. I remember you leaning down to kiss my forehead, and your long blonde hair cascading forward over your shoulder. I remember grabbing your hair with my hand and holding it. I remember that made you laugh, and how beautiful that sounded. I remember that you kissed my nose, and told me that you love me. I remember you gently singing the lullaby you wrote for Eric and me. I remember listening to you and looking into your eyes. I remember feeling something I had no way of understanding at that time. I do now. I felt your love. I felt it flow through my veins.

I still feel your love. I know you feel mine. I know you understand everything I'm feeling now. I am so happy that the world publicly acknowledges who you really are. Before I knew the truth about you, I intuitively knew that truth. I could feel it. No one has had to tell me that you are a Saint. I know you are, have always been, and will always be a Saint, Grandmother.

§§§§

1 April 2078

Uncle Patrick told me the date and that today is Good Friday .   He has also told me what is occurring in Valmondois tonight and tomorrow.   He said that tonight there is a vigil in Gateway Arena, and that thousands of people are expected to attend. Tomorrow, on Holy Saturday, is the Beatification Mass. The Pope is there, and will preside over the Mass.

This is too much for me. I am not extraordinary. I have simply done what I knew God wanted me to do. I always strove to honor him in all I do, foremost because I love him. I owe my incredibly blessed life to him. After all that he has done for and given to me, the least I can do is to live my life for him. After all, I would not have a life were it not for him.

God created me. He gave me life. He gifted me to my beautiful mother and my magnificent father—how I love them so! He brought Matthew and me together on earth so that we could marry and bring life to our precious Eric. Through Eric, we are gifted with our grandsons, Eric and Patrick. My life is so amazingly blessed! Why wouldn't I want to use that life to honor God and to do his work?

I knew from my earliest life in the Unborn Children Sphere that God has a purpose, a destiny, for me, and it never occurred to me to ignore that. He knows what is best for me. He knows more about me than I shall ever know. I trust him completely. I love him completely.

When Uncle Patrick first told me about the canonization process, I admit that it made me uncomfortable. Michael, however, quickly eased my concerns. This is not about me as much as it is about honoring and obeying God. He told me that my life is one example of a life lived entirely in the service of God. My life can serve as a model for people, an inspiration to people, he explained. That did help. Besides, if he and God approve of this, then who am I to disapprove? Doing so would be an act of disobedience itself, and that is unthinkable to me.

§§§§

"Hey, Little One, it's about time I head to earth and get ready for tonight's vigil," Patrick told her as she sat with Eric, Marisol, and Matthew. "Is there anything in particular you want me to wear?" he asked her.

Angilia stood, put her hands on her uncle's shoulders, and said, "It doesn't matter to me what you wear, Uncle Patrick. You will look handsome, as always. Would you please do me a favor, though?"

"Sure thing, just tell me what."

"Tell Eric and the boys how very much I love them. Tell them that I am always with them, and always will be."

"Of course I'll tell them, Little One, but they know that. They've always known that," Patrick told her with a smile.

Eric, Marisol, and Matthew also stood, and they hugged Angilia and Patrick. "None of this is any surprise to me. I've seen how ordained and consecrated you are since your birth. All of this is just what Eric wrote in his diary—public acknowledgment of that. I've always known how very unique and special you are, my beautiful daughter Angilia," Eric told her and kissed the top of her head.

"Your daddy is right, mi hija Angilia. I have seen how sanctified you are as I watched you from Heaven your entire life," Marisol softly said and kissed her daughter's cheek.

"I knew there was something mystical about you from the beginning. I told Eric that when we were in Oxford. I didn't know, or remember, anything about you, but I knew, somewhere in my soul, the truth about you. I realized on our honeymoon in Scotland that, even though I share an incomparable relationship with you, you belong to the world. You do, my Angilia, my Blessed Angilia," Matthew softly said as tears filled his amber eyes.

"Yeah, none of this really surprises the rest of us angels here in Heaven. We've always known the truth about you, Little One," Patrick said, kissed her cheek, and flashed a peace sign as he flew to earth.

§§§§§

"Good evening. I am Joseph Gibbons, and I am coming to you live from outside the Gateway Arena in downtown Valmondois. The Venerable Servant of God Queen Angilia Vigil begins in just over two hours, at 10:00. As you can see, thousands of pilgrims are patiently waiting to enter the arena for tonight's vigil. They are here to pray throughout the night to Queen Angilia, who tomorrow morning at 10:00 becomes Blessed Queen Angilia.

"Valdavian News Network will bring you Venerable Servant of God Queen Angilia's Beatification Mass live from Christ Church Valmondois tomorrow. The mass has drawn record numbers to Valmondois, and will be attended not only by pilgrims from around the world, but by heads of state. Among the guests attending the mass tomorrow are the President of the United States, the President of France, the President of Spain, the Prime Minister of Canada, the President of Zimbabwe, the President of Italy, the Prime Minister of Australia, the Prime Minister of New Zealand, as well as the five men who formed the Queen Angilia Guild and promoted her cause.

"The Pope himself will preside over the Beatification Mass, during which he will proclaim Venerable Servant of God Queen Angilia as Blessed Angilia. This has been the fastest beatification process in modern history, the previous record being the beatification process of Mother Teresa in 2003. After tomorrow's mass, Blessed Queen Angilia's cause has but one more stage to complete before her canonization. That stage is the scientific and theological proofs of a second posthumous miracle attributed to Blessed Angilia's intercession. Once that second miracle passes both the scientific and theological tests, it will be placed before the Pope for his approval. When he gives his approval, Blessed Angilia's canonization will move forward, and she will be declared Saint Angilia.

"Tonight's vigil will be led by Archbishop Murphy, who traveled from Rome, and will be attended by King Eric II, his sons Princes Eric and Patrick, and his granduncle Prince Patrick. We will return to our live coverage of the Venerable Servant of God Queen Angilia Vigil shortly before it begins. Thank you for joining us."

§§§§

The Royal Family, with Leigh and Yvonne, arrived at Gateway Arena at 9:00 that evening to welcome as many people as they could. The sight of Angilia's son, grandsons, and uncle deeply touched everyone, all of whom clamored to touch them. The arena doors opened at 9: 15, and people began filling the seats on the main level. It did not take long before the second level and the balcony began to fill, as well.

The Royal Family continued to greet people as they filed into the arena. Shortly before 10:00, the Royal party entered the arena. As they made their way up the center aisle, people continued to reach for them. The four Royal men shook as many hands as they could before they reached their reserved seats in the front row. There, they were greeted by the Guild members and Archbishop Murphy.

Archbishop Murphy stepped up on the stage at 10:00, at which time he welcomed everyone to the Venerable Servant of God Queen Angilia Vigil. At that moment, a large banner depicting a smiling Angilia was revealed at center stage. The crowd erupted in cheers at the site of their beloved Queen Angilia. Chants of "God Bless the Venerable Servant of God Queen Angilia" filled the arena for several moments. Prince Patrick pulled his handkerchief from his jacket pocket and dabbed the tears from his eyes. Eric put his arm around his son in support; he, too, became quite emotional. Prince Eric in turn put his arm around his father, sensing how emotional the weekend was for him.

Uncle Patrick took that moment to give them Angilia's message. "Hey, guys, Angilia asked me to tell you tonight how very much she loves you. She also told me to tell you that she is with you, always and forever. I told her you know that, and she nodded but said she just wanted me to tell you that tonight especially."

Prince Patrick grabbed his great-granduncle in a tearful hug, and said, "Tell her how very much I love her, too."

Prince Eric stood and hugged his Uncle Patrick also. "Ditto. Tell her how much I love her."

"Add me to the list, Uncle Patrick. Tell Mommy how very, very much I love her."

"Sure," Patrick replied just as Archbishop Murphy led the thousands of people in the first prayer of many said that night. The four members of the Royal Family held hands as they prayed unceasingly for hours. Many people began praying on their own, with thousands of voices raised in prayer to Angilia. By 1:30, the arena was filled with a mixture of joyous and somber prayers in unison. Hundreds of people cried as they prayed, while others sang gospel songs.

The sights and sounds mingled to create one of the most emotionally-charged events the Princes had ever experienced. It all became too intense for the sensitive Prince Patrick, and he began crying. Those sitting behind him could not help but notice, and many of them placed their hands on his shoulders and back. Their intention was to comfort him, but he was so overcome by emotion that he cried even harder. Prince Eric reached over and held his brother's hand, an act of love that made other people cry.

It was at that moment that Eric told Leigh and Yvonne that it was time for them to leave. He knew how extraordinarily poignant the next day would be for him and especially for his sons, and he did not want them to become emotionally exhausted. "Patrick and Eric, I think it's time we go home and try to get at least a little rest before the mass begins tomorrow. The last thing your grandmother wants is for you to become upset or ill over this. Come on," Eric told his sons. Prince Eric agreed, and Prince Patrick nodded.

"Yeah, that's probably the best thing. You go home and get some rest, and I'll see you tomorrow. I'm going to stay here for the rest of the vigil," Uncle Patrick told them. Eric thanked him, and gave him a hug of gratitude.

Eric put his arm around Prince Patrick as they walked down the center aisle of the arena and left. Prince Eric, Leigh, and Yvonne followed them. At home on the third floor, Prince Eric helped his brother take off his suit and get ready for bed.

Prince Eric knew how much things such as the vigil affected his brother, and his love made him want to help Prince Patrick. Unbeknownst to them, Angilia watched them from Heaven with an overabundance of love for them. As Prince Eric hugged his brother before he went next door to his own suite, they felt a familiar warmth envelop them. "Oh, Grandmother, I love you," Prince Patrick said through his tears as the twins embraced.

§§§§

Eric and his sons awoke very early Saturday morning. They knew how overwhelming and poignant that day would be for them, and none of them could sleep much. Instead, they showered and dressed, after which Eric went to the kitchen for a cup of coffee. He was soon joined by Prince Eric and Uncle Patrick.

"Hey, guys. The vigil ended just about an hour ago, so I came here to change into Little One's favorite suit. How are you guys?"

"We're okay," Eric replied. "This is all extremely emotional for us all, especially Patrick. But we're all right."

"It is a bit overwhelming, but we all realize what this really means. Grandmother's work on behalf of God is immortalized forever. That is pretty awesome, and it shows that people respond to her," Prince Eric said just as his brother entered the kitchen.

"Yes, it does. Everyone recognizes Grandmother's piety. All of this goes back to something she once said about you, Uncle Patrick. She said that your singing career had a purpose. She said people were drawn by your handsome looks, your charm, and your talent, but then people were drawn to God through you, just by how you live. The same is true about Grandmother," Prince Patrick said.

"That's beautiful, Patrick. It's also very true. Mommy never preached or forced her beliefs on other people. She just lived her life, and that is what taught people how to live godly lives. She was always just herself, a servant of God, and that is what today is all about," Eric said.

§§§§

The Royal Family, Leigh, and Yvonne arrived at Christ Church Valmondois one hour before the Beatification Mass began. Valmondois was standing room only as people packed practically every square inch in order to see Angilia's beatification. Large screens had been set up throughout Valmondois so that the pilgrims could witness the mass. Eric, his sons, and his granduncle spent a few moments greeting people before they entered the church.

The church itself was already filled to capacity, and they welcomed invited guests and pilgrims alike as they made their way to the front of the church. There, they greeted their lifelong friends Shannon, Nicole, Darlene, Scott, and Billy, all of whom had what Angilia had perpetually called happy tears in their eyes. As usual, Darlene openly wept, and she grabbed Eric in a hug with one arm. She now used a cane, as she had become rather feeble at 85. "Oh, Eric, I can just imagine how proud your handsome grandfather is as he watches our Angilia's Beatification Mass," she said, not seeming to care that the whole world heard her. Eric smiled, thanked her, and then greeted the Queen Angilia Guild.

Archbishop Murphy briefly spoke to the Royal Family, directing Prince Eric, Prince Patrick, and Patrick where to go stand with the others who were in the processional. They would carry the reliquaries and place them on the altar for veneration. They would also carry the reliquaries to His Holiness for blessing during the mass. At the end of the mass, they would carry the reliquaries in the recessional. The three men hugged Eric before they joined Reverend Emerson and the other holy men who would participate in the processional.

As the processional began, the church pianist began playing Gounod's "Ave Maria." Patrick, Prince Eric, and Prince Patrick led the processional as they held the reliquaries. The three men stopped before a special altar that had been built for the mass, and placed the reliquaries on top. They bowed their heads in reverence before they joined Eric in the pew. Deacons, Bishops, Archbishops, and other clergy followed. They slowly walked past the altar, stopping to bow in veneration. Reverend Emerson, Pope Romanus, and his Magistri Caerimoniarum Apostolicarum, his Masters of Apostolic Ceremonies, completed the processional.

Pope Romanus stopped at the altar to give his veneration to the reliquaries. He knelt to his knees in prayer, and then lit incense within a thurible. He waved the incense above the reliquaries as a symbol of purification and sanctification. Prince Patrick removed his handkerchief and dabbed tears from the corners of his eyes at that moment. Eric patted his son on the shoulder in solidarity. Next, Pope Romanus stood at the foot of Angilia's coffin with his head bowed for a moment. He knelt and kissed her coffin, an act symbolic of his recognition of her sanctity.

Reverend Emerson took his seat to the left of the altar, while Pope Romanus was assisted to his chair, which had been placed at the head of the apse. Pope Romanus stood until the hymn concluded, and then he sat upon his chair. One of the Magistri Caerimoniarum Apostolicarum removed the Pope's mitre and replaced it with a skullcap.

Reverend Emerson stood and went to a microphone to the left of the altar. "Holy Father, we welcome you to Valmondois. Your service to God inspires and influences thousands, and you have blessed Valdavia with your presence. We are honored to have you preside over the Beatification Mass of Venerable Servant of God Queen Angilia, whose own service to God maintains a strong influence over all. May God bless you always."

Pope Romanus presented a golden chalice to Reverend Emerson, who in turn gave a leather-bound volume of Angilia's memoir, <u>My Life In Heaven and Earth</u>, to Pope Romanus.

The Pope stood for the prayer of the mass. "In the name of the Father, and of the Son, and of the Holy Spirit, peace be with you. My Brothers and Sisters, in order to prepare ourselves to celebrate the sacred mysteries, let us call to mind our sins. I confess to almighty God, and to you, my brothers and sisters, that I have sinned through my own fault, in my thoughts and in my words, in what I have done, and in what I have failed to do; and I ask blessed Mary, ever virgin, all the angels and saints, and you, my brothers and sisters, to pray for me to the Lord, our God. May almighty God have mercy on us, forgive us our sins, and bring us to everlasting life. Amen." One of the Magistri Caerimoniarum Apostolicarum replaced the Pope's mitre at that moment.

Everyone repeated the Amen. The choir then sang one of King Eric I's favorite hymns, "I Vow to Thee My Country," one of the emotional high points thus far.

Archbishop Clancy, head of St. Joseph's Church in Valmondois, stepped to the microphone. "Most Holy Father, the

Archbishop of Valmondois humbly requests Venerable Servant of God Queen Angilia be proclaimed Blessed." Archbishop Clancy bowed and resumed his seat.

Next, the Archbishop of Paris, Cardinal Jéan Beau, stepped to a microphone to the right of the altar. His participation symbolized the eternal connection between France and Valdavia. Cardinal Beau, as the head of Cathédrale Notre Dame de Paris, represented the nation of France at Angilia's Beatification Mass. He was honored with the task of providing a detailed biography of Angilia, which highlighted her obedience and service to God throughout her a very public life.

After Cardinal Beau took his seat, Pope Romanus stood for the climax of the mass. "Acceding to the request of our brother Bernard Clancy, Archbishop of Valmondois, and of many other of our brothers in the episcopate and many faithful, and after consultation with the Congregation for the Causes of Saints, by our apostolic authority we declare that the Venerable Servant of God Queen Angilia shall henceforth be invoked Blessed, and that her feast shall be celebrated every year on the 17 of November in the places and according to the norms established by church law. In the name of the Father, and of the Son, and of the Holy Spirit. Amen."

At that moment, a fanfare resounded, and it seemed that the whole nation of Valdavia erupted in thunderous cheers, screams, and applause. Even those inside the church stood and applauded. Angilia's family and friends were overcome with a plethora of emotions. Darlene once more openly wept, but she was not the only one. Shannon, Nicole, and Yvonne also cried, and even Scott and Billy shed tears. Billy and Yvonne had known Angilia their entire lives, while the COC friends had met her 66 years earlier.

What had begun as a request for her to become their Christ on Campus sponsor and advisor had forged friendships that lasted the rest of Angilia's life. Shannon, Billy, and Yvonne even worked for the Royal Family. Angilia had befriended Billy when he was four years old and besotted with her. She had been Yvonne's godmother, the one woman above all whom Nicole wanted to give that honor. A lifetime of memories and emotions flooded them at the moment that their friend was proclaimed Blessed Queen Angilia.

Prince Patrick and Prince Eric could not help but cry, their love for their grandmother so immense that their hearts overflowed. They had learned about God and learned to love God by listening to their grandmother tell them about his wondrous work, blessings, and love for them. How could they not love God when they had learned about him from one of his angels?

Eric bowed his head as the enormity of his mother's status became reality. He had loved her completely from the beginning of his life. She felt such a part of him that at times it was almost too much to feel. Eric never fully understood this feeling, and he could never truly articulate it, but he did know that it was real. It consumed his soul.

Uncle Patrick sat between his great-grandnephews, his arms around them, and beamed. He loved his niece tremendously, and had since he had met her 101 years earlier. Angilia was Patrick's savior. She instantly erased his fears about what came after death. One look at the beautiful angel who was his Spirit Guide showed him what happened—eternal life, pure and splendid. Angilia had made that abstract a concrete reality for the teenager.

The applause inside the church lasted for more than 15 minutes as Pope Romanus smiled. Although the cheers and applause outside continued, when the church grew quiet, the choir sang a hymn that had been written especially for Angilia's Beatification Mass, "Blessed Angel on High."

Prince Patrick looked up at the Stations of the Cross that had been in the church for more than 100 years. He stared at the 12th Station of the Cross—Jesus dying on the cross—and recalled his grandmother telling him about Jesus' murder and suffering. He prayed his thanksgiving for that gift while tears filled his eyes and love filled his heart.

Blessed Angel on high we see

The life we should live under God,

The service that will set us free.

Blessed Angel, behind you we plod.

Blessed Angel for us intercede.

Carry our prayers before dear God

So that he will meet our urgent needs.

Blessed Angel behind you we trod.

Blessed Angel, you teach us grace

In the face of trials and sorrows

So that Holy God maintains first place.

Blessed Angel, to God all we owe.

Blessed Angel for us be the light

That guides us to Holy God above,

Forever shining oh so bright.

Blessed Angel, our beacon of love.

After the hymn, Uncle Patrick, Prince Eric, and Prince Patrick stood. Uncle Patrick was escorted to the altar, where he picked up the reliquary containing the bullet and the bone fragment. He carried the reliquary to the Pope's chair and knelt before him. The pope lifted the reliquary while Patrick held it, and he venerated it with a kiss. He then placed his hand on Patrick's head and blessed him. Patrick kissed the Pope's hand in reverence. He then stood, returned the reliquary to the altar and stood to the side until his great-grandnephews finished.

Prince Eric was then escorted to the altar, where he picked up the reliquary containing his grandmother's hair ribbon. He, too, knelt before the Pope's chair, where the Pope venerated the reliquary with a kiss. He then placed his hand on Prince Eric's head and blessed him. Prince Eric kissed the Pope's hand, as well. Prince

Eric walked to the altar, returned the reliquary, and stood beside Uncle Patrick.

Prince Patrick was likewise escorted to the altar, and he picked up the reliquary containing the piece of his grandmother's blouse. Like his uncle and his brother, he knelt before the Pope's chair. Pope Romanus had noticed Prince Patrick's emotionalism, and he gently clasped the young man's hands as he lifted the reliquary for the veneration. He placed one hand upon Prince Patrick's head and blessed him, but then placed both of his hands on Prince Patrick's shoulders and quietly told him, "May God continue to bless you." Prince Patrick was moved, and he kissed both of the Pope's hands. With tears shining in his eyes, Prince Patrick returned the reliquary to the altar, and then joined his brother and his uncle to return to the Royal Family's pew.

The entire congregation stood and sang the hymn "Glory to God in the Highest" with the choir. As he sang, Eric silently offered his thanksgiving to God for his family. He knew how blessed he was, and like his mother, he never took his blessings for granted.

At the conclusion of the hymn, everyone remained standing, and the Pope stood. "Let us pray," he commanded. Everyone bowed their heads. "Oh God, Bestow upon Blessed Queen Angilia the light of your heavenly kingdom, and through your grace grant peace in your church. Grant that through your grace and the power and example of Blessed Queen Angilia's intercession and example we may belong to the fullness of your love, through the gift of your Son Jesus Christ and the glory of the Holy Spirit, and know that there is one God forever and ever. Amen."

At that moment, the now-76-year-old Jack Cornwell stepped to the pulpit. Angilia's prayers had led to his cure from lung cancer in 2036. Jack's wife Tammy and their daughter smiled from the pew, forever aware of how blessed they and Jack were. "I would like to read Psalms 5, which was one of Blessed Queen Angilia's favorite chapters in the Bible. *'(To the chief Musician upon Nehiloth, A Psalm of David.) Give ear to my words, O LORD, consider my meditation. Hearken unto the voice of my cry, my King, and my God: for unto thee will I pray. My voice shalt thou hear in the morning, O LORD; in the morning will*

I direct my prayer unto thee, and will look up. For thou art not a God that hath pleasure in wickedness: neither shall evil dwell with thee. The foolish shall not stand in thy sight: thou hatest all workers of iniquity. Thou shalt destroy them that speak leasing: the LORD will abhor the bloody and deceitful man. But as for me, I will come into thy house in the multitude of thy mercy: and in thy fear will I worship toward thy holy temple. Lead me, O LORD, in thy righteousness because of mine enemies; make thy way straight before my face. For there is no faithfulness in their mouth; their inward part is very wickedness; their throat is an open sepulchre; they flatter with their tongue. Destroy thou them, O God; let them fall by their own counsels; cast them out in the multitude of their transgressions; for they have rebelled against thee. But let all those that put their trust in thee rejoice: let them ever shout for joy, because thou defendest them: let them also that love thy name be joyful in thee. For thou, LORD, wilt bless the righteous; with favour wilt thou compass him as with a shield.'"

After Jack took his seat, a soloist in the choir then sang the hymn "Holy God, We Praise Thy Name." Psalms 5 was indeed one of Angilia's favorite chapters. She had often read it to her grandsons, especially when they were quite young. Prince Patrick smiled as he recalled sitting attentively listening to her, her voice so resonant with emotion. She did not just read the chapter to Prince Patrick and Prince Eric, but had also explained its meaning and significance to their lives. She had taught them how to live godly lives, which Prince Patrick considered the most important lesson his grandmother had taught him.

After the hymn, 50-year-old Charlie Britt went to the pulpit. Angilia's intercession, her prayers, had led to his cure from bone cancer in 2038. "I will read Proverbs Chapter 3, which was written by King David's son Solomon. Angilia always had an affinity for David and Solomon, and she learned quite a lot from their wisdom. *'My son, forget not my law; but let thine heart keep my commandments: For length of days, and long life, and peace, shall they add to thee. Let not mercy and truth forsake thee: bind them about thy neck; write them upon the table of thine heart: So shalt thou find favour and good understanding in the sight of God and man. Trust in the LORD with all thine heart; and lean not unto thine own understanding. In all thy ways acknowledge him, and he shall direct thy paths. Be not wise in thine own eyes: fear the LORD, and depart from evil. It shall be health to thy navel, and marrow to thy bones. Honour the LORD with thy substance, and with the firstfruits of all thine increase: So shall thy barns be filled with plenty, and thy presses shall burst out with new wine. My son, despise not the chastening of the LORD; neither be weary of his correction: For whom the LORD loveth he correcteth; even as a father the son in whom he delighteth. Happy is the man that findeth wisdom, and the man that getteth understanding. For the merchandise of it is better than the merchandise of silver, and the gain thereof than fine gold. She is more precious than rubies: and all the things thou canst desire are not to be compared unto her. Length of days is in her right hand; and in her left hand riches and honour. Her ways are ways of pleasantness, and all her paths are peace. She is a tree of life to them that lay hold upon her: and happy is every one that retaineth her. The LORD by wisdom hath founded the earth; by understanding hath he established the heavens. By his knowledge the depths are broken up, and the clouds drop down the dew. My son, let not them depart from thine eyes: keep sound wisdom and discretion: So shall they be life unto thy soul, and grace to thy neck. Then shalt thou walk in thy way safely, and thy foot shall not stumble. When thou liest down, thou shalt not be afraid: yea, thou shalt lie down, and thy sleep shall be sweet. Be not afraid of sudden fear, neither of the desolation of the wicked, when it cometh. For the LORD shall be thy confidence, and shall keep thy foot from being taken. Withhold not good from them to whom it is due, when it is in the power of thine hand to do it. Say not unto thy neighbour, Go, and come again, and to morrow I will give; when thou hast it by thee. Devise not evil against thy neighbour, seeing he dwelleth securely by thee. Strive not with a man without cause, if he have done thee no harm. Envy thou not the oppressor, and choose none of his ways. For the froward is abomination to the LORD: but his secret is with the righteous. The curse of the LORD is in the house of the wicked: but he blesseth the habitation of the just. Surely he scorneth the scorners: but he giveth grace unto the lowly. The wise shall inherit glory: but shame shall be the promotion of fools.'"*

When Charlie returned to his seat, the choir sang a hymn written by Saint Thomas Aquinas, "Panis Angelicus." Prince Eric smiled at Uncle Patrick, who took ahold of the young man's hand. The Beatification Mass was both beautiful and emotional for everyone present or watching around the world. However, no people were as affected as were Angilia's son, grandsons, and uncle.

Eleanor Hale, now 23 years old, next walked to the pulpit. It was due to Angilia's prayer that Eleanor could walk. Eleanor had been unable to walk from birth until one summer day in 2069, months before Angilia's death. That day, her Queen had prayed to God that he heal Eleanor and enable her to walk. He did. So it was that a beaming, emotional Eleanor attended Blessed Queen Angilia's beatification with her sister Bess, who had witnessed the miracle in 2069. "I will read Matthew 5, from Jesus' Sermon on the Mount. Angilia always loved the wisdom, instruction, and truth in this sermon. *'And seeing the multitudes, he went up into a mountain: and when he was set, his disciples came unto him: And he opened his mouth, and taught them, saying, Blessed are the poor in spirit: for theirs is the kingdom of heaven. Blessed are they that mourn: for they shall be comforted. Blessed are the meek: for they shall inherit the earth. Blessed are they which do hunger and thirst after righteousness: for they shall be filled. Blessed are the merciful: for they shall obtain mercy. Blessed are the pure in heart: for they shall see God. Blessed are the peacemakers: for they shall be called the children of God. Blessed are they which are persecuted for righteousness' sake: for theirs is the kingdom of heaven. Blessed are ye, when men shall revile you, and persecute you, and shall say all manner of evil against you falsely, for my sake. Rejoice, and be exceeding glad: for great is your reward in heaven: for so persecuted they the prophets which were before you. Ye are the salt of the earth: but if the salt have lost his savour, wherewith shall it be salted? it is thenceforth good for nothing, but to be cast out, and to be trodden under foot of men. Ye are the light of the world. A city that is set on an hill cannot be hid. Neither do men light a candle, and put it under a bushel, but on a candlestick; and it giveth light unto all that are in the house. Let your light so shine before men, that they may see your good works, and glorify your Father which is in heaven. Think not that I am come to destroy the law, or the prophets: I am not come to destroy, but to fulfil. For verily I say unto you, Till heaven and earth pass, one jot or one tittle shall in no wise pass from the law, till all be fulfilled. Whosoever therefore shall break one of these least commandments, and shall teach men so, he shall be called the least in the kingdom of heaven: but whosoever shall do and teach them, the same shall be called great in the kingdom of heaven. For I say unto you, That except your righteousness shall exceed the righteousness of the scribes and Pharisees, ye shall in no case enter into the kingdom of heaven. Ye have heard that it was said by them of old time, Thou shalt not kill; and whosoever shall kill shall be in danger of the judgment: But I say unto you, That whosoever is angry with his brother without a cause shall be in danger of the judgment: and whosoever shall say to his brother, Raca, shall be in danger of the council: but whosoever shall say, Thou fool, shall be in danger of hell fire. Therefore if thou bring thy gift to the altar, and there rememberest that thy brother hath ought against thee; Leave there thy gift before the altar, and go thy way; first be reconciled to thy brother, and then come and offer thy gift. Agree with thine adversary quickly, whiles thou art in the way with him; lest at any time the adversary deliver thee to the judge, and the judge deliver thee to the officer, and thou be cast into prison. Verily I say unto thee, Thou shalt by no means come out thence, till thou hast paid the uttermost farthing. Ye have heard that it was said by them of old time, Thou shalt not commit adultery: But I say unto you, That whosoever looketh on a woman to lust after her hath committed adultery with her already in his heart. And if thy right eye offend thee, pluck it out, and cast it from thee: for it is profitable for thee that one of thy members should perish, and not that thy whole body should be cast into hell. And if thy right hand offend thee, cut it off, and cast it from thee: for it is profitable for thee that one of thy members should perish, and not that thy whole body should be cast into hell. It hath been said, Whosoever shall put away his wife, let him give her a writing of divorcement: But I say unto you, That whosoever shall put away his wife, saving for the cause of fornication, causeth her to commit adultery: and whosoever shall marry her that is divorced committeth adultery. Again, ye have heard that it hath been said by them of old time, Thou shalt not forswear thyself, but shalt perform unto the Lord thine oaths: But I say unto you, Swear not at all; neither by heaven; for it is God's throne: Nor by the earth; for it is his footstool: neither by Jerusalem; for it is the city of the great King. Neither shalt thou swear by thy head, because thou canst not make one hair white or black. But let your communication be, Yea, yea; Nay, nay: for whatsoever is more than these cometh of evil. Ye have heard that it hath been said, An eye for an eye, and a tooth for a tooth: But I say unto you, That ye resist not evil: but whosoever shall smite thee on thy right cheek, turn to him the other also. And if any man will sue thee at the law, and take away thy coat, let him have thy cloke also. And whosoever shall compel thee to go a mile, go with him twain. Give to him that asketh thee, and from him that would borrow of thee turn not thou away. Ye have heard that it hath been said, Thou shalt love thy neighbour, and hate thine enemy. But I say unto you, Love your enemies, bless them that curse you, do good to them that hate you, and pray for them which despitefully use you, and persecute you; That ye may be the children of your Father which is in heaven: for he maketh his sun to rise on the evil and on the good, and sendeth rain on the just and on the unjust. For if ye love them which love you, what reward have ye? do not even the publicans the same? And if ye salute your brethren only, what do ye more than others? do not even the publicans so? Be ye therefore perfect, even as your Father which is in heaven is perfect.'"*

Once Eleanor was seated, Pope Romanus gave a heartfelt sermon on the importance of the date and of Angilia's life. "Dear Brothers and Sisters in Christ, this day that has brought us together in Valmondois is an auspicious one. First of all, it is Holy Saturday, that day between Jesus' Crucifixion and Resurrection. On this day, Jesus' dead body lay in his tomb wrapped in linen. A heavy stone had been rolled before the entrance. Faithful kept a vigil, praying to God. They could not know the miracle that would confront them the next morning. Mary Magdalene was the first to encounter the resurrected Jesus. He was not dead. His earthly life and Crucifixion served as the preparation for and the proof of eternal life. God sent his only Son to bear the burden of our sins, to pay the ultimate price, for us. Because of Jesus' sacrifice, we have the gift of eternal life.

"Few people exemplify the belief in that gift more than Blessed Queen Angilia. Throughout her life, she carried that truth in her soul. She never feared death, for she knew that she would never die. If she taught us anything, it is that a life spent in obedience and service to God is rewarded with eternal life in Heaven. Blessed Queen Angilia's life is an exemplary model for all people who seek intimacy with God. From Blessed Queen Angilia we can learn how to turn our lives over to God and to trust him unwaveringly. May the life of Blessed Queen Angilia serve as an inspiration to people everywhere for generations to come."

Pope Romanus went to the altar, where he prepared and blessed the wafers and wine for communion. He was the first to take communion, after which an Archbishop instructed everyone to observe two minutes of quiet reflection. At the conclusion of the reflection, Pope Romanus led a responsory. The Pope then returned to his chair and sat.

This portion of the mass was the prayers of the faithful for Blessed Queen Angilia. Six different nations were represented by delegates who had been sent by their local Archbishops. Each would speak a prayer for Angilia in his or her native language. A gentleman from France was the first to pray at the pulpit. He was followed by a man from Spain, a woman from Germany, a woman from Africa, a woman from Japan, and a man from Greece. Between each of their prayers, a soloist from the choir led a brief responsory.

Pope Romanus then spoke a prayer. "Almighty God and Mighty Father, hear our prayers we bring to you. Amen." The six international delegates bowed to the Pope. The choir then sang Schubert's "Ave Maria," one of Angilia's favorite hymns.

Following the hymn, offerings to God for the communion were brought to Pope Romanus for his veneration. At Eric's recommendation, the family's closest friends were chosen for this honor. Shannon was the first to carry a sterling silver pyx containing unleavened bread. She knelt, and the Pope venerated the offering by kissing the pyx. He then placed his hand on her head and blessed her. She kissed his hand in gratitude, and then placed the pyx on the altar.

Nicole and Yvonne carried pyxes containing unleavened bread. The Pope venerated their offerings by kissing the pyxes. He placed his hand on Yvonne's head, blessed her, and she kissed his hand. Pope Romanus then placed his hand on Nicole's head and blessed her, after which she kissed his hand. Together, mother and daughter walked to the altar, where they placed the pyxes.

Billy next knelt before the Pope with a pyx that contained unleavened bread as well. The Pope kissed the pyx, venerating it, and then blessed Billy by placing a hand on his head. Billy kissed Pope Romanus' hand, and then placed the pyx on the altar.

Leigh next carried a gold pitcher containing wine. He, too, knelt before the Pope, who venerated the offering by kissing the pitcher. The Pope then blessed Leigh. Leigh kissed the Pope's hand, and then walked to the altar, where he placed the pitcher.

Finally Scott and Darlene carried the last two offerings, also containing wine. Scott assisted his wife in kneeling before Pope Romanus. He venerated the offering by kissing the pitchers. He then smiled at Darlene and placed his hand on her head to bless her. She openly sobbed when he did so, and Scott placed an arm around her. Darlene kissed the Pope's hand and thanked him. He smiled again in reply. The Pope placed his hand on Scott's head, blessing him. Scott helped Darlene stand, and they walked to the altar, where they placed their offerings with the others.

They stood with their five friends, faced the Pope, and bowed. Pope Romanus nodded in acknowledgement and then walked to the altar with his two *Magistri Caerimoniarum Apostolicarum*. One of them removed the Pope's mitre and placed his skullcap on his head. The Pope then took the thurible and venerated the offerings with incense. He then prayed, "Oh God, we pray that our offerings are accepted and in your favor. Amen." He then led a responsory.

The choir and congregation stood to sing the hymn "Anima Christi (Soul of My Savior)." Pope Romanus then read a short blessing in Latin, after which the church bell tolled three times while the Pope held a gold goblet containing wine aloft. The choir next sang the hymn "Hosanna." Pope Romanus read another blessing while he waved the thurible of incense, and then the bell tolled three more times. The Pope held the goblet while reading another blessing, and the bell tolled three times.

Pope Romanus then knelt on a kneeler before the offerings and prayed. The Pope stood and led a responsory, after which two Archbishops read prayers. When they finished, Pope Romanus said, "Let us pray," and the congregation stood. "Let us pray with confidence to our Lord," he commanded, and led those gathered in The Lord's Prayer, Psalms 23. The Pope then instructed everyone to perform the Sign of Peace. Everyone hugged those around them. Eric, Prince Patrick, Uncle Patrick, and Prince Eric turned to face those behind them, and they hugged them. The four men even left their pew to hug those in the further pews.

Finally, the choir began singing another Aquinas hymn, "Adoro te devote," and everyone returned to their seats. Bishops went into the congregation with pyxes filled with the bread and chalices of wine so that everyone could partake of the Eucharist. Other Bishops went outside to offer Eucharist to those gathered near the church.

The Pope gave communion to the holy men on the apse, and then he moved to a specially-built kneeler where he gave the Eucharist to Blessed Queen Angilia's family and close friends, beginning with her son, King Eric II. Prince Eric, Prince Patrick, and Uncle Patrick followed, and then Darlene, Scott, Billy, Shannon, Nicole, Yvonne, and Leigh received Eucharist from the Pope.

Pope Romanus returned to his chair until Eucharist concluded, and he smiled as he watched people partaking of Jesus Christ in this symbolic way. While communion continued, the choir sang the hymn "For the Glory of the Lord." After communion, an Archbishop instructed everyone, "Let us reflect upon this experience of partaking the body and the blood of Christ." Another two minutes of silence was observed.

At the end of the two minutes, the Pope stood. "Let us pray." The congregation stood. "Oh God, Let us do as Christ commanded. Through communion, through partaking of the bread and the wine, we remember Jesus Christ, his life, works, Crucifixion, and Resurrection. We examine ourselves, so that we are attuned to our shortcomings and sins, and can strive to confess them and to repent of them. We proclaim the Lord's death until he returns, the Second Coming prophesied in the book of Revelation. We participate in the body of Christ, coming together as one body, the Church he founded.

"As we reflect upon today's communion, let us look to the example of Blessed Queen Angilia. Her life was spent in constant remembrance of Jesus Christ, in self-examination and confession of her sins and repentance of those sins, and of becoming part of the body of Christ. She openly acknowledged Christ as the Son of God, her Savior, and her example. Her life was lived upon the Commandments of God in the Old Testament and the Commandments of Jesus in the New Testament. May her life of devotion and service serve as an example to all people.

"Brothers and Sisters in Christ, we have beatified Queen Angilia today. By doing so, we acknowledge that Christ lived in Angilia and she lived in Christ. She bound her life to his. She strove to honor God the Father, God the Son, and God the Holy Spirit. She wrote in her diary at the age of 11, when she received her Doctor of Philosophy degree from the University of Oxford, the following:

'Today I received my DPhil from Oxford. Daddy, Roger, Susan, and Daniel were there in the theatre. They have been part of my life from the moment I was born. I love them so very much. I love Daddy with all of my being. Daddy, Roger, Susan, and Daniel were not the only ones there to support

me today. I felt God there, too. I felt his hands guiding me, supporting me, as he has done for all of my life, in the Unborn Children Sphere, the Angels Choir, and here on earth. He is always with me. He lives in my heart and in my soul. I want nothing more than to please my two fathers—God and Daddy. My prayer is that my life is spent in such a way that I do honor them both.

How sinful it would be to honor one and not the other. God created me, and I owe my life to him. My favorite Bible verse says it best: I John 4: 19. 'We love him, because he first loved us.' Of course I love and honor God.

God gave Moses the Ten Commandments. All of them are important and are to be obeyed. The fifth commandment is especially dear to my soul: 'Honour thy father and thy mother: that thy days may be long upon the land which the Lord thy God giveth thee.' I have loved Daddy from the time Great-grandfather told me about him when I was in the Angels Choir. I loved him beyond measure when I saw him for the first time that day Uncle Patrick died. God, in his infinite wisdom, proclaimed me as Uncle Patrick's Spirit Guide. God is the one who sent me to Daddy on that heartbreaking day, allowed Daddy to see me, and thus God forged our impenetrable bond.

My life is devoted to God and to Daddy. Who I am and everything about me is due to them, my two fathers. I love them both beyond mere words, but they know. They see it and they feel it within me. I pray that my life is in complete honor of and obedience to them.'

"Angilia wrote that the evening of her graduation day in 2007. While the world celebrated her prodigious achievements, she gave the glory and honor to the two men closest to her—God, her heavenly Father, and King Eric I, her earthly father. In doing so, she upheld two of God's Ten Commandments, the first and the fifth.

"May we learn from and follow Blessed Queen Angilia's example every day. Rather than fall prey to the deadly sin of pride, remember from whom your talents, deeds, and achievements come—God."

Pope Romanus led a responsory while the choir once more sang "Ave Maria." After the responsory, the Pope took his sceptre, a gold cross, and stood before the congregation. Those on the apse began filing out, and once they had all left, the Pope went to the altar. There, he knelt before the reliquaries once more, and then knelt at the foot of Angilia's coffin. Uncle Patrick, Prince Eric, and Prince Patrick stood, walked to the altar, and picked up the reliquaries. They went to one of the side chapels, where they joined Reverend Emerson, Archbishop Murphy, and the other clerics who had participated in Angilia's Beatification Mass.

Finally, Pope Romanus stood and kissed Angilia's coffin before he left the apse. At that moment, those in the church could hear the applause of the several thousand pilgrims gathered outside of the church. People inside the church began lining up to speak with Eric, and he devoted that time to attendees he would not see later that day. Heads of State, members of the clergy, and friends had been invited to the palace for a formal banquet that afternoon.

Meanwhile, Prince Eric, Prince Patrick, and their great-granduncle Patrick officially presented the reliquaries to Reverend Emerson. An altar to Blessed Queen Angilia would shortly be built in Christ Church Valmondois, which would become the official place of worship and prayer to her. "Thank you, Patrick, Eric, and Patrick. The church is honored to house these relics, and we know that they will be items of reverence, devotion, and reflection for pilgrims," Reverend Emerson told them.

Before he left, Pope Romanus spent several minutes with the Princes. "Your grandmother is a beautiful example of a godly woman. She taught you well. You are fine, godly young men, and I have been pleased to meet you." He turned his attention to Uncle Patrick and said, "Your presence today is but one of the many miracles that surround Blessed Queen Angilia."

The Pope then told one of the Bishops that he wished to speak with King Eric, so the Bishop relayed the message to Eric. He excused himself from a throng of pilgrims and went to the side chapel. Pope Romanus immediately grasped Eric's arms. "My son, what a glorious day to share with you and your family. I have been quite impressed by your core of strength during what must be one of the most emotional experiences of your life. You are clearly your mother's son."

"Thank you, Your Holiness. You're right on both counts. This is an extraordinarily emotional experience. I inherited my faith from my mother, and that is what gives me my strength. Without God, I know I would crumble and falter. My family and I have been so incredibly honored to have you preside over my mother's Beatification Mass."

"It has been my honor to do so. I chose to preside over Blessed Queen Angilia's beatification, because she remains such a perfect example of a life devoted to God." The men kissed one another's hands before the Pope and his Magistri Caerimoniarum Apostolicarum bid everyone farewell. The Pope would return to The Vatican that afternoon.

Eric reminded Reverend Emerson, the Queen Angilia Guild members, Archbishop Murphy, and Archbishop Clancy about the banquet. They all promised to be at the palace within a couple of hours. On the Royal Family's way out, Eric also reminded the Heads of State and their close friends, who all promised to be there soon.

The Royal Family and Leigh greeted more pilgrims in the church, although many were once more filing past Angilia's coffin. The men finally made their way to the church door, which prompted screams and cheers. The Royal party crossed the street and spoke with as many people as they could until Leigh told them it was time to get ready for the banquet. "Thank you all for your support and for sharing today with us. We truly appreciate it," Eric said in a loud, clear voice before he, his sons, granduncle, and Leigh walked to the palace, where they briefly spoke to those on the mall.

Inside the foyer, Eric, Prince Eric, and Prince Patrick took deep breaths. What a weekend! First the vigil and then the two-hour Beatification Mass. The day was far from over, though, as they prepared to host over 100 people at the banquet. "We best freshen and gather our thoughts before people begin arriving," Eric told his sons. The three men went to their second-floor suites, while Leigh checked with the kitchen staff, maids, and butlers that all was ready and under control. He was able to grab 10 minutes to collect his thoughts before he went to Eric's suite.

Soon, Leigh and the Royal Family were in the fifth floor ballroom, waiting for the guests to arrive. Billy arrived first, thinking he would help. "Thank you, Billy, but you are a guest. Get something to drink and just relax and enjoy yourself," Eric told him.

Soon, Nicole, Yvonne, Shannon, Scott, and Darlene arrived together. They hugged Eric, Prince Eric, Prince Patrick, and Uncle Patrick—except for Darlene. When she got to Uncle Patrick, her face turned bright red and she looked flustered.

Patrick smiled and said, "This has been such a great honor for Angilia today, hasn't it, Darlene?"

"Yes, it really has," she said, relaxing. "I'm so happy for her. I just wish I could give her a big hug right now."

"Well, I'll pass it on to her," Patrick said and held his arms open. Darlene hugged him—for the first time—and did not seem to realize she had until she pulled away and looked at him.

"Please do," she said, cleared her throat, and fanned her face. Prince Eric and Prince Patrick smiled at one another. They had seen Darlene faint and get agitated over their great-grandfather and Uncle Patrick dozens of times over the years. Not much had changed.

Charlie Britt arrived with Eleanor and Bess Hale, and they all warmly greeted Eric, Price Eric, Prince Patrick, and Uncle Patrick. "Thank you for inviting us to this celebration, Sir. We were so honored to be asked to attend Blessed Queen Angilia's Beatification Mass," Bess said and curtseyed.

"I am the one honored to have you here, my dear. You and your sister are proof of God's miracles," Eric replied.

"I know," Eleanor said, "but the miracle wouldn't have happened without Blessed Queen Angilia's prayer that July day. I had prayed for years, and so did Bess, but it took Angilia's prayer to God on my behalf to cause me to walk. I owe her more than I can ever repay."

"No, you don't, Eleanor. You just live your destiny and honor God, and you will do all that is required of you. Fulfilling your destiny is what God wants for you," Prince Patrick told her.

"I will. I'm in college now to become a teacher. I'm following your grandmother's example," Eleanor said. Prince Patrick hugged Eleanor, already knowing that their destinies merged. Prince Patrick would open his university, and he would ask Eleanor to be one of the first professors. Everything was already falling into place.

Jack and Tammy Cornwell then greeted the Royal Family, and thanked Eric for inviting them. "Your mother's prayers cured me, and I also owe her a debt of gratitude. I was cured so that I could fulfill my destiny, a huge part of which is our daughter Angilia," Jack told Eric with a huge smile.

Eric looked at the dark-haired woman who stood with Jack and Tammy, and his eyes filled with tears. "It's so lovely to meet you, Angilia," he told her through the lump in his throat as he clasped her hand. Eric turned to Jack. "Thank you for honoring my mother in this way."

"My daughter's name is Erica, after your grandfather," Angilia told Eric. "I know how much Blessed Queen Angilia loves her father, and that is her second name after him, so it seemed the perfect name for my daughter."

"Thank you. This is extraordinary to learn on this day," Eric said. He hugged Jack, Angilia, and Tammy.

More guests arrived and greeted the Royal Family. Soon the ballroom with filled with people, all of them talking about the morning's mass. Kings, Queens, Prime Ministers, Presidents, Archbishops, Bishops, and Reverends comfortably talked. All were impressed by the morning's mass and by Angilia herself. Charlie, Jack, and Eleanor were popular guests, as everyone wanted to hear about their miraculous cures.

Uncle Patrick was the most sought-after attendee, for everyone knew his story and how he and Angilia had first met. The fact that he was an angel whom they could see, touch, and talk with was proof that Angilia's memoir was indeed true. Patrick graciously answered many questions about death and Heaven, and he even posed for dozens of pictures with the guests. During a brief lull, he told Eric, "I get that people have questions, and part of my duty is to answer them honestly. That's never a problem. But I find it a hoot that they want my picture."

"I don't, Uncle Patrick. You're the one person who has known Mommy the longest. 101 years. That's more than many people can wrap their brains around. You are proof of immortality," Eric said with a smile.

Finally, everyone took their seats for the evening meal, and butlers served the guests. Before they ate, Father Fisher led them all in a prayer of thanksgiving. Eric felt the enormity of the day's importance suddenly sink into his soul, and he found himself fighting tears. So did Prince Patrick and Prince Eric, as well as many who had been deeply affected by the mass.

That night, alone in his suite, Eric stood on his sitting room balcony and looked up at the gleaming stars. "Oh, Mommy, I love you so. This has been such an amazing but overwhelming experience for me and the boys. Your holiness is truly public, more than ever. We always knew it, we always saw it, but the whole world knows and sees it now. You are truly one of God's Supreme Angels, and I am so grateful that you are my Mommy. I love you."

§§§§

The following morning, the Royal Family arrived at Christ Church Valmondois at 7:00. The church had remained open to pilgrims until 6:30, at which time the doors had been closed. A guard on duty at the doors bowed and opened the doors for Eric, Prince Eric, Prince Patrick, and Uncle Patrick. The four men entered, and were greeted by Reverend Emerson.

The Royal Family stood next to Angilia's coffin once more and prayed. Each of them kissed the coffin before Eric unlocked the Royal Vault. The military pallbearers carried Angilia's coffin into the Vault and placed it in its tomb. They then lifted the heavy lid atop the tomb, which Eric vowed would never be opened again. The soldiers saluted and stood at attention.

Angilia's son, grandsons, and uncle bowed their heads in prayer. "I love you, Grandmother," Prince Patrick said through the tears that choked him. Eric and Prince Eric put their arms around

126

him, and Uncle Patrick smiled at the sight. He knew their love and support were strong, and he also knew that they had inherited that love and support from his brother Eric and his niece Angilia.

Eric thanked the soldiers, who saluted Angilia and left. They had diligently guarded their Queen's coffin throughout its public viewing, not just because it was their duty, but because they loved and respected her. The Royal Family then left, and Eric locked the Vault. They thanked Reverend Emerson for his assistance and compassion during Angilia's beatification and promised to return shortly for the Easter services.

They spent the time before the service doing a walkabout near the church, where hundreds of people still stood. Many of them had waited to greet the Royal Family that morning, and as usual, they were not disappointed. In fact, many of them were touched that the Royal Family had spent so much time with the people over the past several days.

"Thank you for remembering us," a woman in the crowd told Eric when he shook her hand. "You have no idea what this means to us, you really don't. This is one of the most important weeks in your family's history, and you all have taken a big part of that time meeting with us. That is just what your Blessed mother used to do, you know. She was famous for her lengthy walkabouts. You are so much like her, it warms my heart. Her legacy lives in you and in your beautiful sons. I love you all, and I love your mother."

§§§§

Uncle Patrick told me about the Beatification Mass, every detail. I did not watch it, even though Daddy, Mommy, Matthew, and the rest of the family did. I understand why it was done, and what its true significance is, but I felt it was wrong of me to watch it. To me, that would have been vain, and that is not a trait I wish to possess, so I do all I can keep it at bay.

Instead, I found a quiet spot near a brook where I sat drawing, the best I could, the beauty of God's Heaven. I wasn't alone for long. Tom sought me out, and he sat with me as we listened to the gentle flow of the water and to the singing of the birds. Tom Greenfield, the man who entered my life as part of God's plan for me.

We talked for a long while, and Tom told me that I should never have in any way felt guilty for the plane accident. "It was supposed to happen, Angilia. That was my time to die. That was not your time to die. God had many more years planned for you, you know that. Had you gotten on that plane, God's destiny for you would have been destroyed. You were not meant to be there. You would not have stopped it from happening. You couldn't have."

I told Tom that I had realized that years after the accident. Had I died in that plane crash, Eric and his sons would have never been born. That would have been a devastating tragedy. Even now, I do not like to ponder that. I told Tom that he, like Uncle Patrick, was placed in my life at the time determined by God. There is a divine purpose to everything in our lives.

Tom and I smiled at one another, and then we sang together for the first time in such a very long time. We sang some of our favorite hymns, and we were soon joined by the band! They accompanied us as they had always done. What a glorious life we have in Heaven! We are surrounded by God, our families, our friends, and boundless beauty and peace. What more could we need or want?

§§§§

"Welcome to this glorious Mother's Day service. As you know, Mother's Day was founded 66 years ago by Blessed Queen Angilia and proclaimed a national annual holiday by her father, King Eric I. Every fourth Sunday in June has since been set aside to do as the fifth of God's Ten Commandments instructs us to do— honor our mothers," Reverend Emerson said at the start of the June 26, 2078 church service.

After Reverend Emerson led the congregation in prayer, he bowed to Eric, who walked to the pulpit. He would deliver that day's sermon. "Today is a very special day to all of us, for today is our opportunity to publicly acknowledge our love and gratitude to our mothers. Each one of us owes our mothers far more than we could ever repay with mere material gifts. However, we can most certainly repay that debt with our love. Love is the most cherished and priceless gift we can give another.

"My mother loved everyone, and she lived her love. Her love shone in everything she did. We all felt her love. One person, however, shared a one-of-a-kind love with her. My father. You

128

know the story of how they met on this earth in 2012, in the midst of tragedy. You know by now that she instantly recognized him as her friend from the Unborn Children Sphere. You know that he was besotted with her from that moment he rushed to her side, and that he quickly fell in love with her. You know that he gave her a promise ring on her 17th birthday in 2013, and proposed to her on Christmas Day 2015.

"You know that my parents married in this church 61 years ago today. June 26, 2016 was also Mother's Day. That morning, my mother spoke about her mother, Queen Consort Marisol. She had never met her mother, but she knew her mother. My grandfather made sure of that. In fact, on my mother's engagement day, which was also her 20th birthday, my grandfather gave her the tiara that he had had made for his fiancée to wear on their wedding day. My mother wore that same tiara on her wedding day, and in doing so symbolically carried her mother with her.

"Such acts were common for my mother. She often paid tribute to my grandmother by wearing her jewelry or clothes. Those simple acts were her way of tangibly having a part of her mother with her. She told me on her coronation day that this was her way of making her mother part of the event. She also told me that by wearing her mother's pieces, she kept her mother alive for other people. For example, the diamond brooch my mother wore on her coronation gown had been worn by her mother on her coronation gown in 1992. In 2029, many people recognized that brooch, as well as its significance. They understood that their new Queen was paying homage to her mother, Queen Consort Marisol.

"So today, honor your mother even if she is no longer with you on this earth. Carry something of hers with you at all times, as a constant tangible reminder of her. Write her a letter or talk to her, and somehow tell her what she means to you. If ever my mother has taught us anything, it is that both life and love are eternal."

§§§§

The summer passed rather uneventfully after Angilia's Beatification Mass, with the exception of Darlene's 86th birthday on July 21. Scott hosted a party at their home, which Billy, Nicole,

Yvonne, Shannon, Eric, Prince Patrick, and Prince Eric attended. Darlene could not walk any longer—she was confined to a wheel chair—but she truly enjoyed her party with her closest friends there.

Eric presented her with a one-of-a-kind lap shawl made from the finest Scottish wool. It was in the Bruce tartan, which thrilled her. "This reminds me of that story Angilia told us at that slumber party at the palace. Ooh, how exciting it was to learn all about her three ancestors, Robert the Bruce, King Edward I, and William Wallace. I've never forgotten that. She never claimed to have a favorite of the three, but I could just tell by the way her eyes sparkled when she talked about him that she was partial to Robert the Bruce."

"You're right, Darlene. She was. Dad knew it, and that's why he chose Scotland for their honeymoon. He surprised her with trips to Robert's birthplace and his burial places. She always kept the snow globe of Turnberry Castle that Dad bought her there. It's still on the white bookshelf in her sitting room," Eric shared.

"Angilia had the most beautiful rooms I've ever seen. That suite of hand-painted furniture is just gorgeous. Sure, she was born a princess, but that room was created from her parents' love for her. She never changed a thing. That says a lot about not just how appropriate her suite was for her, but about her adoration of her parents. Her suite was a symbol of their love for her and of her love for them," Nicole said as tears filled her eyes. Yvonne and Shannon put their arms around her.

"I remember that bookshelf. On the top shelf, she had some of her most important treasures, like a late-19th century tin commemorating her great-great-grandfather's coronation. And that plate for her parents' wedding. Oh, King Eric will always be the most handsome man ever," Darlene said in her very familiar dreamy tone.

Everyone smiled and hugged Darlene. She was still the same as she had been when she entered the DeBruce Martineau family's lives in 2012. She had long gone from irritating to charming. Somehow her consistency kept things rather normal in an ever-changing world.

"I will use this shawl proudly, knowing that it is the tartan of my King Eric's Scottish ancestors. Thank you, dear Eric," Darlene said to the man she had known since his birth. Eric hugged his lifelong friend, knowing in his heart that she would not be with them much longer.

§§§§§

"Good morning, and welcome to the early morning edition of Valdavian News. I am Candace Shore, and this is Thursday, November 17. Today is the triple birthday of King Eric II, Prince Eric, and Prince Patrick. Today is also the anniversary of King Eric I's birth 124 years ago. Today also marks the first Feast Day of Blessed Queen Angilia.

"Christ Church Valmondois opens shortly, at 6:00, for today's celebration. The altar to Blessed Queen Angilia was recently completed, and serves as a place for people to pray and to worship. The altar houses the three reliquaries that contain the relics of Blessed Queen Angilia—the bullet which Dr. Taylor removed from her aorta in 2012 and a bone fragment he saved from that surgery, a piece of the blouse she was wearing when she was shot, and her favorite pink hair ribbon. Hundreds of people have already visited the altar since it was unveiled two weeks ago.

"Many thousands of people are expected to visit Christ Church Valmondois today to celebrate the godly life and works of the Blessed Queen Angilia. The formal celebration will last most of the day, from 6:00 A.M. until 6:00 P.M. As part of today's reflective and prayerful nature, most people will fast, an act of penance for their sins.

"King Eric is expected to attend today's religious celebration at Christ Church Valmondois, while his sons Eric and Patrick will attend the religious celebration at University Church of St. Mary the Virgin in Oxford, England. That is the church which their grandmother attended when she was a professor at the University of Oxford from 2007 until 2012."

§§§§§

Just as Eric's mid-morning meeting ended, his private phone rang. It was Scott. "Eric, I hate to bother you, but Darlene is dying." Eric could hear the tears in Scott's voice.

"I'm coming, Scott," Eric immediately said. He told Leigh and Yvonne where he was going, and Yvonne asked if she could go with him. Leigh would stay and handle the calls, messages, and guests.

When they arrived, Nicole answered the door and hugged them. "Scott called me a while ago. Darlene had trouble swallowing and breathing this morning, so he called the nurse. She's in there now, but it's just a matter of time. We're keeping Darlene comfortable and talking to her. She's in and out of consciousness, but does seem to hear us."

Eric put his arms around Nicole and Yvonne and walked to the bedroom with them. Yvonne stifled her cries when she saw her friend lying there so frail, wan, and seemingly lifeless. Eric walked to Scott and hugged him.

"Darlene is the only woman I've ever loved, Eric. She was always this lovable child-woman. I don't know what I'll do without her," Scott said and cried against Eric's shoulder.

"I know, Scott. I know." Eric held Scott until they heard Darlene moan. The nurse checked her heart and pulse, and then arranged the blankets around Darlene. Eric noticed that around her shoulders was the Bruce tartan he had given her, and he smiled.

Eric leaned down, kissed Darlene's cheek, and said, "Hello, Darlene. I came to visit you."

She opened her eyes and gave him a weak smile. "I'm glad you did, Eric. This is the last time you'll see me, on this earth anyway."

Yvonne and Shannon could not help crying, and Darlene looked at them. "Come here, and give me a hug," she told her friends. Shannon, Nicole, and Yvonne hugged and kissed her, but could not stop crying.

"It's okay. I've had a long and happy life. It's my time. I love you all." She reached for Scott, and he sat facing her. She held his hand in both of hers. "I love you most of all, Scott." She closed her eyes and lay unmoving for a long while.

Suddenly, she opened her eyes and smiled. Her voice was soft and halting as she spoke. "My grandmamma's here. She's my Spirit Guide. She's taking me to Heaven very soon. That means I have to leave you, but I'll be waiting for you." Her eyes glistened and she appeared excited. "This means I'll see my King Eric again."

Scott smiled and kissed his wife one last time just before Darlene died. Nicole, Yvonne, and Shannon cried. Scott bowed his head in prayer as Eric put his hands on Scott's shoulders. "Darlene finally gets what she's been waiting for for 14 years," he commented through his tears.

§§§§

May 8, 2079

Darlene died today. She was such a devoted and loyal friend to my family for 67 years. She was one of Mommy's closest friends and supporters. Darlene was always there whenever Mommy needed her. Darlene was one of those rare people who would do anything for Mommy—or for any of us, for that matter. I know how much Mommy valued Darlene's friendship. Mommy told me once that Darlene was one of the real friends in her life. I know that.

Darlene was a true sweetheart through it all. Scott said today that she was a child-woman, and he's right. She never really stopped being that teenage girl who attended Mommy's sleepover in 2012. How often I heard about that, mostly from Darlene! Her legendary crush on Grandfather became well known that night, and it just seemed to grow deeper with each passing year.

How often I saw her blush, become unsettled, or faint when she was near him! So did Eric and Patrick, from their earliest years. They didn't understand it all when they were young—they thought Darlene had an illness. So did Grandpa that night of the sleepover when Darlene fainted several times. We all soon realized that she simply (or not so simply) admired Grandfather more than most people do. I look back now and find it rather charming.

I will miss Darlene's kindness, friendship, laughter, tears, and, yes, her fainting spells. But I know I'll see them again someday. Darlene said this afternoon that her grandmamma was her Spirit Guide and would take her to Heaven—where she would soon see her King Eric again. Oh, how I look forward to Uncle Patrick telling me about that!!

§§§§

"Oh, Daddy, I do love you so," Angilia said, leaned up, and kissed his cheek. Marisol, Patrick, Matthew, Mitchell, and Katherine smiled as they sat nearby, forever touched by Eric's and Angilia's extraordinary bond.

Without any warning, someone grabbed Eric from behind in a huge hug, and enthused, "So do I! You are as handsome as ever, my King!"

"Darlene!" Angilia declared, surprised to suddenly see her friend. "You're here!"

"Yes. Grandmamma just brought me. I had to come find you first," she told Eric.

"Me? What about your family, Darlene?"

"Oh, they'll be here. They're not going anywhere. I told Scott, Nicole, Shannon, Yvonne, and Eric just before I came here that my dream would finally come true. And it has," she gushed, still holding Eric.

She suddenly seemed to realize that she was hugging him when she noticed that her face was mere inches from Eric's. "I'm flattered, Darlene, but I'm not going anywhere, either," Eric said as Darlene's face became red.

"I hope not," she mumbled as she fainted.

"Oh, good grief," Eric said. "Here? She still does that here?"

Patrick giggled, reminded of Darlene's perpetual adoration of his brother and how she had once raved about seeing Eric again

134

in Heaven when she died. Scott had teased her about fainting in Heaven, and sure enough, she had.

"I don't believe it. I just don't believe it. I thought that would never happen here, I really did. Idol worship and all of that. But I guess some things just don't change even here," Mitchell said as Katherine laughed against his shoulder.

"Is this the girl who has a puppy love for you, mi marido?" Marisol asked Eric.

"Yes," he replied, looking as uncomfortable as ever. "I best take her to her family," he said as he stooped to pick her up.

"No! If she opens her eyes and realizes she's in your arms, I don't know what will happen," Mitchell urgently said.

"I don't either. She's already dead, so it won't kill her. It might turn her into a zombie of some sort, though—you know, in a constant state of lovesickness from which she can't awake," Katherine said. Mitchell, Matthew, and Patrick laughed.

"It's not funny. It's never been funny. Is this going to happen for all of eternity?" Eric asked, looking rather distraught at the thought.

Angilia hugged her father. "Oh, Daddy, this could be like that slumber party all over again. I'm so sorry."

"Nah, I'm sure she'll get over it. Eventually," Patrick said with a giggle.

Eric rolled his eyes, and Mitchell stood. "I'll carry her to her family. Maybe they can find a way to deal with Darlene's chronic condition."

§§§§

17 November 2079

Grandmother, it was 10 years ago today that you left this world and went to Heaven. My love for you has only grown in magnitude over the past

135

decade. One decade. How I miss you! I always will. I know that, God knows that, and you know that.

I also know that you are not dead. You will never be dead. You are immortal. You live forever and ever. When my body dies, I will be with you again! I will be with you, Grandfather, Great-grandfather, and I will meet Mommy and Great-grandmother! What a glorious, beautiful promise! How I do look forward to that.

Before that, though, I have much to do here on earth. I know my destiny, and I will make it happen! I will open that university. I know what it will be called, and how perfect that name is for Valdavia's first university. In 2081, Eric and I earn our Bachelor's Degrees, mine a BEd. I am focusing on education administration so that I can become as knowledgeable and prepared as possible as I enter my graduate work, getting both a MEd and a DPhil in education administration. I want to do this. I <u>have</u> to do this. I told you this years ago, and I clearly remember how you glowed and hugged me.

Today is very special, Grandmother, because it is also your Feast Day. Thousands of people are in Valmondois for the celebration in the church. Eric and I don't have Friday classes this term, so we both came home to attend the celebration with Dad. That will be so very special, because it is also our shared birthdays. I said it to Uncle Patrick nine years ago, but it is such a beautiful feeling that you share this day with Great-grandfather, Dad, Eric, and me. We are eternally connected, and this is just one more layer added to that.

I love you, Grandmother,

Patrick

§§§§§

Angilia approached God's throne, and the Seraphim bowed and let her pass. She neared his throne, as always, with her head bowed, and knelt before him. Her hands were clasped in front of her in reverence. She never spoke to God directly until he spoke. She knew she did not have to tell him why she had come, because he already knew. Still, in such situations, she felt it necessary to speak directly to God.

"I know why you are here, Angilia. You have prayers to place before me, prayers that people sent to you so that you could bring them to me. You may relay them to me."

"Thank you, dear God. I do have prayers for you that were sent to me. These are not the first prayers from Alexander Najera that I bring you. At the time Uncle Patrick told me that I would be beatified, Alexander Najera first prayed to you through me, and I came to you with his prayers," Angilia said.

"Yes. Alexander prayed for his daughter Hope's cure."

"Yes, he did. He fasted and prayed for one week nonstop. Hope had a rare form of brain stem cancer, and all of the doctors who were treating her or who were consulted about her case told Alexander and his wife Maria that Hope would die soon. After Alexander's prayers, her cancer went into remission, but now has returned. Alexander is fasting and praying to me ceaselessly from Christ Church Valmondois, while his wife stays with Hope in the hospital in Mexico. Maria is praying to me from her daughter's hospital room, and she asks for Hope's cure, as well. She wants Hope to grow into the woman she dreams of becoming, a teacher, a wife, and a mother.

"The oncologists have told Alexander and Maria that this time Hope will certainly die soon. She is only 11 years old, and her dream is to be a teacher. Alexander has prayed for her cure so that she can grow up and live the life she aspires to live. That is what I pray to you to consider, dear God. If it is in your will and destiny for Hope, please cure her of this deadly cancer. Please let her live a long, fruitful, productive life that honors you and serves others. This I pray to you, with love and respect, my beloved God," Angilia said, her voice filled with emotions.

"I have heard the prayers of Alexander and Maria that you have brought before me. I will do what is best and right for Hope. You may rise, Angilia, with my gratitude for your unwavering faith," God told her.

CHAPTER 5

Angilia sat playing piano duets with Gabriel, watched by her family and friends. They were all there, including Abraham Lincoln, Robert the Bruce, Tom, Sam, Tim, John, Greg, Joe, Mr. Brennan, Randy Meadows, William, and Darlene. They were each enchanted, and so were other angels, including Michael, who soon joined the audience. As the duets continued, more people drifted nearby to listen, likewise entranced.

Marisol put one arm around Eric and her head on his shoulder. "This is so beautiful, Eric. Our Angilia is such an astounding angel."

"I know, darling. I've known since she was a baby. She has always awed me," Eric told her softly.

"Apparently, she awes someone else, too," Marisol whispered. She nodded toward Matthew, who sat staring at Angilia with those ever-present love-struck eyes. Eric smiled and hugged his wife, realizing more than ever that little really had changed between their lives on earth and in Heaven.

Angilia and Gabriel began playing a glorious aria, one so exquisite that everyone sat completely enthralled. Without warning, though, a high-pitched voice began singing pseudo-Italian words in accompaniment. "No! It can't be!" Roger exclaimed.

It was.   Miss Yost, doing her best Maria Callas impersonation, made a grand entrance and stood front and center. Everyone was stunned. Susan, as always, grabbed Daniel's arm. Eduardo looked at Bonnie with what could best be described as a pained expression. Mitchell knew he would get no sympathy from Katherine, so he simply put his arms on his knees and leaned forward, refusing to watch. Chef Antoine shook his head, disbelief evident on his face.

Juanita and Katherine, however, hugged one another in joy. They had always been partial to Miss Yost. Matthew also smiled, delighted. He had always liked Miss Yost. Roger sat ramrod straight, apparently in shock. Marisol covered her mouth with her hand, stifling her giggles.

"So, is this the infamous Miss Yost?" Marisol managed to whisper in her husband's ear.

"Oh, yes. Miss Yost is definitely one-of-a-kind," Eric quietly replied.

"Let us all be grateful for that," Robert the Bruce said from his seat beside Eric. "A choir of her would indicate that we are not in Heaven."

That comment, which was heard by quite a few people in the audience, elicited several giggles, chortles, and agreements. Thankfully, the aria soon ended. Miss Yost took a grand bow, holding out her black dirndl skirt and rainbow apron as she did so. Roger, Daniel, Susan, Mitchell, Alejandro, Eduardo, Antoine, and Robert grimaced at the sight.

Angilia leapt from her piano bench, and ran to Miss Yost. She gave the self-proclaimed world's favorite music teacher a hug. Angilia then stunned nearly everyone by asking, "Isn't Miss Yost absolutely fantastic? Please show her our appreciation."

Angilia applauded, which forced everyone else to do likewise. Miss Yost smiled her toothy smile and made yet another grandiose bow in gratitude. When she stood, she truly stunned everyone by saying, "I have many more operatic marvels in my repertoire with which I can entertain you."

Nearly everyone looked horrified. Robert the Bruce took charge, as only he could. He stood and walked to Miss Yost. He gallantly kissed her hand, which made her giggle like a schoolgirl, and tactfully said, "While I am sure we would all enjoy that, I dare say the performances would mean more were they scattered throughout eternity, one at a time."

Almost everyone thanked God, literally, at that moment for Robert's command. Miss Yost took his comment as the greatest compliment she had ever received. "Oh, yes, you are so correct, Your Majesty, yes you are. Why should I regale you in one sitting, when I can regale you for all eternity?"

Most everyone groaned, although Eduardo reminded them, "Wouldn't you rather have her in small chunks than for what *feels* like eternity?"

"If those are my only options, then one aria at a time is, of course, the best option," Roger said. "It's the only one I can survive even here." Marisol stifled her laughter again as Eric rolled his eyes.

§§§§

Eric took a break from writing a proposal and went to his office window. He smiled as he looked at the fluffy spring clouds in the sky, and his hand unconsciously covered the pendant he constantly wore under his clothes. "Oh, Mommy, three years ago, the boys and I sat in church for your Beatification Mass. What an emotional and beautiful mass it was for you. I can't ever forget one moment."

At that moment, Eric's private telephone rang, and he cleared his throat before he answered. "Archbishop Murphy, how nice to hear from you. I was just reflecting on my mother's Beatification Mass and how emotional and lovely it was."

"Yes, it was, Sir. Ironically, I'm calling to give you some news about Blessed Queen Angilia.

"News?"

"Yes, Sir. In November, the Bishop and the Archbishop members of the Congregation for the Causes of Saints gave an affirmative vote on your mother's cause for canonization and forwarded the cause to Pope Romanus for his vote. His Holiness carefully reviewed and studied Blessed Queen Angilia's cause. He has spent the past four months doing so, wanting to make the absolute correct decision. He has done so. He has given his affirmative vote. Your mother's Canonization Mass will occur on November 17, this year, at St. Peter's Square in the Holy See."

Eric was stunned. He quickly sat in his chair. "My mother will become Saint Angilia?"

"Yes, Sir, on November 17, Pope Romanus will declare Blessed Queen Angilia as Saint Angilia. His Holiness will make the announcement today. I wanted to let you know in advance, Sir," Archbishop Murphy said.

"Thank you, Archbishop Murphy. Thank you. This has all happened so fast. I understood that two miracles have to be proven before someone can be canonized."

"Indeed. Two miracles have been authenticated as being caused by Blessed Queen Angilia since her death. Both cases were thoroughly scrutinized, studied, and verified, scientifically and theologically."

"That really doesn't surprise me, of course, knowing what I do about my mother. But the speed with which this whole process has progressed does surprise me. This is really happening?"

"Yes, Sir, it is."

"I need to tell my sons before the news breaks, if you will please excuse me. Thank you so much for calling, and God bless you."

Eric called Prince Patrick first, and told him the news. "Grandmother will soon be Saint Angilia! I knew she would be proclaimed a Saint, I did! How could she not be?"

Eric heard the excited exclamations of his son's classmates, and he smiled. "Where are you, Patrick?"

"I'm on my way to class with some friends. The best thing I can do to honor Grandmother is to go to class, learn as much as I can, and do my best. Final exams are at the end of the month, and then Eric and I graduate. That gets me one step closer to fulfilling my destiny. This news has just given me another push."

"I'm so proud of you, son. You go to class, and I'll talk to you soon. I love you, Patrick."

Prince Patrick's friends surrounded him, all talking at once, and hugged him. "This is awesome, Patrick, it really is," Edward Stiles said. Patrick's other friends echoed Edward's comments.

Patrick beamed, thanked them, and then said, "We better get going, or we'll be late for class."

§§§§

Eric next called Prince Eric, who had just finished a class and was heading to the library, and told him the news about his grandmother. "This is for real? Wow, this is amazing! Grandmother will officially be declared a Saint!" Prince Eric excitedly said.

"This is very real, Eric. When Archbishop Murphy called me a short time ago, I told him that I was amazed at how fast this process has moved. Your grandmother's Canonization Mass is on her Feast Day this year in St. Peter's Square. Pope Romanus will issue the announcement soon, so I wanted to call you and Patrick before he does."

"Thank you, Dad. I'm half tempted to go to my apartment and watch the announcement, but I was just on my way to the library to finish my research project. This is the main assignment for the semester in my executive law class, and I know Grandmother would want me to work on that, so that's what I'm going to do. I've worked too hard to make a big mistake now," Prince Eric told his father.

"I'm so proud of you, Eric. Patrick was on his way to class when I called him. He told me the same thing, that he was going to do the right thing and go to class. You're right, your grandmother and I both want you to do your best and focus on your education. You go finish your project, and I'll talk to you later. I love you, Eric."

§§§§§

At 4:00 that afternoon, the Valdavian News Network anchor, Jason Fuller, interrupted the regular programming for a special live announcement from the Vatican. Eric had turned on the news earlier, after he called his sons, so that he would see the announcement live. He turned up the volume, and stared at the screen.

Pope Romanus stood at a podium in a room filled with Cardinals and supporters of Blessed Queen Angilia's cause. He read the announcement in Latin, in which he declared that she would be proclaimed Saint Angilia on November 17, 2081. He spoke of her virtues and sanctity as the chief reasons for her canonization.

Cardinal Rossi, Prefect of the Congregation of the Causes of Saints, then read a brief biography of Angilia, which emphasized her service and impact both within and beyond the Christian world. He reminded people that she had loved everyone, Christian or not, just as God commanded all people to do. Angilia's impact, therefore, truly was global.

Immediately after the live announcement, Jason Fuller introduced his portion of the special program. "What an amazing, remarkable announcement! Blessed Queen Angilia becomes Saint Angilia on November 17. Joining me to help us understand the vast importance of the Canonization Mass is Archbishop Clancy, the Archbishop of Valmondois. Welcome, Archbishop Clancy."

"Thank you for inviting me, Jason. This is indeed a remarkable announcement from Pope Romanus. If we look at previous beatifications and canonizations, we realize that Queen Angilia's is the shortest canonization process in the Church's modern history. Queen Angilia was beatified just three years ago, and today the Holy Father announced her canonization date," Archbishop Clancy said.

"That is indeed incredible," Jason said. "I understand that two miracles must be attributed to Angilia's intercession since her death, one of them since her beatification. So obviously, the Catholic Church has verified these miracles, correct? How do they verify such miracles, Archbishop Clancy?"

"Indeed, Jason. Two posthumous miracles have been attributed to Blessed Queen Angilia's intercession. The Church requires that miracles credited to those whose causes for sainthood are in progress be verified as true miracles. Most such miracles in the modern world involve medical cures. In these cases, the cures cannot be due in any way to medical intervention or treatment. To verify this, the scientific committee studies the case and confirms that medical intervention or treatment did not cause or contribute to the cure. That often involves examining the person's medical records and speaking with that person's doctors regarding any treatments or medications provided. These miracles must also be verified by the theological committee, who substantiates that the sick person, or someone on that person's behalf, prayed unceasingly to the Saint candidate, asking him or her to take the prayers before God. That is what we mean by intercession. So both posthumous miracles in Blessed Queen Angilia's cause have been verified both scientifically and theologically," Archbishop Clancy explained.

"What are the two miracles that have been verified for Blessed Queen Angilia?" Jason asked.

Archbishop Clancy nodded and then explained both miracles. "As people might recall, the first miracle was verified before the-then Venerable Queen Angilia could be declared Blessed Queen Angilia. That miracle occurred in March 2070, when Gwen Jordan was cured of her metastasized breast cancer. She, her husband, and her two children prayed unceasingly to Venerable Queen Angilia for Gwen's cure. Gwen's oncologists had given her just a few months left to live, and deemed her cancer untreatable.

"Gwen had stopped receiving radiation, chemotherapy, or any medications whatsoever, according to her oncologists. Her cancer had not responded to these treatments, the oncologists said, so the treatments were ceased in order to enable Gwen to live the remainder of her life as comfortable as possible. It was after the treatments had proven ineffective that Gwen and her family began praying to Venerable Queen Angilia.

"Within weeks, the oncologists treating Gwen found her tumors shrunken, and eventually gone. They thoroughly tested Gwen, even removing lymph nodes for biopsy, and found that she no longer had cancer. The evidence was found to be conclusive by both the scientific and theological committees."

"What a story of true faith and the power of prayer," Jason said. "In fact, Gwen Jordan has issued a statement following Pope Romanus' announcement. *'My family and I remain eternally grateful to Blessed Queen Angilia for her intercession. We know beyond doubt that she is the one who prompted my healing, my cure, by taking my prayers directly to God. When all was hopeless, when I was told I had a short time left to live, I knew that there was one person I could turn to for help—Venerable Queen Angilia. Queen Angilia had prayed for people throughout her life, and her prayers had led to many cures and recoveries. I trusted her. My family trusted her. We prayed to her, praying that I be cured of cancer so that I can be here, on earth, for my children and future grandchildren. Queen Angilia is a mother and a grandmother, and I knew that she would have special empathy for me and my family. She did. She does. In 11 years, I have not had a recurrence of cancer. I am cured, thanks to the intercession of Blessed Queen Angilia.'* What a powerful testimony, Archbishop Clancy."

"It most certainly is. Gwen Jordan is living proof of the power in Blessed Queen Angilia's intercession. So is the second miracle. Alexander Nejara came to Valmondois in 2076 to pray for his daughter Hope. Mr. Nejara prayed at the statue of Queen Angilia for one week nonstop, during which time he also fasted. His wife Maria remained beside Hope's hospital bed, also praying to Queen Angilia.

"Hope Nejara had been diagnosed with one of the most fatal forms of juvenile cancer, diffuse intrinsic pontine glioma, a brain stem tumor. As in Gwen Jordan's case, Hope Nejara's cancer proved unresponsive to radiation and chemotherapy. Surgery was not an option, due to the risks involved. So Mr. Nejara made a pilgrimage to Valmondois to pray at Queen Angilia's statue.

"Hope Najera's cancer went into remission, which of course the family considered a miracle. Unfortunately, however, Hope relapsed. Her cancer returned. In 2079, Mr. Nejara made another pilgrimage to Valmondois, where he fasted and prayed at the altar to Blessed Queen Angilia in Christ Church Valmondois. Before he was able to return home, his wife Maria called him with the astounding news that Hope's tumor had vanished. Mr. Nejara flew home to Mexico as quickly as possible, and anxiously sat with his wife while their daughter Hope underwent multiple tests to confirm that her cancer had vanished.

"After two weeks of testing, Hope Nejara's oncologists, as well as outside oncologists who were consulted, verified that young Hope did not have diffuse intrinsic pontine glioma. Just as in Gwen Jordan's case, both the scientific commission and the theological commission scrutinized her case, and found that Hope Nejara's cancer was cured not by medical means but as a result of Blessed Queen Angilia's intercession," Archbishop Clancy informed the audience.

"What an amazing story. As you were speaking, my producer informed me that the Nejara family gave a live statement in Mexico a short time ago. We have footage of that we would like to share with our viewers," Jason Fuller said.

People around the world watched as Alexander, Maria, and Hope Nejara publicly shared their testimony. Alexander Nejara cried as he told of his fasting and praying to Queen Angilia on both occasions, and how his love for his daughter was his driving force. Alexander said, "When they told Maria and me that our Hope would die, I did not accept that. I could not accept that. I did the only thing I knew would work, the only thing I could do. I traveled to Valmondois, Valdavia. I made a pilgrimage there so that I could pray to Queen Angilia, a woman whose prayers often heal people. Her prayers healed people during her life on earth, and they still do from her life in Heaven. Blessed Queen Angilia is a Saint, with or without any church's declaration."

When the camera returned to the news studio, both Jason Fuller and Archbishop Clancy were smiling. "That is what today's announcement by Pope Romanus is all about. Blessed Queen Angilia's canonization symbolizes and publicly proclaims her holiness, her existence in Heaven, and her intimate relationship with God," Archbishop Clancy stated.

§§§§§

Eric, Leigh, Yvonne, and two security guards flew to Oxford, England for Prince Eric's and Prince Patrick's graduation. Eric had seen them when he had gone to the University on March 8 for the annual scholarship ceremony. He had spent that weekend with them. Now he returned to share their graduation.

During the two-hour flight, Eric reflected upon his sons' 24 years of life and what they had accomplished. Prince Eric would be the next King de Valdavia, and he had spent his teenage and young adult years preparing for that role. Prince Eric had majored in politics with the goal of learning as much as possible for his future job. After his graduation, Prince Eric would return to Valmondois and take on patronages and more duties. He had told his father that he wanted to do so, because he considered it on-the-job training. Eric was proud of his oldest son, and he understood, for he had done the same thing after his college graduation.

Prince Patrick would continue his education at the University of Oxford, earning both his BEd and his DPhil in education administration. He had talked to his father more fully about his plan to open Valdavia's first university. He had mentioned knowing what he would call the university, although he had not told anyone its name. He had told Eric that this was more than his dream. This was his destiny, his life's purpose. He had to do this, he said, because it was what he was born to do. Eric was so gratified by Prince Patrick, because his son did not have to work so hard—Patrick wanted to work that hard. He chose to pursue this path.

Both of his sons had inherited their great-grandfather's and their grandmother's strength, dedication, will, faith, and belief in destiny. He saw so much of his grandfather and his mother in both of his sons. He knew that their legacy would live forever, passed down to the generations who followed them. More than ever, Eric understood the DeBruce Martineau legacy, its meaning, and its lasting impact.

§§§§

The summer proved busy for the Royal Family as they continued to work tirelessly for the people of Valdavia. King Eric II had stepped into the patronage of his grandfather's Open Heart Foundation after his coronation. He had also become the Patron of Randy Meadows' foundation, Star of Hope, of which his mother had been the Patron. He continued the work that mattered to them, the vital work of making life better for people who suffer.

Now that he had graduated, Prince Eric became a full-time working member of the Royal Family. He regularly performed duties and attended charity functions. He became the Patron of the Athletic Association of Valdavia, commonly known as AAV, of which his great-granduncle Patrick had been the first Patron. Prince Eric also became Patron of a foundation his grandmother had founded, Light Within. That foundation was important to Prince Eric, because it had been extremely important to both his grandmother and his paternal great-grandmother Katherine, and its mission was to help people.

Prince Patrick enthusiastically became the Patron of a foundation his grandmother had founded when she was in graduate school. Learning for Life was extremely imperative and symbolic to Patrick, because its mission was to promote global and lifelong education and to work with outreach programs and organizations so that learning opportunities were available for as many people as possible. Prince Patrick also became the Patron of his grandmother's Tom Greenfield Foundation, founded on the 25th anniversary of Tom's death, with the goal of bringing musical instruments and education to children across the world, in schools, hospitals, and other organizations.

As the three men dedicated their summer months to nonstop work, the world counted down the days until Blessed Queen Angilia's Canonization Mass. Prayer cards had been created for Angilia, and her son and grandsons carried copies in their jacket pockets every day. Their friends Nicole, Shannon, Scott, Billy, Charlie, Jack, and Eleanor were understandably excited and thrilled about Angilia's impending sainthood. They all planned to attend her canonization in Rome. In fact, Yvonne smiled as she shared her mother Nicole's elation with her best friend Eric, telling him how much Nicole looked forward to sharing the experience. Eric hugged her, knowing how much his mother's canonization meant to her friends. He even prayed with her, thanking God for their friends.

§§§§

"Eric, is it all right if I go to my mother's house for a while?" Yvonne asked a couple hours after breakfast one day.

"Of course, Yvonne. Is anything wrong?"

"I don't know. Mom hasn't answered her phone since yesterday, and I'm worried about her. I just want to check on her and make sure everything's all right."

"Do you want me to go with you?" Eric asked.

"Can you? I'm almost afraid to go alone. It isn't like Mom to ignore her phone," Yvonne said, the anxiety evident on her face.

"Of course I can, Yvonne. Let me just tell Leigh where we're going," Eric said, stood, and went across the hall to Leigh's office. Within minutes, Eric drove them to the Alexander home, where Yvonne rang the doorbell. There was no answer, even after Yvonne pounded on the door, so she unlocked it with her key.

"Mom? Are you here?" Yvonne asked several times as she went from the living room to the kitchen to the sunroom. She looked at Eric frantically, more afraid than ever that something was wrong. They had seen Nicole's car in the driveway, so it was not possible that she had driven anywhere.

Yvonne next checked the basement, where the laundry room was, but no one was there. She then quickly went from room to room looking for her mother, as Eric closely followed. When they entered William's study, Eric's heart sank and Yvonne shrieked a pained, "Mom!"

150

As Yvonne stood with her hands over her mouth, Eric quickly knelt beside Nicole. He felt for a pulse and checked for breathing and a heartbeat. He did not detect any, and he called for an ambulance. He performed CPR until the EMTs arrived, and they immediately examined Nicole. After several minutes, one of them looked at Eric and Yvonne and said, "I'm so sorry. There is nothing we can do for Mrs. Alexander."

Yvonne began crying inconsolably, and Eric hugged her close to him. He, more than anyone, understood how she felt. The EMTs said they would take Nicole's body. Eric thanked them, but asked, "May we have some time alone with Nicole first?" The two men nodded, and respectfully waited in the living room.

"Oh, Eric, my mother is gone. What am I going to do without her?"

Eric held his friend, understanding that Yvonne needed to grieve. He held her while she cried for nearly one hour. Yvonne then sat next to her mother's body on the floor, and stroked Nicole's hair off of her face. "You are so beautiful, Mom. I know you're not really gone. I know that you're with Dad in Heaven, and that someday I'll be with you again. I will miss you and love you until then." Yvonne kissed her mother's cheek, and stood. She looked at Eric and said, "I'm ready."

Yvonne and Eric went to the living room, and told the EMTs where to take Nicole's body. Like William, Nicole wished to be cremated, so the EMTs transported her body to the crematorium. After the ambulance left, Yvonne went to her parents' bedroom, where Nicole kept William's urn, and tenderly picked it up. She looked at Eric, and he nodded in understanding, knowing that she wanted to keep her father's and her mother's urns with her.

The next day, Eric drove Nicole to the crematorium, where she got her mother's urn. Shannon, Scott, Billy, and Leigh were waiting for Eric and Nicole in the palace foyer when they returned, and they all gathered around Yvonne with love. The lifelong friends went into the palace chapel, where they held a memorial service for Nicole. Each of them shared their memories and love of her, all of them remembering her compassion, her love of life, and her devotion to her family and friends.

"I was born knowing Nicole," Eric shared. "Nicole quickly became one of my mother's closest, most loyal friends in 2012. Sixty-nine years of friendship and love. Their friendship and love remained strong and constant, and gave birth to the lifelong friendship and love between Yvonne and me. That is the legacy of love that will burn eternally, from this world to the next."

Nicole Danielle Taulbert Alexander

11 March 1993

9 October 2081

Blessed is he that waiteth

--Daniel 12:12

§§§§§

"Angilia!"

"Nicole!" Angilia greeted her friend with a huge hug, as Nicole and William walked upon Angilia, her family, and Darlene. Matthew also stood and welcomed Nicole to Heaven. "Oh, it's so wonderful to see you, Nicole," Angilia said as she held Nicole's arms.

"I've missed you, Angilia, I really have. You were right. Heaven is the most beautiful place anyone could imagine. My mother was my Spirit Guide, and now I know what you and Patrick meant all those years. Seeing my mother and having her escort me here is the most beautiful thing I have ever experienced," Nicole said and then kissed her friend's cheek in gratitude.

At that moment, Eric stepped forward and welcomed Nicole with a hug and that charming dimpled smile. Eric said hello to William while he smiled. Darlene, as always, fell into a faint at Eric's feet. "Are you kidding? This is just like that slumber party!" Nicole exclaimed.

"Oh, yes it is, unfortunately," Mitchell said as he once more revived the love-struck Darlene. "Darlene, why don't you return to your grandmama now," Mitchell commanded.

"But I'm in Heaven. All I wanted when I came to Heaven was to see my King Eric. I want to stay here," Darlene pouted.

"I thought you, William, and Angilia could show me around Heaven," Nicole suggested.

"I won't be much of a guide. I haven't really gone anywhere except, well, except, you know, here," Darlene stammered.

"Well, then, why don't we both get the tour of Heaven from William and Angilia," Nicole said as she linked her arm through Darlene's.

"Well, okay, if I must. But I really don't think I'll ever go very far from my King Eric," Darlene matter-of-factly said.

"Don't be silly, Darlene. You are in Heaven! Why would you stay in one place for all of eternity?" Nicole asked while she pulled Darlene along beside her as the four friends prepared for their tour.

Angilia stood on her toes, kissed her father's cheek, and said, "I'll see you soon, Daddy. I love you."

"So will I. So do I," Darlene said as she looked over her shoulder at Eric as Nicole walked her away.

Marisol walked up behind Eric, put her hands on his shoulders, smiled, and said, "Mi pobre marido. I know how uncomfortable this makes you, but I feel sorry for Darlene. She is in love with a man with whom she knows she could never have a romantic relationship. Oh, I know she loves her husband Scott. But you, mi marido, are her ideal man, her dream man. She means no harm, and she cannot control her feelings. I think Darlene is sweet. She is like a love-struck teenager in a woman's body."

Eric smiled, turned, and kissed his wife. "I love you, Marisol."

§§§§§

On Saturday, November 15, 2081, the Royal airplane departed the Valmondois airport for Rome, Italy. On board were Eric, Uncle Patrick, Prince Eric, Prince Patrick, Leigh, Yvonne, Billy, Shannon, Scott, Charlie, Eleanor and her sister Bess, Jack and Tammy, their daughter Angilia, and six security officers. Angilia's Canonization Mass would take place on Monday. As excited as they were, all of them were cognizant that William, Nicole, and Darlene would not be physically present as they had wanted to be. Still, the Royal party did know that the three friends would be with Angilia in Heaven during the mass.

Uncle Patrick did not need to travel on the airplane, but he chose to, so that he could be with his grandnephew and great-grandnephews and support them. He noticed that his namesake great-grandnephew wrote in his diary during most of the two hour flight. Angilia's canonization was overwhelming and highly emotional to everyone who knew her, especially her son and grandsons.

Uncle Patrick recognized quite a lot of himself in Prince Patrick, especially in the young man's introspection and sensitivity. Whereas Uncle Patrick had publicly masked those parts of himself, Prince Patrick never had. Uncle Patrick had also felt things deeply, and he expressed those feelings through his poetry. His great-grandnephew, however, wrote it all in his diaries. Angilia had done both, and Uncle Patrick considered her a sort of fusion of himself and Prince Patrick.

As the plane neared Paris, Prince Patrick put away his diary and pen, and looked out the plane window. They were up among the clouds, and Prince Patrick watched them, as if searching for something—or someone. Uncle Patrick moved into the seat next to Prince Patrick, and leaned his head over the young man's shoulder. "Heaven is among the clouds, Patrick," Uncle Patrick softly said as he pointed upwards. "She's up there, probably watching us at this moment. She, your grandfather, your great-grandfather, your mother, your other great-grandparents—they are all there together. I know you never met all of them, but you will someday. They know you and Eric, though, and they love you both."

"I know. I feel Grandmother near me a lot. I feel her soul. I don't see her, but I don't have to see her to know that she's with me. It's enough to feel her, Uncle Patrick," Prince Patrick whispered. Uncle Patrick put his arms around his great-grandnephew and smiled.

§§§§

"Welcome. I am Dana Fisher, and I am reporting live from St. Peter's Square today as Valdavian News Network brings you uninterrupted coverage of Blessed Queen Angilia's Canonization Mass. What a glorious day it is in Rome, as we await the start of the mass. Even though the temperatures are cool, the sun is shining brightly, as if in celebration with the world.

"Local police estimate that 800,000 pilgrims fill St. Peter's Square and the surrounding areas. That number, of course, does not include all of you who are watching or listening to the broadcast across the globe. We do know that 150 Cardinals, 1000 Bishops, and 100 government delegates are attending today's Canonization Mass. Many of the government delegates are arriving, including the King and Queen of Spain, the King and Queen Consort of England, the Prince and Princess of Monaco, the President of France, the President of Zimbabwe, the President and First Lady of the United States, the Prime Ministers of Great Britain, Canada, Australia, New Zealand, Japan, Israel, and the Netherlands, the King of the Netherlands, the President of Italy, and the President of the People's Republic of China.

"One question we posed to an official at the Vatican is whether the government delegates attending are all Catholic. The Cardinal we spoke with told us not all of them are, but that is not a prerequisite for attending Blessed Queen Angilia's Canonization Mass. He told us that everyone who attends does so out of respect for and to honor the life and work of Blessed Queen Angilia.

"The Canonization Mass is beginning, as we hear one of the four choirs here today singing a hymn in Latin." A few minutes later, Dana Fisher commented, "A Cardinal has just led the first responsory, and we hear the bells of St. Peter's ringing. The choir performs another hymn as more crowned heads and government delegates arrive. As the choir sings, a Cardinal welcomes these invited guests. We now see the Cardinal greet three people who received healing miracles as a result of Queen Angilia's prayers. First we see the Cardinal welcome Eleanor Hale and her sister Bess, and then Charlie Britt, and finally Jack Cornwell, his wife Tammy and daughter Angilia, who was named after the Queen.

"The last of the invited guests to be greeted are Blessed Queen Angilia's family. Her grandson Prince Eric shakes the Cardinal's hand and speaks with him, followed by his twin brother Prince Patrick, both of whom turn 25 years old today. Next the Cardinal greets Blessed Queen Angilia's paternal uncle Patrick, who everyone knows by now died 104 years ago. Finally, the Cardinal welcomes and talks with Blessed Queen Angilia's son, King Eric II, whose 60th birthday is today. The four men are dressed in black suits with red and white ties, the Valdavian national colors. We know how ecstatic and emotional they are today as their beloved Angilia becomes Saint Angilia.

"We will now bring you, uninterrupted, the Canonization Mass of Blessed Queen Angilia in its entirety."

The Sistine choir sang a chant, Litany of the Saints, during the processional as Cardinals carried candles, crosses, and Holy books. As they neared the altar, they removed their mitres, revealing their skullcaps, as they bowed and then stood at their seats to the left of the altar. Pope Romanus was the last to enter, carrying his crucifix scepter, followed by his two Magistri Caerimonarum Apostolicarum. The Pope went to the altar, where one of his assistants removed his mitre, revealing his skullcap. The Pope bowed and offered the liturgy for the Eucharist, during which he venerated the Eucharist by waving a thurible of incense over the altar. When he finished, his mitre was replaced and he was handed his crucifix scepter. Pope Romanus walked to a statue of the Virgin Mary, which he venerated and kissed. Afterward, he walked to his chair, where he stood and said a prayer in Latin to bless the Canonization Mass.

Unlike at the Beatification Mass, there would be three petitions made by three Cardinals from the Congregation of the Causes of Saints for Blessed Queen Angilia's canonization before the Pope would make the proclamation of holiness. The first to speak was Cardinal Rossi, prefect of the Congregation of the Causes of Saints. "Most Holy Father, Holy Mother Church earnestly beseeches Your Holiness to enroll Blessed Queen Angilia among the Saints, that she may be invoked as such by all the Christian faithful."

Pope Romanus then prayed, "Dear Brothers, let us lift up our prayers to God the Father Almighty through Jesus Christ that through the intercession of the Blessed Virgin Mary and all the Saints, he may sustain with his grace the act we now solemnly undertake."

A Cardinal instructed everyone to observe two minutes of silence, for prayer, after which Pope Romanus said, "We ask you Lord graciously to accept the prayers of your people that our devoted service may be pleasing to you and contribute to the growth of your Church through Christ our Lord."

The second petition was then spoken by another Cardinal from the Congregation of the Causes of Saints. "Most Holy Father, strengthened by unanimous prayer, Holy Church more earnestly beseeches Your Holiness to enroll her child among the Saints."

Pope Romanus then prayed, "Let us then invoke the Holy Spirit, the giver of life, that he may enlighten our minds and that Christ our Lord may not permit his Church to err in a matter of such importance."

The Pope then stood with his hands folded before him in prayer, as the choir sang a ninth century hymn, "Veni Creator Spiritus" ("Come Creator Spirit"). The entire audience also stood during the hymn. At the hymn's conclusion, Pope Romanus took his seat for the third petition.

"Most Holy Father, Holy Church, trusting in the Lord's promise to send upon her the spirit of truth, who in every age keeps the Supreme Magisterium immune from error, most earnestly beseeches Your Holiness to enroll her, your elect, among the Saints."

Pope Romanus then made the proclamation of holiness. "For the honor of the Blessed Trinity, the exultation of the Catholic faith, and the increase of the Christian life, by the authority of our Lord Jesus Christ, and by the Holy apostles Peter and Paul, and our own, after due deliberation and frequent prayer for divine assistance, and having sought the counsel of many of our brother Bishops, we declare and define Blessed Queen Angilia be Saint, and we enroll her among the Saints, decreeing that she is to be venerated as such by the whole Church. In the name of the Father, and of the Son, and of the Holy Spirit."

A wave of applause began before the Pope finished his proclamation and continued during the hymn, Psalm 32. Eric, Prince Eric, Prince Patrick, and Uncle Patrick bowed their heads in prayer. They were all overcome by their emotions. Eric put his hand on Prince Patrick's shoulder when the younger man wiped his tears with a handkerchief. As the hymn ended, Prince Patrick smiled at his father, his brother, and his great-granduncle.

As they had at Angilia's Beatification Mass, they would carry the reliquaries to Pope Romanus for his blessing, the difference being that the twins would carry one reliquary together. The third reliquary would be carried by a very special person.

Accompanied by two Cardinals, Prince Eric and Prince Patrick carried the reliquary containing the piece of their grandmother's blouse to Pope Romanus. They knelt before him, and he kissed the reliquary in blessing. He then smiled fondly at both young men, and placed his hands upon their heads to bless them. Both of them kissed the Pope's hand. The Princes walked to the altar, where they placed the reliquary upon a special table that had been built to its left.

The Cardinals accompanied them to their seats, and then escorted Uncle Patrick to Pope Romanus' chair as he carried the reliquary that contained Angilia's hair ribbon. Patrick knelt before the Pope, who blessed the reliquary with a kiss, and then placed his hand on Patrick's head to bless the angel of God who knelt before him. Patrick kissed the Pope's hand, and then walked to the altar, where he placed the reliquary alongside the one his great-grandnephew's had placed there.

Perhaps the most emotional moment of the Canonization Mass occurred next. Young Hope Nejara, escorted by two Cardinals, carried the reliquary that contained the first-class relics, the bullet and the bone fragment that Matthew had saved. Hope knelt before the Pope, and he blessed the reliquary by kissing it. Pope Romanus then placed his hand atop Hope's head, and blessed her. She cried when she kissed his hand, and he patted her cheek and spoke with her for a moment. No one knew what Pope Romanus said to her, but Hope smiled and nodded in return. She then carried the reliquary to the table, and placed it with the other two.

Next, others who been touched, directly or indirectly, by Angilia's prayers, carried bouquets of yellow and white flowers to the reliquary table. They placed the bouquets around the reliquaries, and bowed in prayer. Candles were lit and placed on the table, as well. A deacon venerated the reliquaries by waving a thurible of incense over and around them.

Cardinal Rossi made the formal request of Pope Romanus, saying, "Most Holy Father, in the name of the Holy Church, I thank Your Holiness for making this proclamation, and humbly request that you decree that the apostolic letter concerning the active canonization be drawn up."

Pope Romanus' mitre was removed, and he stood for the singing of the hymn, "Gloria." When the hymn concluded, the Pope said, "Let us pray. God of everlasting mercy, who in the very recurrence of All Saint's Day, kindle the faith of the people you have made your own. Increase, we pray, the grace you have bestowed, that all may grasp and rightly understand in what font they have been washed, by whose Spirit they have been reborn, by whose blood they have been redeemed. Through our Lord Jesus Christ your Son who lives and reigns with you in unity with the Holy Spirit our God forever and ever. Amen."

Eric stood and walked to the lectern for the first gospel reading. "Matthew Chapter 7. *'Judge not, that ye be not judged. For with what judgment ye judge, ye shall be judged: and with what measure ye mete, it shall be measured to you again. And why beholdest thou the mote that is in thy brother's eye, but considerest not the beam that is in thine own eye? Or how wilt thou say to thy brother, Let me pull out the mote out of thine eye; and, behold, a beam is in thine own eye? Thou hypocrite, first cast out the beam out of thine own eye; and then shalt thou see clearly to cast out the mote out of thy brother's eye. Give not that which is holy unto the dogs, neither cast ye your pearls before swine, lest they trample them under their feet, and turn again and rend you. Ask, and it shall be given you; seek, and ye shall find; knock, and it shall be opened unto you: For every one that asketh receiveth; and he that seeketh findeth; and to him that knocketh it shall be opened. Or what man is there of you, whom if his son ask bread, will he give him a stone? Or if he ask a fish, will he give him a serpent? If ye then, being evil, know how to give good gifts unto your children, how much more shall your Father which is in heaven give good things to them that ask him? Therefore all things whatsoever ye would that men should do to you, do ye even so to them: for this is the law and the prophets. Enter ye in at the strait gate: for wide is the gate, and broad is the way, that leadeth to destruction, and many there be which go in thereat: Because strait is the gate, and narrow is the way, which leadeth unto life, and few there be that find it. Beware of false prophets, which come to you in sheep's clothing, but inwardly they are ravening wolves. Ye shall know them by their fruits. Do men gather grapes of thorns, or figs of thistles? Even so every good tree bringeth forth good fruit; but a corrupt tree bringeth forth evil fruit. A good tree cannot bring forth evil fruit, neither can a corrupt tree bring forth good fruit. Every tree that bringeth not forth good fruit is hewn down, and cast into the fire. Wherefore by their fruits ye shall know them. Not every one that saith unto me, Lord, Lord, shall enter into the kingdom of heaven; but he that doeth the will of my Father which is in heaven. Many will say to me in that day, Lord, Lord, have we not prophesied in thy name? and in thy name have cast out devils? and in thy name done many wonderful works? And then will I profess unto them, I never knew you: depart from me, ye that work iniquity. Therefore whosoever heareth these sayings of mine, and doeth them, I will liken him unto a wise man, which built his house upon a rock: And the rain descended, and the floods came, and the winds blew, and beat upon that house; and it fell not: for it was founded upon a rock. And every one that heareth these sayings of mine, and doeth them not, shall be likened unto a foolish man, which built his house upon the sand: And the rain descended, and the floods came, and the winds blew, and beat upon that house; and it fell: and great was the fall of it. And it came to pass, when Jesus had ended these sayings, the people were astonished at his doctrine: For he taught them as one having authority, and not as the scribes."*

Eric bowed his head and returned to stand at his seat for the singing, by a male soloist, of the hymn "Hallelujah." After the hymn, Uncle Patrick walked to the lectern for his gospel reading. "Hebrews Chapter 11. '*Now faith is the substance of things hoped for, the evidence of things not seen. For by it the elders obtained a good report. Through faith we understand that the worlds were framed by the word of God, so that things which are seen were not made of things which do appear. By faith Abel offered unto God a more excellent sacrifice than Cain, by which he obtained witness that he was righteous, God testifying of his gifts: and by it he being dead yet speaketh. By faith Enoch was translated that he should not see death; and was not found, because God had translated him: for before his translation he had this testimony, that he pleased God. But without faith it is impossible to please him: for he that cometh to God must believe that he is, and that he is a rewarder of them that diligently seek him. By faith Noah, being warned of God of things not seen as yet, moved with fear, prepared an ark to the saving of his house; by the which he condemned the world, and became heir of the righteousness which is by faith. By faith Abraham, when he was called to go out into a place which he should after receive for an inheritance, obeyed; and he went out, not knowing whither he went. By faith he sojourned in the land of promise, as in a strange country, dwelling in tabernacles with Isaac and Jacob, the heirs with him of the same promise: For he looked for a city which hath foundations, whose builder and maker is God. Through faith also Sara herself received strength to conceive seed, and was delivered of a child when she was past age, because she judged him faithful who had promised. Therefore sprang there even of one, and him as good as dead, so many as the stars of the sky in multitude, and as the sand which is by the sea shore innumerable. These all died in faith, not having received the promises, but having seen them afar off, and were persuaded of them, and embraced them, and confessed that they were strangers and pilgrims on the earth. For they that say such things declare plainly that they seek a country. And truly, if they had been mindful of that country from whence they came out, they might have had opportunity to have returned. But now they desire a better country, that is, an heavenly: wherefore God is not ashamed to be called their God: for he hath prepared for them a city. By faith Abraham, when he was tried, offered up Isaac: and he that had received the promises offered up his only begotten son, Of whom it was said, That in Isaac shall thy seed be called: Accounting that God was able to raise him up, even from the dead; from whence also he received him in a figure. By faith Isaac blessed Jacob and Esau concerning things to come. By faith Jacob, when he was a dying, blessed both the sons of Joseph; and worshipped, leaning upon the top of his staff. By faith Joseph, when he died, made mention of the departing of the children of Israel; and gave commandment concerning his bones. By faith Moses, when he was born, was hid three months of his parents, because they saw he was a proper child; and they were not afraid of the king's commandment. By faith Moses, when he was come to years, refused to be called the son of Pharaoh's daughter; Choosing rather to suffer affliction with the people of God, than to enjoy the pleasures of sin for a season; Esteeming the reproach of Christ greater riches than the treasures in Egypt: for he had respect unto the recompence of the reward. By faith he forsook Egypt, not fearing the wrath of the king: for he endured, as seeing him who is invisible. Through faith he kept the passover, and the sprinkling of blood, lest he that destroyed the firstborn should touch them. By faith they passed through the Red sea as by dry land: which the Egyptians assaying to do were drowned. By faith the walls of Jericho fell down, after they were compassed about seven days. By faith the harlot Rahab perished not with them that believed not, when she had received the spies with peace. And what shall I more say? for the time would fail me to tell of Gedeon, and of Barak, and of Samson, and of Jephthae; of David also, and Samuel, and of the prophets: Who through faith subdued kingdoms, wrought righteousness, obtained promises, stopped the mouths of lions, Quenched the violence of fire, escaped the edge of the sword, out of weakness were made strong, waxed valiant in fight, turned to flight the armies of the aliens. Women received their dead raised to life again: and others were tortured, not accepting deliverance; that they might obtain a better resurrection: And others had trial of cruel mockings and scourgings, yea, moreover of bonds and imprisonment: They were stoned, they were sawn asunder, were tempted, were slain with the sword: they wandered about in sheepskins and goatskins; being destitute, afflicted, tormented; (Of whom the world was not worthy:) they wandered in deserts, and in mountains, and in dens and caves of the earth. And these all, having obtained a good report through faith, received not the promise: God having provided some better thing for us, that they without us should not be made perfect."*

Patrick said a silent prayer and returned to his seat, but he stood with everyone while the hymn "We Walk by Faith" was sung by a choir. Next, two Deacons would sing the same gospel, the first Deacon in Latin and the second Deacon in Greek. The Deacons carried the two holy books to the lectern, where the first Deacon placed his book on the lectern and venerated it with a thurible of incense. He then sang I Peter 1 in Latin. When he finished, the second Deacon placed his book on the lectern and venerated it with the thurible of incense. He sang I Peter 1 in Greek.

When they finished, the Deacons carried the holy books to Pope Romanus for his veneration. Following that, four choirs joined their voices and sang the solemn response, Psalm 117.

Pope Romanus then spoke the homily at the lectern that was placed before his chair. "At the heart of this day are obedience and faith. Throughout Scripture, God the Father and God the Son teach us the virtues and rewards of obedience and faith. In Isaiah 1:19, we are told that '*If ye be willing and obedient, ye shall eat the good of the land.*' And in the New Testament, John 14:15, Jesus tells us, '*If you love me, keep my commandments.*'

"Saint Angilia possessed perfect obedience to and faith in God. She acknowledged him as her Heavenly Father, her creator, and her teacher. She publicly said many times that she loved God, and that her desire was to do his will. She obeyed his Ten Commandments, using them to guide her life. When she did, or thought she had, broken one of the Commandments, she prayed for God's forgiveness, and she repented of her sins.

"King Solomon, whom Saint Angilia admired for his wisdom, wrote Proverbs 3:5. '*Trust the Lord with all thine heart; and lean not unto thine own understanding.*' In Mark 9:23, Jesus Christ declares, '*if thou canst believe, all things [are] possible to him that believeth.*' Saint Angilia's faith was extraordinary in its depth and consistency. Her faith never wavered, remaining steadfast even in the face of threat and danger. At the time of the assassination attempt on her life in 2012, Saint Angilia wrote in her diary that no matter what happened she knew that God was in control. She trusted God to take care of her father, King Eric I, the one she thought was in imminent danger. Saint Angilia had faith that God would do his will.

"That belief in God, that obedience and faith, are at the core of Saint Angilia's intercessions. Those for whom Queen Angilia prayed when she was alive say that her prayers always included the heartfelt request that God do his will and bidding. She knew that there was a greater purpose and meaning behind God's destiny for each of us, and that was a consistent element of her prayers of intercession.

"If we take but one lesson from the life of Saint Angilia, let it be that obedience to and faith in God remain the surest, sturdiest shields we can wear. Obedience and faith will carry us through whatever trials and tribulations, struggles and sadness assault us, because, no matter the outcome, we remain safe in the arms of God."

Those gathered at St. Peter's Square applauded at the end of Pope Romanus' homily. A Deacon commanded everyone to observe two minutes of reflective silence, after which the Pope said a prayer in Latin. A responsory hymn was sung before the Prayers of the Faithful. Representatives from five countries said prayers for Saint Angilia in their native languages: Spanish, Arabic, English, Chinese, and French. Pope Romanus then prayed for God to bless everyone in the name of his Son Jesus Christ.

The Offertory Procession, the gifts of bread and wine, began as a hymn was sung in Latin by a choir. Pope Romanus walked to the altar, and his miter was removed before he prayed and venerated the offerings with a thurible of incense. The Pope knelt on a kneeler, from where he prayed for and venerated those in the audience who would receive the bread and wine. He then walked around the altar and into the front rows of the audience and venerated the audience with the thurible of incense, as well. The Pope led a responsory prayer for communion in Latin, after which another hymn was sung in Latin. During the hymn, Pope Romanus bowed his head in prayer before the altar.

He said another Latin prayer to bless the bread and wine and to ask that God bless the Eucharist. After that prayer, two Bishops prayed in Latin. Another responsory hymn was sung, followed by the singing of the hymn "Amen," which Pope Romanus sung while he bowed his head in prayer. Priests began going into the crowd, to give communion to the people, while the Pope greeted the religious men near the altar.

Pope Romanus bowed his head in prayer before he received Holy Communion. The Pope then gave communion to Angilia's family—Eric, Prince Patrick, Prince Eric, and Uncle Patrick. He next gave communion to Cardinals and Bishops seated to the left of the altar near Angilia's family. Bishops finished giving Communion to the Holy men, while the priests gave communion to as many people as possible. After several minutes of communion, a cardinal commanded everyone to observe two minutes of prayerful silence, at which time the Pope said a prayer in Latin.

Pope Romanus began the conclusion of the Canonization Mass by thanking those who had come. He first greeted the pilgrims, many of whom had journeyed long distances to attend, thanked them for their faith, and offered his desire that God protect and bless them. He thanked the Cardinals, Bishops, priests, and other Holy men and women who had come, many of whom had participated in the mass. He thanked the Cardinals who were members of the Congregation of the Causes of Saints. He finished by thanking Saint Angilia's family, saying, "King Eric II, Prince Eric, Prince Patrick, and the Divine Angel Patrick are the true heirs of the Church's newest Saint, Saint Angilia, whom we have commemorated today."

The final prayer of Saint Angilia's Canonization Mass was spoken in Latin by Pope Romanus, the Regina Caeli prayer to Saint Mary, the mother of Jesus. "Let us pray: O God, who gave joy to the world through the resurrection of thy Son our Lord Jesus Christ, grant, we beseech thee, that through the intercession of the Virgin Mary, His Mother, we may obtain the joys of everlasting life: Through the same Christ our Lord. Amen." After the prayer, the Pope once more walked to the statue of Saint Mary, where he bowed his head in reverence and then tenderly touched the statue with his hand. When he finished, he made the sign of the cross while a choir sang the hymn "Hallelujah." After the hymn, a fanfare sounded as the Pope walked to the altar, which he venerated with a kiss.

A soloist performed a song Angilia had written and recorded for her first album when she was six years old. Even then, as a world-renowned prodigy, Angilia's work honored God. The crowd applauded and cheered throughout the song, as the lyrics rang true and touched their hearts. Eric and Uncle Patrick put their arms around Prince Eric and Prince Patrick as the four men radiated joy.

Before me stretches my destiny,

Decided long before my birth by God,

That I shall forever willingly trod.

This true life path is my reality

And forevermore my necessity,

One that leaves my entire being awed.

This path that is narrow and never broad.

This path has been mine for eternity.

The force directing my walk is the Word,

That which I believe with all of my soul,

That in the beginning of my being stirred,

That created me a complete and whole

Child whose Holy Father she so treasured

And whose virtues she would ever extol.

The Canonization Mass officially ended at that moment. Pope Romanus went to Angilia's family and spoke with them for several moments. As he held Eric's hand in both of his, he said, "Saint Angilia is such an inspirational Christian. How blessed your life has been with her as your mother and your teacher. I can tell through my relatively brief interactions with you, that you have inherited Saint Angilia's faith and obedience. May God truly bless you, my son."

"Thank you, Your Holiness. Your belief in and support of my mother's cause was a constant source of peace for me," Eric said before he kissed the Pope's hand.

Pope Romanus took Prince Eric's hand and told him, "Your grandmother, Saint Angilia, believed that God ordained her father and her son as the Kings de Valdavia, due to their virtuous qualities.

You were born heir to the throne, and I can see that you have inherited those qualities. You will become a King de Valdavia in the mold of your great-grandfather and of your father, with the unwavering faith of your grandmother. May God continue to bless you throughout your life and reign."

"Thank you, Your Holiness. I have learned a lot from my father, as well as from my great-grandfather and my grandmother. She is the one, more than anyone else, who taught me how to live a godly life just by watching her live her life. I learned from her example, and I can see now how very many people also learned from her life," Prince Eric said and kissed the Pope's hand.

Pope Romanus turned to Prince Patrick and smiled as he took hold of the young man's hand. "I hear that you are one step closer to opening that university of yours. I see quite a lot of your grandmother shining from within you, my son. You and she steadfastly believe that this is your destiny. I agree. Your brother Eric was born to be King de Valdavia, but you were born to serve people in this way. It is as if these two parts of your grandmother's compassion and public service split into the two of you, in legislation and in education. May God always bless you."

"Thank you so much, Your Holiness," Prince Patrick said as tears filled his eyes. "That is exactly what I told my grandmother when I was seven years old, that God destined me to help people in this way, just as she had. She is the noblest woman I will ever know, in every sense of the word. Thank you." Prince Patrick somehow managed to restrain his tears as he bent to kiss the Pope's hand.

Pope Romanus finally turned to Uncle Patrick, and clasped his hand. "I know the miracle it is to see you, to touch you, and to talk with you. Like most people, I know your story. It is a story like Saint Thomas' that reiterates faith and belief. God allowed your recordings and manifestations so that people would hear you and see you, and therefore believe in eternal life. Your niece Saint Angilia's holiness is proved through the prayers she takes to God and through the miracles that result. God does bless you and Saint Angilia, and he will do so for all eternity."

CHAPTER 6

“ **D** ad, do you know what's going on? The morning news is buzzing about some important announcement from the church this morning,” Prince Eric asked as he entered his father's dressing room one morning.

Eric looked confused as he finished tying his navy blue tie. “No, Eric. Which church?”

“Ours—Christ Church Valmondois.”

“Reverend Emerson hasn't mentioned anything important to me. I suppose we'll find out soon,” Eric said, patted his son's shoulder, and walked downstairs to the dining room with him.

There, Prince Patrick, Leigh, and Yvonne greeted Eric with similar questions. No one knew what the important announcement was, but they were all curious. They knew it was nothing to do with Reverend Emerson retiring or leaving his position. He had mentioned on Christmas Eve—just nine day earlier—how much he enjoyed his work and his parishioners. The Royal household would simply have to wait for the announcement and learn the news with everyone else.

Just after breakfast, as Eric entered his office, he received a telephone call from Reverend Emerson. “Eric, if at all possible, I'd like you and your sons to be here at the church in two hours for today's special announcement. Archbishop Clancy and Father Fisher will also be in attendance."

Eric's brain was swirling, wondering why both religious men would attend the announcement. Perhaps something had suddenly happened that had forced Reverend Emerson to resign or retire. "Is everything all right, Reverend Emerson?"

"Yes, Eric, everything is just fine. This is a very important announcement, though, and we would like you and the Princes to be present."

"Of course, Reverend Emerson. We had planned to visit the Royal Vault today anyway. We always do on my mother's birth date, you know."

"I know, Eric. Lots of people have already been here this morning to pray, light candles, or leave flowers at Saint Angilia's altar. I look forward to seeing you, Patrick, and Eric."

Eric quickly informed his sons, Leigh, and Yvonne that they were expected to attend the announcement at the church soon. They became more curious than ever as they completed a few tasks prior to leaving. They were greeted by well-wishers on the mall as they left the courtyard and began their walk to the church. Soon, they noticed the large crowds gathered outside the church, including members of the local and international press.

"This must be some important announcement for this many people to show up," Prince Eric commented.

"Yeah. This is how it was during Grandmother's canonization process," Prince Patrick added, reminding everyone of the intense public and press interest during those years.

The Royal Family was cheered when they arrived, and they waved to everyone before they entered the church. Inside, they greeted Reverend Emerson, Archbishop Clancy, and Father Fisher. Eric was relieved to see Reverend Emerson smile as they shook hands, taking that as a positive sign. "I must say, you've certainly generated quite a lot of interest for a Saturday morning," Eric told Reverend Emerson with a smile.

"This hasn't been the easiest secret to keep. Not everything goes unnoticed by everyone, especially since this is the home church of Saint Angilia. There are several visitors to the church every day, so people do notice each little move or change. Still, I think we managed to pull this off without anyone knowing exactly what we were doing," Reverend Emerson said with a wink.

"Well, I certainly don't know what's going on," Eric said. "I did notice that the sign out front is being replaced, but that isn't too unusual. The last time the sign was replaced was when I was six years old, so it's about time for a replacement."

Prince Eric smiled at his father and said, "I say so, too. Fifty-four years is a long life for a sign."

"Ouch. Are you saying I'm old, son?" Eric grinned.

"No, not you, Dad. The sign. The sign is old."

"Nice save," Prince Patrick teased his brother. The men giggled before Reverend Emerson reminded them that the announcement would be made soon.

Eric and his sons took a few moments to pray before the altar, and then walked outside with Reverend Emerson, Archbishop Clancy, and Father Fisher. A podium had been placed near the front entrance, and Reverend Emerson stepped to the microphone. "Welcome. Archbishop Clancy, Father Fisher, and I are pleased that you could join us on this beautiful Saturday morning for this exciting announcement. This is something we are so pleased and honored to make public and to share with you, especially today. To make the formal announcement, I welcome to the podium the Archbishop of Valmondois, Archbishop Clancy."

Archbishop Clancy smiled, shook Reverend Emerson's hand, and greeted the public and the Royal Family. "Good morning. Reverend Emerson is correct. We are quite pleased about today's announcement, and I am sincerely honored to be the one to share this news with you. The idea for this actually was brought to me a few years ago, but was not something we could pursue at that time.

"We did pursue this as soon as possible, and we chose today to make this official. This date is significant and symbolic for two reasons. First, his Majesty King Eric I died 17 years ago, in his daughter's arms. King Eric died on his daughter's birthday. Saint Angilia was born 86 years ago today.

"Saint Angilia's inaugural Father's Day sermon is legendary by now. In that sermon, Saint Angilia compared her father, King Eric de Valdavia, to King David of Israel. King Eric, in his wisdom, followed David's lead and made his child his co-monarch. Both Solomon and Angilia reigned for 40 years. The first three years of Solomon's reign were spent as his father's co-monarch. The first 36 years of Angilia's reign were spent as her father's co-monarch. The many parallels between King Eric and King David and between Queen Angilia and King Solomon have been mentioned and commemorated numerous times over the past few decades.

"These four monarchs are cemented in history as the most godly, wise, empathetic, compassionate, and beautiful. We know how true those qualities are for Queen Angilia in particular. She would not have been canonized as Saint Angilia were her godliness, wisdom, empathy, and compassion not used in the service of God. Her entire existence, as we know, is spent in obedience to God and in helping others.

"What better way to honor that than by renaming Christ Church Valmondois." At that moment, Father Fisher removed a black velvet sheet from the church sign, and people erupted in cheers. Prince Patrick grabbed his father's arm, and began crying. Prince Eric hugged his father as tears also filled his eyes. Eric placed his hand over his heart—over the holy pendant hidden under his shirt—and felt his love and emotions overflow his veins.

Archbishop Clancy finally was able to speak again as the cheers subsided. "A new plaque commemorates this occasion," he said as Reverend Emerson removed a black velvet curtain from a plaque on the church wall near the door. Archbishop Clancy read the plaque aloud as people began crying and praying.

Saint Angilia Church

Dedicated 3 January 2082

The 86th Anniversary of the Birth of

Angilia Erica Charity DeBruce Martineau Taylor

§§§§

Angilia and Tom sat alone next to a brook, playing guitars and singing gospel songs. As they finished "The Lord's Prayer," Tim, John, Greg, and Joe joined them. As if on cue, the four musicians' instruments appeared, and the band immediately launched into a song that Tom had taught Angilia, "O Come Angel Band." Soon Patrick joined them, and sang "I Love to Tell the Story" and "Just As I Am" with them.

Midway through "Just As I Am," Eric walked nearby, and leaned against a tree. Angilia smiled up at him as she sang, and motioned for him to join them. He put his hands upon his daughter's shoulders, and sang with her, Patrick, and Tom. That was the first time that the four of them had sung together, and Angilia smiled up at her father, uncle, and friend in joy.

In fact, all eight friends could not stop smiling as they continued with "It Is No Secret (What God Can Do)." It was not long before Darlene heard Eric, and she ran to the brook. She stood motionless, staring at Eric with her perpetually wide eyes.

"Isn't this just beautiful?" Marisol suddenly asked as she walked up behind Darlene and put her hands on Darlene's shoulders.

"Uh-huh," Darlene muttered. "He surely is."

Marisol stifled her giggle, and patted Darlene's shoulder. She led Darlene to a log closer to Eric, Angilia, Patrick, and the band. Soon they were joined by Matthew, his parents, Marisol's parents, and Eric's parents and grandparents. Angilia beamed when she saw her family, especially her great-grandfather Stefan. He rarely left his choir, the Principalities, in the Angel Realm. He still served as an Overseer, teaching and training those angels who had purposes for being in the Angel Realm—just as he had prepared Angilia to become Uncle Patrick's Spirit Guide.

Stefan smiled and nodded to Angilia, delighted to see and to hear his great-granddaughter and his two grandsons together in Heaven. Angilia noticed that Stefan tapped his foot as she, her father, her uncle, and Tom sang "Amazing Grace." Angilia felt her father squeeze her shoulder, telling her without words how exquisite it felt to have their family around them.

The final song they performed was one they had all known since their childhoods—"Jesus Loves Me." When the song ended, Stefan walked to Angilia, gently pulled her into a hug, and said, "Yes, he most certainly does, my darling. He always has, and he always will." Stefan smiled at his grandsons, his family, and their friends. "He loves all of you," he smiled.

Darlene began crying, and Stefan reassured her, "Jesus' love is so beautiful, I can understand your tears, my child."

"No. I mean, yes, his love is beautiful, but that's not why I'm crying. It's King Eric. His performance was so beautiful. He is so beautiful. It's just too much," Darlene sobbed.

Patrick and Tim snickered, but Angilia shushed them. Eric sighed, and said, "This is too much. Is this really going to happen for the rest of eternity?"

"Darlene, your admiration of my grandson is really fine praise for God, who created Eric the way he is. In fact, the glory for each of us and our existence goes to God alone," Stefan lectured.

"Oh, I know, Your Majesty. I praise God every time I look at King Eric. Believe me, I do," Darlene gushed.

"That's fine, my child. Continue to praise God and to focus on him, and you will be doing the right thing," Stefan told Darlene. Stefan then turned to Eric, clasped his shoulders, and whispered, "I will pray for you, Eric, and I will pray for Darlene."

"Good luck, Grandfather. I've been praying for Darlene for years. It's hopeless," Patrick said.

"Nothing is hopeless in Heaven, not even Darlene's infatuation," Stefan winked.

"I pray not," Eric said.

"I do, too, but Heaven hasn't met anyone like Darlene before. I think we've got our work cut out for us," Patrick admitted as he patted his brother's back.

§§§§§

After the Royal party returned to the palace following the annual Father's Day church service, Eric, Prince Patrick, Prince Eric, Leigh, and Yvonne settled in the sitting room. Prince Patrick suddenly turned on a movie network, only to see a classic movie from 143 years earlier just beginning. He smiled as he watched the opening scene of Dorothy Gale and Toto running home after school, a scene he had first watched with his grandmother.

Prince Eric smiled, too, and watched the movie with the same happy memories flooding his mind. Eric watched his sons as much as he watched the movie, enjoying their happiness. "The Wizard of Oz" had been his mother's favorite movie since she had first watched it when she was four years old with her father. She had shared the movie with Eric when he was a toddler, and years later with his twin sons.

More than two hours later, when the movie ended with Dorothy's famous line that *'There's no place like home,'* Prince Patrick softly said, "No, there isn't."

Eric smiled and agreed with his son, who then said, "Dad, Eric, I want to take you to lunch for Father's Day. Today is very special, and I want to spend as much time as possible today with you both."

"That's cool, Patrick. That'll be fun," Prince Eric smiled.

"Yes, it will, Patrick. Let's go," Eric said, and the three men went to Prince Patrick's car. He drove them to Angilia's favorite Italian restaurant, where they shared love, conversation, and laughter for a long lunch.

§§§§§

"Princess darling!"

"Billy! Oh, how wonderful to see you," Angilia exclaimed as she hugged her lifelong friend.

"You are the first person I had to find when I got here. My dad was my Spirit Guide, and he smiled when we arrived. He knew I would seek you out, and he said you would probably be here," Billy said, referring to the brook where Angilia often sat.

Angilia giggled, and Billy cherished the sound he had not heard for almost 13 years. "I've missed you so, Angilia. I knew you were here, and that you were alive, healthy, and happy. I knew I would see you again when I died, or at least I prayed I would. I lived my earthly life so I would spend my eternal life in Heaven with my family and friends. I tried to do my best to do so, and here I am," Billy enthused.

"Oh, Billy, there was never any doubt. I knew in my soul I would see you again. You were always such a true friend to me and Daddy, and then to Matthew and Eric."

"That was easy to do. When you bent down and talked to me at the Christmas tree lighting when I was four, I thought you were an angel. You were so beautiful and kind to me. You singled me out, and our friendship was born. I think I sensed the truth about you that first time we met. I was so young and innocent, untainted by the world, and I saw what few people saw. That's how it was for Natalie when she saw you that day. God let Natalie and me see the truth, even though I didn't take it literally for many years. That's why your autobiography never really surprised me. I knew in my heart that my Princess darling is an angel."

"Oh, Billy, that's beautiful. God brought you into my life for a reason, and I am so grateful for that," Angilia said and again hugged Billy.

"So am I," he smiled.

"Come on. Let's go visit Daddy and Matthew. Roger, Daniel, Susan, Nicole, William, Darlene, Mr. Brennan, and Miss Yost are here, too. They will adore seeing you," Angilia smiled and linked her arm through his.

"Miss Yost? I bet she still sings, too. What else would she do, after all? I mean, music was her whole life."

"Yes, she does sing. She joined Gabriel and me once when we were playing, and she sang an aria. That was such a nice treat," Angilia smiled.

Billy laughed. "I'm sure it was for some people. Miss Yost is a very nice lady, even if her music class was a bit much for middle school. Is it true that in Heaven people can do what they've always wanted to do?"

"Yes, it is. Katherine, for example, finally has her flower garden that she never had time for on earth. Dr. Taylor has his own golf course. My grandmother Matilda enjoys doing her embroidery. She makes lovely pieces. Matthew does his art, just like he did in the Unborn Children Sphere," Angilia explained with a smile. She looked at him and asked, "What have you always wanted to do, Billy?"

Billy smiled broadly, and immediately answered, "I did what I really wanted to do on earth. I got to work for and help Eric and you. That had been my dream since childhood, and it came true. I have no idea what I want to do here, Angilia. My life on earth was just perfect."

"Billy, what a sweet thing to say. You'll figure out what you will do. Your earthly work was all about helping others. You rarely spent time for yourself. Now you have earned your eternal reward. Perhaps you will become an Overseer like my great-grandfather," Angilia pondered.

"Do you really think so? That would be ideal for me. Perhaps I can speak with King Stefan about that. First, though, I want to see Eric and Matthew again," Billy said with a smile as they walked down a golden path.

§§§§§

Prince Patrick awoke quite early for a Saturday morning, feeling the importance of the day before the sun had lit the world. While most people still slept, he walked to the University Church of St. Mary the Virgin. Not only was the church at the heart of the University of Oxford, it was the church his grandmother had attended when she lived in Oxford. Patrick smiled as he entered, picturing his very young grandmother kneeling to pray.

Prince Patrick took a deep breath and knelt in prayer. *Dear God, I pray that in your loving kindness you stand with those of us who earn our degrees today. We each have reasons for being here, for getting our degrees. We have purposes to fulfill. You have long known mine. You have known longer than I have. I know that I was born to do what I am at Oxford to learn. I am meant to open that university. That is how you intend me to help people. You know how much I long to do that. I have to do that. I ask that you continue to guide me on this journey, God, so that I do as you expect of me. Amen.*"

As Prince Patrick still knelt with his head bowed, he felt a gentle, warm breeze encircle him. He knew. "Grandmother," he whispered. Suddenly, he breathed in sharply as he felt a hand on his cheek, a gentle, warm, and soft hand. He stood and opened his eyes, but never saw anyone. Still, he knew it was his grandmother. How very often he had felt her hand caress his cheek when he was a child. It was such a loving, safe touch, one he would forever remember.

"Oh, Grandmother, I love you. I know you are with me always, but to feel you, to physically feel you, is such a miracle, especially today," Prince Patrick softly said as tears trickled from the corners of his eyes.

"Hey, buddy, she knows. She loves you so very much," Uncle Patrick said as he manifested beside his namesake.

Prince Patrick smiled at his great-granduncle, and said, "I know. I've always known. I've always felt her love."

"Hey, Angilia asked me to bring something from her to you today.   Here," Uncle Patrick said, and handed a large manila envelope to Prince Patrick.

"This is from Grandmother?" Prince Patrick asked in amazement.

"Yeah. She wants you to have this, Patrick."

Prince Patrick carefully opened the envelope and pulled out handwritten sheets of parchment. He stared at the first sheet, at his grandmother's familiar slanted cursive script, and felt indescribable elation. The last time he had received something she had written was the birthday card she had given him on his 13th birthday—the same day she had died.

Prince Patrick stood before the church altar and read the 82 pages, never moving except to turn the sheets. Uncle Patrick watched with a smile, knowing that Angilia's tract would serve its purpose. "This is mind blowing," Prince Patrick managed to whisper when he finished reading.

"Yeah. Angilia has written tons of stuff going back to the Unborn Children Sphere and the Angels Choir. She's always written. She wrote this after she died, after she went to live in Heaven with all of us," Uncle Patrick explained. "I told her I should bring that to earth and have it published. She talked with Michael about that, and he agreed with me that it would alleviate peoples' fears of death, about what happens when they die, and about what Heaven is like. So she told me to give it to you."

"Why me? I mean, this is incredible, but I don't know anything about publishing a book."

"Talk to Yvonne. The Press Office published one of Angilia's books years ago, with the proceeds going to Eric's and Angilia's foundations. They can publish and sell this book, and the proceeds will go toward your university. That's what Angilia wants," Uncle Patrick told his great-grandnephew.

Prince Patrick began crying, and he grabbed Uncle Patrick in a tight embrace. "When I was seven, Grandmother told me that my university would go from dream to reality. She told me that it was meant to be, and that she would help me in every way she could. She set up trust funds for Eric and me, which I always knew would be a huge help with funding the university. Now this. This is more than I ever imagined."

"I know. But this will help all people, just like your university will. Nothing about this is coincidence, you know. She wrote this, never expecting it to leave Heaven, but it's meant to be read. People need this. They need the truth. This helps people, including you, because the money goes into your university. See. It's meant to be this way. Everyone benefits," Uncle Patrick smiled.

"Yeah, we do. This is the kind of thing Grandmother always did. Thank you, Uncle Patrick," Prince Patrick said.

"Sure thing. You better go get ready for your graduation. Your dad, brother, and friends will be here soon."

"Right. I'll talk to Yvonne about the book on our flight home. I know she knows, but tell Grandmother I love her more than life," Prince Patrick smiled, repeating a phrase that she had told him numerous times over the years.

§§§§§

8 May 2083

On the plane flight home this evening, I talked with Yvonne about publishing Grandmother's book. Of course she was stunned by the idea at first—a manuscript written in and delivered from Heaven is quite unusual, after all. Still, she agrees that it's a fabulous idea, and she will have the manuscript prepared by her assistant next week, and also have someone in graphics to design the cover. Yvonne said Grandmother's book should be available soon—just a few weeks, maybe three.

I shared the manuscript with Dad and Eric tonight after dinner. They both read it, and they both cried. It's such a true and hopeful piece, and they agree with Uncle Patrick that it will help people tremendously. People who have died and come back to life—whose times for death had not yet come—have written books about their experiences. They described what they saw during their brief time in Heaven and the loved ones there, as well. Those are touching stories, important because they show us what does await us when we die. Well, what awaits those of us who believe in and are obedient to God.

Still, there has never been an account from someone who lives in Heaven, someone who died and stayed there. Grandmother's short but powerful book will be the first of that kind. In fact, Yvonne said it will be ideal to have the manuscript typeset, as usual, but to also scan Grandmother's handwritten pages into the book as well. She said it will make a huge impact for people to see the actual pages, in Grandmother's handwriting. So this will be a facsimile edition, she said. Yvonne herself will scan the parchment sheets tomorrow after church.

When she finishes, I will keep them with me for the rest of my life. I already know that they will be kept protected in my office at my university. When I die, they will be placed in Grandmother's suite here in the palace. Here they will remain for all of Grandmother's descendants to have and to learn from. Just seeing them confirms the truth of eternal life and Heaven.

Grandmother is the most miraculous woman to ever live. She has given all of us so very much, both tangible and intangible. I will never love anyone as I love her. My love for her is unlike any other. I love Dad, Eric, and our friends very much. Grandmother—there is just something extraordinary about her and how she has made me feel since my birth. She touches the depth of my soul in this indescribable way. Magical is the wrong word. Transcendent is the right word. She, and the feeling she brings to me, transcend this mortal world.

I love my life, and I don't want to die without accomplishing my purpose, my destiny. But I'm not afraid to die. When I do, I know what and who I will see. What a beautiful gift Grandmother has given me—given everyone.

§§§§

"Good afternoon, and welcome to the midday news on this pleasant Monday, May 31, 2083. I am Gene Cooke, and I am reporting from outside the Palais Royale de Valdavia. The top story today is the release of a new book written by Saint Angilia. No one can recall such enthusiasm and interest surrounding a book as we have witnessed since 8:00 this morning. That's when the palace Press Office opened and sales of <u>The Splendor of Heaven</u> went live.

"Miss Yvonne Alexander, the palace Press Secretary, has graciously agreed to talk with us for a few moments on what is one of the busiest days the Press Office has ever experienced. Thank you, Miss Alexander. What exactly has been the reaction to Saint Angilia's book?"

"You're welcome, Mr. Cooke. The Press Office began receiving calls and messages two weeks ago when we announced that the book would be released. We have been inundated with calls, messages, and orders for the book since then, to the extent that we have hired additional temporary staff to help us handle the load.

"We went into this knowing that <u>The Splendor of Heaven</u> would generate tremendous interest and excitement, so we were as prepared as we could be. All of us are elated that Saint Angilia's book touches people, and that she continues to inspire and to comfort people," Yvonne stated with a radiant smile from the crowded, noisy mall outside the palace.

"Prince Patrick is the one who spearheaded the book's publication, we understand. All proceeds go toward the funding for the university which he plans to open in Valmondois."

"That's correct," Yvonne said. "In fact, shortly, we will have copies of the book available for purchase on the courtyard. Prince Patrick has agreed to sign copies of the book this afternoon. As you likely know, he wrote the forward, which tells the incredible story of how the manuscript came to him."

"That is quite an incredible story indeed. I know you must return to the Press Office now. Thank you for taking the time to talk with us today, Miss Alexander." Yvonne quickly returned to the Press Office, while palace staff prepared for Prince Patrick's book signing. "Ladies and gentlemen, we anticipate an even more intense public reaction when His Royal Highness makes his appearance soon. We will bring you coverage of his book signing this evening."

§§§§

Prince Patrick signed copies of his grandmother's book throughout the afternoon and evening as a constant stream of faithful and fans filed past a table set up on the courtyard. The last woman to purchase a book told Prince Patrick, "Saint Angilia always spoke of Heaven as this beautiful place full of love. She always made it seem like the only place anyone could want to be. Thank you for bringing this book to us, Patrick."

"Thank you. It's ironic you mention that, because Grandmother wrote something along that theme in this book."

"Would you read it for us, Patrick?" someone asked as the sky grew darker. The hundreds of people still on the mall watching Prince Patrick and taking his picture voiced their desire to hear the passage.

Prince Patrick nodded, opened a copy of the book, and read his grandmother's words:

Love. Love is the heart of all of creation. We were created from God's love. We are the manifestations of his love. The earth upon which we live our physical lives was created from that same love, as a place that provides all we need in order to live those lives. Its beauty and wonder are manifestations of his love. Look around, and you will see his love in the sunrise, in a snowflake, in a soaring bird, in a majestic mountain, in a growing flower. Everything was created from that most perfect love.

So, too, was Heaven. God created Heaven as our eternal home. When we have finished our lives on earth, and if we have reciprocated God's love for us, we will live in Heaven forevermore. Heaven is difficult to describe, for mere words can never capture the awesome wonder, beauty, and peace of Heaven. Heaven is the only place to ever exist where there is no strife, no pain, no sickness, no night, no hunger, no death, and no hatred. Love is all that exists in Heaven. Love fills Heaven and all who dwell here.

God's love for us fills Heaven and us. That love is so powerful and immense that there is no room for any other feeling. That love is the most comforting we will ever know. Heaven contains the most glorious beauty, beauty beyond human comprehension or imagination. True perfection exists only in Heaven, for Heaven is the only place untainted by the evils and ills that plague earth.

You will never feel pain, sorrow, exhaustion, hunger, heartbreak, regret, anger, resentment. You will feel only peace, joy, and love. You will become a new creature made entirely of love. All of the baggage of your earthly life will leave you when you die and enter the gates of Heaven and begin your eternal life. You will still be you, but you will be reborn whole and perfect. Your physical life will end. Your spiritual life will never end. That is your reward for loving God as he loves you. No greater love exists than God's love for each of us, and Heaven is the proof of that love.

CHAPTER 7

That summer, Prince Patrick purchased a 100-acre plot of land in Valmondois. He then met with an architect to discuss the facilities needed for his university. Six buildings were proposed, and by the end of the summer Prince Patrick approved the designs. Work began on all six buildings immediately: administration offices; library; classrooms/laboratories; music/arts/drama; and two dormitories. More buildings would be built once the university was open, but to start, Prince Patrick needed the most essential buildings established.

Once the construction was underway, Prince Patrick applied for the university's license. He then worked on the governance: mission statement, policies, personnel needs, and admissions parameters. Next, he established the disciplines that would be taught: history, sociology, anthropology, geography, economics, government, languages, nursing, English, education, communication, business administration, engineering, mathematics, social work, criminal justice, biology, chemistry, religion, and philosophy. He had to recruit faculty before he applied for accreditation. He needed at least one faculty in each discipline, as they would develop the curricula.

The first person Prince Patrick called was Eleanor Hale, who was on summer break from her high school teaching job. "Eleanor,

I am returning to Oxford soon to complete my studies and earn my DPhil in education. The buildings for the university are being built as we speak. While I am working on my DPhil, I'd like to hire 20 faculty, one in each discipline, who will draft the curricula. That will enable us to apply for accreditation and to begin recruiting students. I know you have a teaching job, but you are the first person I considered. I'd like to talk with you about becoming a faculty in the history department at the university. You don't have to answer yet, but I would like to schedule a meeting so we can at least discuss this."

"I'd be honored and delighted, Your Royal Highness," Eleanor immediately replied. "I have keenly followed the news of your university's construction, and I am amazed at the progress you have already made. I know that this is important to you and to your grandmother. I want to be part of this. I want to help people as much as I can, in her honor."

Once Eleanor convinced Prince Patrick that she was committed to the university, she submitted her resignation at the high school and met with him to begin drafting the history curriculum. Before he had to return to Oxford, Prince Patrick had hired all 20 faculty members, all of whom worked on the curricula in rented offices until the administration building was finished. He left Valmondois in early October knowing that progress on the university was smooth and on schedule.

Michaelmas term lasted from October 10 through December 4, during which time Prince Patrick learned all that his professors had to teach. He also worked on the university's mission statement, revising it numerous times until the holiday break. He returned home after attending the morning church service on December 5, and excitedly caught up with his father and his brother.

That afternoon as they, Leigh, and Yvonne decorated the Christmas tree in the sitting room, Prince Eric told them that he had met someone special. "Giselle was at the charity luncheon last week. We talked for a long time, and I'd like to get to know her better. I want you to meet her."

"Hey, cool, man. You've never brought a girlfriend home before. This sounds serious," Prince Patrick smiled.

"I hope so. She's the first woman I've met who's interested in me, my thoughts and ideas, instead of titles and all of this," Prince Eric said as he gestured a hand around the room, meaning the palace. "Other girls couldn't wait to come here and see the palace and all. They didn't like me as much as they liked my title and address."

"Yeah, I hear you," Prince Patrick replied. "I get that, too, but I'm just not interested right now. I've got important things to do before I want to even think about that. It's gotta be harder for you, though. You're the next King. At least I don't have to deal with that from people."

"I'm sure Great-grandfather and Uncle Patrick dealt with this all the time. I mean, they were among the first superstar princes. Look at all the magazines, newspapers, and posters that Grandmother preserved in the family archives. They were treated like rock stars. That had to be crazy," Prince Eric marveled.

"It was, but the great thing is that neither of them seemed to notice. They didn't pay attention to all of that. They never seemed to notice the girls who threw themselves at them or fainted at their feet. They did their work. They never did realize just how much people loved them. I remember Grandfather was always surprised by the reactions he got. Everyone saw it but him," Eric said as he shook his head.

"Uncle Patrick still doesn't totally get it. He just doesn't see that a lot of the attention really is about him," Prince Patrick added. "To him, it's all about his work for God."

Prince Eric giggled. "That's not why girls still scream when they see him. Sure, they know he's an angel, but he's still Patrick, the heartthrob of the 1970s."

"You know, Mommy said once that Uncle Patrick's physical looks reflected his soul. Despite his reputation as some rebellious bad boy, he lived a godly life. He was beautiful inside, and that was reflected outside in his handsome looks," Eric shared.

"That's why Grandmother is so beautiful," Prince Patrick softly said.

Prince Eric grabbed his brother in a hug as his emotions overflowed, and Eric smiled as he looked at Yvonne, tears in his eyes. Happy tears, as his mother perpetually called them.

§§§§

On Christmas Eve afternoon, Prince Eric drove to Giselle's apartment. As she picked up her purse, she said, "I'm so excited to meet your father and brother, especially today. Christmas is my favorite time of year."

"Mine, too. Dad and Patrick can't wait to meet you, Giselle," Prince Eric smiled as he helped her into his car. "I'm so happy you are attending the midnight service with us."

"So am I, Eric. I remember the first Christmas after my dad and I moved here. Your great-grandfather told the Christmas story, and I just remember how much love was in his voice. I mean, here was this very important and powerful ruler. He seemed so kind and gentle that night, and I was happy that Dad had moved here. I suddenly felt safe here. I wasn't homesick anymore."

"Great-grandfather was so awesome. I'm so grateful for him. I can't tell you how much I love him, Giselle."

"You don't have to, Eric. It shows. I can hear it in your voice. I wish I could have met him."

"So do I. But now you get to meet Dad and Patrick," Prince Eric said as he parked his car in the palace garage. Prince Eric walked around the car, opened Giselle's door, and took her hand as she stood. When they entered through the patio door, Prince Eric guided her to the stairs. "Everyone's in the sitting room," he explained, and linked his arm through hers.

As soon as the couple entered the sitting room, Eric, Prince Patrick, and Leigh stood. Eric noticed his son's huge smile when he introduced Giselle Marie Potok to him. Giselle curtsied, and then said, "I am so honored to meet you, Your Majesty. Eric has told me so much about you, and I've followed your work, so I feel like I already know you."

"Thank you, Giselle. Eric has told us a lot about you, as well. It's wonderful to finally meet you," Eric replied as he hugged her.

"Yeah, it's nice to meet you," Prince Patrick said with a huge smile. He was pretty sure that Prince Eric and Giselle were serious, because Prince Eric had never dated anyone else more than once. None of the women had ever been interested in Prince Eric; they were drawn to his title and wealth. Prince Eric once more told Prince Patrick that Giselle was the first woman who cared about him: his feelings, his thoughts, and his beliefs. Prince Patrick was so thrilled for his brother.

Giselle equally charmed Leigh and Yvonne, who were also happy that Prince Eric had found someone who loved him. They sat with the Royal Family and Giselle in the sitting room for a few hours before dinner, chatting and getting to know the woman who seemed to have captured Prince Eric's heart. At one point, Yvonne asked Giselle about her parents, and recognized the look of sadness in the young woman's eyes.

"My father is enjoying his holiday break from work. He goes back to work on January 3, so this is a nice chance for him to relax. He's worked so hard all of my life, especially after Mom died. He had to take care of me and keep everything together, so he never had time to just break down. I know he probably wanted to, but he never did. I'm sorry. I didn't mean to be such a downer today," Giselle said and gave a small smile to everyone.

"No, don't apologize," Eric gently said. "We understand. My grandfather went through the same thing when his wife died. He had their baby daughter, my mother, to care for, and he really never let his grief take hold of him. He stayed so strong and stoic his entire life. He had to, for Mommy and for the country. There was never time for grief, not really."

"I know. I've thought of King Eric I so often over the years and wondered how on earth he kept it all in check for so very long. I know that Dad has more time for tears and sadness now that I'm on my own. It makes me sad, but I know it's not healthy to hold it in, either. He has to let it out. He has to," Giselle said as she dabbed a tear from her eye.

"Grandfather did, too, at least a couple of times that I know of. Once was when he, Mommy, and Dad toured America and visited a children's hospital. One of the little girls reminded him of Grandmother. She was dark-haired and dying of leukemia. Grandfather and Mommy talked about Grandmother's death that evening, and that's the only time I know of that they cried about her together. Like Mommy always said, grief isn't wrong. She always told us that our grief equals our love."

Giselle nodded. "I believe that. Mom died when I was seven. I was old enough to understand what happened. She was on her way home from work when a drunk driver hit her car. She was killed instantly. At least that's what the coroner told us. I hope so. I pray she didn't suffer." Giselle began weeping, and Eric held her while she cried.

Finally, she stopped and dried her eyes. "Thank you. I've never said any of that out loud before. I never talk about her. I don't want to hurt Dad."

Yvonne leaned forward and held Giselle's hand. "It won't hurt him. Memories keep her alive for both of you, and you should share them. It will help. Mom and I talked about Dad a lot after he died, and we laughed far more than we cried."

Giselle smiled and said, "Thank you, Yvonne. I think I'll bring her up when Dad comes over for Christmas tomorrow. Christmas was Mom's favorite holiday. She made it so special, and there are so many memories we can share."

"That's the best way to celebrate Christmas, Giselle," Prince Eric smiled at her. "Great-grandfather and Grandmother are such a part of Christmas. In fact, the gingerbread palace we always display at Christmas was given to Grandmother when she and Grandfather were in America in 2046." Prince Eric walked with Giselle to the table where the gingerbread palace had been displayed every Christmas for 37 years.

"This is amazing," Giselle marveled, and squealed with delight when she opened the front door to see the miniature King Eric in the foyer. "I've never seen anything like this. I bet your Grandmother adored this, Eric," she smiled up at him.

"She did indeed. She had the museum staff preserve this, and we've treated it with care. I just hope it lasts many more years."

"Oh, wouldn't it be just incredible if your children are able to enjoy this, too, Eric," Giselle exclaimed. Eric and Prince Patrick smiled at one another. How remarkable that Giselle instantly understood the emotional importance of something as simple as a gingerbread house. They were certain that Prince Eric had found his one and only love.

§§§§

Prince Patrick checked the progress of his university's development before he returned to Oxford in mid-January 2084. King Eric flew to Oxford for the annual Eric DeBruce Martineau Scholarship for Musical Excellence—the 72nd ceremony—on Monday, March 13. He spent the weekend with his son, who attended the ceremony as usual at the end of each Hilary term.

The men returned home the following day, and Prince Patrick wasted no time in checking on his university's construction. He then spent his six-week break meeting with the faculty, discussing the curriculum. He went back for the Trinity term in late April knowing that all was going well and on schedule. When Trinity term ended, he spent his long 15-week summer break working nonstop on his university.

After making sure the accreditation application was filed, Prince Patrick hired a Board of Regents. The 14-member Board, appointed from professionals in various fields, met bimonthly during Prince Patrick's summer break. They approved of the University's mission statement and curriculum plan, and also began fundraising and major gift cultivation to assist not only with the operating costs but with the establishment of scholarships.

Prince Patrick's final break prior to attaining his DPhil began in early December 2084. He met with the Board of Regents twice during the six-week break and once with the faculty. Assured that all was well with the University, he relaxed and enjoyed the Christmas holiday with his family—and Giselle, who brought her father to Christmas Eve dinner and the midnight church service as a guest of the Royal Family.

Mr. Potok had met Eric several times and King Eric a few times, but enjoyed meeting Prince Patrick and getting to know the family. He, too, was quite certain that his daughter and Prince Eric would marry. Their love was evident to all who saw them together, as both fathers delightedly discussed.

"I admit that I was stunned when Giselle told me that she was in love with Eric. The idea never entered either of our minds, but it just happened without warning. I had my doubts, I'll tell you. This isn't a life for everyone, what with all of the scrutiny and criticism. But Eric loves my daughter, and he has gradually been introducing her to the lifestyle. I couldn't ask for a better son-in-law," Charles Potok said to King Eric.

"I feel the same about Giselle. She and Eric do love one another, and that will carry them through anything. Love is the only thing that truly matters in any relationship, Charles. I'm delighted to have you and Giselle with us for Christmas."

"Thank you, Eric. It's wonderful to have an extended family. It's been just Giselle and me for so long. I have a feeling we'll be celebrating something besides Christmas this time next year," Charles said with a wink.

§§§§

In what seemed the blink of an eye, Prince Patrick completed his graduate studies and faced his graduation on March 10, 2085. The Royal plane arrived in Oxford for the ceremony carrying King Eric, Prince Eric, Giselle, Charles Potok, Leigh, and Yvonne. They all joined the audience in giving Prince Patrick a rousing standing ovation as the shadow of his grandmother's own Oxford legacy loomed over the University. No one felt that more than Prince Patrick as he stood in the same Sheldonian Theatre that 11-year-old Angilia had in 2007. Although her tenure as a Professor of Literature had lasted a mere five years, its influence was still felt. Prince Patrick longed to impact people as she had done; she was his inspiration in founding his university.

That evening, after the celebratory dinner, Prince Eric joined his brother in the privacy of his apartment. "I'm so proud of you and so happy for you, Patrick. This is the moment you've worked hard for, and this is the ticket to your dream coming true." Prince Eric hugged his brother for several moments before stepping to the window and looking at the darkening sky. "I know this is your day, but I have something to share with you."

Prince Patrick smiled and grabbed his brother in a hug. "Congratulations, Eric."

"I haven't told you yet."

"I know. You don't have to, though."

"I want to. You're the first person to know. I asked Giselle to marry me yesterday, and she said yes. We're engaged!"

"This is such wonderful news today. Thank you for telling me first. Dad and Mr. Potok will be thrilled. So will Grandmother. I felt her spirit all day, and I know she's watching us."

§§§§§

"Oh, Matthew, isn't this just beautiful?" Angilia asked her husband as they watched their grandsons that evening. "Our little Eric is such a wonderful man, so godly and kind, and now he's engaged to marry his one true love."

"Yes, my darling. I pray that he and Giselle are as happy as we were," Matthew exclaimed and hugged his wife.

"Excuse me, Angilia and Matthew. I don't mean to intrude, but I've been watching them today, too, and I'm just as ecstatic about Eric and Giselle. I'm Frances Potok, Giselle's mother. She and Eric love each other so much. They will be very happy as long as they hold onto their love and faith, as I know they will."

"Oh, Frances, it's so wonderful to meet you," Angilia said and hugged Mrs. Potok. "Giselle is a fabulous woman, and I know how much love she gives to Eric. I'm so happy for them."

"So am I," Matthew smiled. "Our families are now one for all time," he added and hugged Frances.

CHAPTER 8

The Royal party returned to Valmondois on March 13, the day after the scholarship ceremony, and prepared for the engagement announcement. Mr. Potok and Giselle arrived at the palace early on Thursday morning, where Prince Eric and Giselle went to the chapel to pray before the onslaught of attention. At precisely 9:00 that morning, Leigh posted the formal announcement on the palace gate. When he read it aloud, the euphoric screams of those gathered on the mall were heard inside the palace.

15 March 2085

With the utmost happiness and love, His Majesty King Eric II announces the betrothal of his beloved son Prince Eric de Valdavia to Miss Giselle Marie Potok. Miss Potok is the daughter of Mr. Charles Albert Potok and the late Mrs. Frances Sarah Potok of London, England.

King Eric, Mr. Potok, and Prince Patrick are delighted by the betrothal, and to the impending union of their families. The wedding of Prince Eric and Miss Potok will occur on 26 June 2085 in Saint Angilia Church.

By 9:30, when Prince Eric and Giselle came onto the courtyard, the crowd on the mall had grown substantially. The happy couple posed for pictures and greeted people for two hours before returning to the palace for the official engagement photographs. When Yvonne released the pictures early that afternoon, she smiled as she recalled King Eric's and Julianne's engagement in 2051—34 years earlier. The Royal Family had suffered more than its share of tragedy and heartbreak throughout its history, but they had always maintained their faith and love. Yvonne saw that plainly in the lives of her best friend and his sons, and she knew that Angilia and her father were smiling as they watched Prince Eric's engagement day.

§§§§

"Oh, this is just so romantic and happy. I can't believe little Eric is grown and engaged," Darlene gushed as the family and their friends watched the engagement day proceedings from Heaven.

"My little boy is such a fine man, that's for sure. I am so grateful that he and Giselle have found each other," Julianne smiled.

"So am I, my dear," Marisol added, hugging her granddaughter-in-law.

"Everything is just so perfect and beautiful, just as God planned it all," Angilia said with tears in her eyes and her hands clasped over her heart. Matthew smiled and kissed her, as did Mr. Brennan.

"It most certainly is, Angilia. Your engagement was the last I witnessed on earth, you know. I remember how thrilled and honored I was when you and Matthew had my 100th birthday at the Palais, and then surprised me by having your engagement portraits taken that day. I was the only person outside of the Palais who knew that your engagement would be announced on your birthday two days later. That is one of the happiest memories of my life," Mr. Brennan smiled with utter joy. "I watched your son's engagement and wedding from this seat of honor, and now I watch your grandson's."

Angilia beamed and hugged her beloved friend. "I am so grateful that God brought you into our lives, Mr. Brennan. You are such a very special and dear friend, and I thank you for your gift of friendship."

Eric smiled, as well, and put his arms around his daughter and his friend. "I do, too, Mr. Brennan. We love you."

"And I love all of you. I am so honored to know you all. I watched your family from afar for nearly all of my life, and the day I met my King and my Princess was the ultimate highlight for me. Or so I thought. I had no idea on your 16th birthday that you would become my friends, and that I would be gathered here with all of you for the engagement of the current Prince Eric de Valdavia," Mr. Brennan added.

"Well, we are honored to know you, too, Arthur," Angilia's great-grandfather Stefan replied. "I must say, it is a pleasure to have someone with whom to discuss history. You and my grandson Eric lived through a remarkable amount of history."

Mr. Brennan smiled at Eric and said, "Yes, we did indeed. But now we all live through history for all eternity. We witness it all from the best place to exist. Heaven. Our precious Saint Angilia is the one who taught me more about the splendors of Heaven than anyone else ever did, as I am sure many of you can testify."

"You bet we can, Mr. Brennan," William agreed. So did Nicole, Darlene, Billy, Roger, Susan, Daniel, and Eduardo.

"She sure did," Patrick softly said and kissed his niece's cheek. "As unsure as I was about what would happen after my death, this one girl changed everything the minute I died. She appeared as my Spirit Guide, and I knew I was okay. I knew everything would be just fine, and it was. Forever and ever."

§§§§§

"Good morning, and welcome to our live coverage of the Royal Wedding of Prince Eric and Giselle Marie Potok on this glorious Tuesday, June 26, 2085. I am Stacia Fields, hosting Valdavian News Network's coverage from outside Saint Angilia Church where the wedding will begin in two hours.

"It's been a long time since the last Royal Wedding. 34 years ago today, Prince Eric's parents married in this same church, which was then named Christ Church Valmondois. King Eric was Prince

Eric when he and Julianne Renée LeRoy became husband and wife. Their marriage lasted only five years and five months when Julianne died during childbirth. His Majesty has never remarried, just as his grandfather, King Eric I, never remarried after the death of Queen Consort Marisol.

"All of us wish a long and happy union for Eric and Giselle, one that mirrors that of the groom's grandparents, Saint Angilia and Matthew, Duc de Valmondois. I see that the wedding guests are beginning to arrive, with Scott Ransdale among the first. Mr. Ransdale was a close friend of Saint Angilia's and one of the Duc's best men when he wed Angilia in 2016. Mr. Ransdale is assisted by two caregivers, as he is now in his 90s. How thrilling for him and for the Royal Family that Mr. Ransdale is able to share this day with them.

"We also see dignitaries and heads of state, including the Presidents and First Ladies of the United States and of France, the Prince and Princess of Wales, and the Prime Minister of Israel. As we watch the arrival of the guests, let me tell you that the crowds gathered outside the church and on the mall have grown substantially overnight. They all long to see the Valdavian Royal Family, as well as Miss Potok as she becomes a member of this family.

"As we near the last decade of the 21st century, today harkens back to the grandeur and ceremony of Valdavia's earliest years and reminds us that fairy tales really do exist and come true in this all-too-often unpleasant world. How often we have seen evidence of love and happiness through the lives of our much-loved Royal Family."

§§§§

At 11:00 sharp, King Eric's horse-drawn carriage left the palace. Sitting across from him were his best friends, Leigh and Yvonne, who had supported him and Julianne on their wedding day. Although they had protested, Eric had insisted that they travel to the church with him. They were thrilled to do so, as Eric otherwise would have made the journey alone. Neither of them wanted that.

Ten minutes later, Prince Eric and his best man, his brother Prince Patrick, left the palace grounds in the second carriage of the procession. The screams were deafening when the handsome and very popular young men appeared. People lining the route tossed roses, held banners, waved flags, and shouted well-wishes. Princes Eric and Patrick, dressed in morning suits and looking dapper, smiled and waved throughout the fifteen-minute ride to the church.

When they stepped out of the carriage and turned to wave at those standing across from the church, those inside could not help but hear the screams and shouts. Prince Eric promised everyone, "Giselle and I can't wait to greet you as husband and wife. Thank you for sharing today with us." Prince Patrick's smile seemed a mile wide at the response his brother received, and he joyously waved before the Royal men entered the church for their jubilant walk up the aisle.

As they walked up the aisle, they greeted friends, neighbors, dignitaries, and heads of state before they reached the Royal Family's pew. There, they hugged Scott, Leigh, Yvonne, and their father. "I'm so happy, Dad. This is the happiest day of my life."

"I know, son. The day your mother and I married 34 years ago today was the happiest day of my life until the only day that could eclipse that. The day you and Patrick were born is by far the happiest day of my life. The two of you are the reason I was created. I love you both more than I can say."

"We love you, Dad," Prince Eric said through his tears.

"Yeah, we do. More than life," Prince Patrick added, repeating the phrase his grandmother had often said, and hugged his father.

Ten minutes later, the carriage bearing Giselle and her father arrived, and the screams outside alerted those inside the church. Prince Eric smiled at Prince Patrick as he anticipated her arrival at the altar. In just over one hour, they would be pronounced man and wife by Reverend Emerson, and a new chapter in the story of their lives would begin. Prince Patrick patted his brother's back as the pianist began playing one of Angilia's piano pieces, to which Giselle and her father would walk up the aisle.

Prince Eric inhaled sharply at his first sight of Giselle beside her father. She had told him she would wear her mother's wedding gown from February 14, 2055, a romantic lacy gown perfect for a real-life Cinderella. The heirloom veil was held in place by the same tiara his mother had worn with her wedding gown. Charles Potok smiled at his daughter when he saw the look of love on Prince Eric's face. He squeezed her hand when he saw the same look on Giselle's face. She squeezed his hand in reply as they reached the altar to stand beside Prince Eric.

The centuries-old Christian wedding ceremony brought tears to many peoples' eyes that day as they witnessed an indisputable fairy-tale. The handsome Prince Eric de Valdavia had his Giselle, Princess de Valdavia, and their true love was more than evident. Charles Potok sat beside King Eric after giving his daughter to Prince Eric. The two men hugged during the signing of the register, now bound in friendship through their children.

Charles joined King Eric, Leigh, and Yvonne in the second carriage for the return to the palace and the celebratory luncheon and reception. The two fathers beamed at the ecstatic reaction their children received not only on the journey through Valmondois, but during the balcony appearances before the luncheon. Giselle was adored, because she was the woman who brought love and happiness to Prince Eric. Just as people had loved Marisol, Matthew, and Julianne, people loved Giselle.

That love was evident in the cheers she received from her fellow Valdavians and from Prince Eric's father and brother. The couple's love was evident when they shared their first dance as husband and wife to the same song chosen by the groom's grandparents in 2016 and his parents in 2051—Elvis Presley's timeless love ballad, "Can't Help Falling in Love." Prince Patrick put his arm around his father, understanding the emotional impact of that moment.

"I know Mom is watching Eric and Giselle right now and smiling with love. So are Grandmother, Grandfather, and Great-grandfather. They're never far away," Prince Patrick said and hugged his father. Indeed, Julianne, Angilia, Matthew, Eric and the rest of their family were smiling with love filling their beings as they watched Prince Eric and Giselle. Life was perfect on earth and in Heaven.

§§§§

The first year of Prince Eric's and Giselle's marriage passed happily, busily, and relatively uneventfully. Giselle quickly went from accompanying her husband on engagements to a full schedule of solo engagements. Soon after their honeymoon, Giselle became the Royal Patron of the Musée National de Valdavia, a post her late mother-in-law had held.

The young couple celebrated their first anniversary in part at the museum for their first portrait unveiling. King Eric, Mr. Potok and Prince Patrick attended the ceremony, which followed the tradition established by King Eric I when his first portrait as King de Valdavia was unveiled in 1992. Those attending the unveiling purchased tickets, the proceeds of which were split between the Prince's and Princess' patronages.

The Royal Family returned to the Musée at the end of September 2086 for a very special fundraiser for The Athletic Association of Valdavia. Matthew had become its Patron after his marriage, its first Royal Patron since Angilia's Uncle Patrick. Prince Eric was the organization's current Patron, and he was thrilled that the day's event benefitted such a meaningful cause.

The museum's director, Dr. Vince Newton, began the festivities at 5:00 that evening. "Welcome, and thank you so very much for attending this tribute to His Royal Highness Matthew, Duc de Valmondois on this sunny September Monday. His Royal Highness was born 100 years ago today, on September 30, 1986." Dr. Newton smiled as the crowd applauded.

"As you well know, His Royal Highness was a talented artist, and the Musée is honored to house the His Royal Highness The Duc de Valmondois Collection. We are even more delighted that his son King Eric and grandsons Prince Eric and Prince Patrick have donated twelve of the Duc's paintings to the collection. It is my honor to welcome His Majesty to the podium." Dr. Newton bowed when Eric stepped to the podium and smiled at the crowd.

"Thank you all for attending this unveiling of my father's later paintings. These were painted during the last five years of his life, and I think you'll agree that there is a sense of calm in these pieces. My sons and I decided to donate these twelve paintings in conjunction with the 100th anniversary of my father's birth as the most appropriate way to honor him.

"My mother was and still is the absolute love and light in my father's life, that's undeniable. Art, however, was his passion, his inherent profession. If you are familiar with my mother's memoir, you know that when she and my father met in the Unborn Children Sphere he spent most of his time drawing and painting. Art is what my father was meant to do, and I hope you agree that he excelled at his profession." The audience cheered their agreement, which made Prince Patrick, Prince Eric, and Giselle smile.

"Thank you," Eric continued moments later. "My sons and I agreed in particular that among the dozen paintings we donated today is the last painting my father did. He wrote about it in his diary. It's a forest scene with sunshine and deer. He wrote that my mother would like it, for she has an affinity for animals and nature. I know she does like it, and I also know that she is just as thrilled as my sons and I that the painting is here for everyone to enjoy. Patrick and Eric."

The twins stepped forward and pulled the gold cords that revealed the expanded Duc de Valmondois gallery. The gasps and applause were proof that people did enjoy Matthew's paintings. Throughout the fundraiser, people told the Royal Family how much they loved and remembered Matthew and how they enjoyed his art. By the end of the benefit, €3,500 had been raised for the AAV.

Patrick smiled and hugged his niece as they watched from Heaven. "Happy birthday, Matty," Patrick said with a wink, reminding Matthew of the first time Patrick had called him that—on his and Angilia's wedding day. What a glorious life Matthew had. He silently thanked God as he kissed his wife and hugged Patrick.

§§§§§

26 June 2087

With the utmost joy, Their Royal Highnesses Prince Eric de Valdavia and Giselle, Princess de Valdavia announce that they are expecting their first child. Her Royal Highness is in excellent health, as is her baby. They are both under the care of Dr. Joshua Timmons. The baby is due to be born in January 2088.

His Majesty King Eric, His Royal Highness Prince Patrick, and Mr. Charles Potok are thrilled by this news, and they look forward to welcoming the new member of their family.

§§§§

"What a beautiful start to the year, darling," Prince Eric said, and then kissed his wife and newborn son. "I love you and Stefan so very much."

"I love you, my dear, and our precious son. I never knew anyone could be this happy," Giselle said as she smiled at their tiny son cradled in her arms.

Both grandfathers and the uncle soon joined the happy couple and the dark-haired boy. "2088 really has begun perfectly. Our family is small and love-filled, as Mommy used to say so often. We are so blessed," Eric said through his tears as he tenderly caressed his grandson's cheek. Baby Stefan cooed, opened his eyes, and looked at his grandfather with blue-grey eyes.

Charles Potok put his arm around Eric and smiled. "Yes, we are indeed. Despite the pain and heartbreak we've had, we are so fortunate. God sure is good to us."

"Yes, he is," Prince Patrick softly agreed. "Life is as perfect as it can be."

§§§§

1 January 2088

Their Royal Highnesses Prince Eric de Valdavia and Giselle, Princess de Valdavia are ecstatic to announce the birth of their son. Prince Stefan Eric Matthew was born at 12:07 this morning. He weighed 7 pounds 8 ounces, and is 21 inches tall. Prince Stefan and Giselle, Princess de Valdavia are both in excellent health, and will return home tomorrow.

Prince Stefan's grandfathers, King Eric II and Mr. Charles Potok, are immensely happy to welcome their first grandchild. Equally delighted is the baby's uncle, Prince Patrick. The Royal Family looks forward to the happiness and love which Prince Stefan will bring to them every moment.

§§§§

"Oh, Great-grandfather, how glorious that my first great-grandchild bears your name!" Angilia gleefully exclaimed and kissed King Stefan. She turned to her husband and her father and said, "And both of your names, too. He is so perfect." She kissed both men, and then grabbed her daughter-in-law in a hug. "You are a grandmother now, Julianne. Stefan will know you and love you so very much."

Julianne nodded through her happy tears. "I know, Angilia. He will know all of us. Eric and our sons will make sure of that. None of us will ever be forgotten, because you and your father taught our family just how important our history really is. You both helped us all come to know our ancestors. Little Stefan will do the same for his children someday."

"That's such a beautiful thought, Julianne. History is not just in the past. It's constant. We live it every moment. Life is eternal, yet time constantly moves forward in this synergy of change and consistency. That's how it's always been and always will be," Eric said, his arms around his daughter and his grandfather. "This little baby boy is our future. He will carry our legacy into the next century. Everything truly is perfect."

CHAPTER 9

"King Eric's 20th Jubilee week begins tomorrow, November 14, 2089, with the National Service of Thanksgiving at Saint Angilia Church. His Majesty's Jubilee follows the tradition begun with his grandfather King Eric I's 20th Jubilee week in August 2012. The Jubilee will continue on Monday with various entertainments and the chance to meet and greet His Majesty in King Eric Celebratory Park. On Tuesday will be the Children's Tribute in Gateway Arena. Thursday is the charity luncheon to benefit his grandfather's Open Heart Foundation. Friday will be one of the perennial favorites of any Jubilee week, the Garden Party at the Palais Royale de Valdavia. Finally, on Saturday, the week concludes with the Tribute Concert at Gateway Arena. Needless to say, everyone looks forward to this chance to show our appreciation and gratitude to His Majesty.

"There are no Jubilee events scheduled for Wednesday, November 17. That day is particularly reverent, as it is the Feast Day of Saint Angilia. His Majesty has requested that, in lieu of gifts or tributes to him, people instead honor the charitable work of his mother on that day in particular. Needless to say, that is a most appropriate request, given that Wednesday is the 20th anniversary of Saint Angilia's death."

§§§§§

The Royal Family continued the custom of greeting parishioners at the entrance to the church on Sunday morning. Everyone wished Eric well, thanked him for his service, and were delighted to see his soon-to-be 33-year-old sons alongside him. Next to her husband, Giselle held 22-month-old Prince Stefan, who watched everyone with abundant curiosity. Eric was thrilled that his grandson was the star of the day, charming everyone with his excited kicks and baby babbles.

Scott was assisted into the church by his nurse; he used a wheelchair, as he had become frail after a hip fracture. Eric warmly greeted his lifelong friend, who hugged him and asked Eric to pray for him. "I don't have much longer to live, I know that. I'm ready to leave here and go to Heaven. Most of my friends are there. My Darlene is there, and I miss her so. It will be nice to get out of this wheelchair and be free to walk and run again, like I used to, Eric. My old age is not as vibrant as your grandfather's was, I must admit," Scott added with a smile.

Eric smiled in return, and said, "Most people's aren't, Scott. But I dare say you'd give me a run for the money if you hadn't had that nasty fall. I'm just grateful you weren't even more seriously injured than you were. Come, join us," Eric said and pushed Scott's wheelchair to his family's pew. He knew that Scott would not live much longer, but he also realized that Scott had lived a full and happy life. There were no regrets, just love and gratitude.

§§§§

King Eric, Prince Eric, Giselle, and Prince Patrick were humbled by the reactions and greetings they received as they mingled with people in King Eric Celebratory Park on Monday. One woman kissed Eric's hand and told him, "I was on the mall the day your grandfather died, so grief-stricken and upset. Then your mother surprised everyone by coming out and talking with us. She put us first, even though her heart was broken. She comforted us. Then you and your sons joined her, and I will never forget how you kept your arm around her as you spoke with us. I told you two young men how much of King Eric I saw in you," she looked at the twins. "I do. I see your grandmother Saint Angilia in you, too.

They live in you three men, and in this little boy," she said as she smiled at Prince Stefan. "They will live forever, that's for certain."

"Thank you, Ma'am," Eric said as he clasped her hand. "If my mother taught us anything, it is the gift of eternal life."

"Yes, she did. More than that, she taught people how to earn that gift," the woman said.

"Thank you. My grandmother is the most incredible woman I will ever know. She continues to bless my life, and I am so grateful for her," Prince Patrick said through the tears that choked him.

"We are blessed by her, too," a man in the crowd added. "She still works on our behalf, taking our prayers to God. Her soul must be made of pure love."

"Well, we know Saint Angilia was touched by God, but she had the best teacher possible in King Eric," another man added. "He is as much a saint as his daughter. He cared for our well-being more than any other monarch anywhere. You've inherited that from your grandfather and your mother, Sir. You've taught that to your sons, and they will teach it to their children. That's what life is all about. Helping people, caring for people. That is your family's legacy."

The crowd gathered in the park applauded in agreement as the sun shone down on the statues of King Eric I and Saint Angilia. Giselle smiled as she held Prince Stefan, who reached a hand toward his great-grandmother's statue. Prince Patrick kissed his nephew's cheek and could not stop his tears of joy and love. Stefan did not know Angilia's story, the truth about her, but he seemed to sense it, and the symbolism of his act deeply touched all who witnessed it that day. That evening, Prince Patrick wrote an account of the moment in the family history book that his grandmother had begun when she was a child. Stefan would share that account with his grandchildren many years later.

§§§§

Eric and Prince Patrick both awoke very early on Thursday morning. Eric showered and dressed, and then went into his grandfather's sitting room. Alone in the early morning, with the golden red of sunrise tinting the room, Eric sat on the sofa. He had held his mother there 20 years earlier as she died. Or rather, as her earthly life had ended. She had not died, he reminded himself. She would never die.

"Oh, Mommy, I love you so," Eric softly said. "I love you, and I miss you. I understand how you felt after grandfather died. I live waiting to reunite with you in Heaven."

Eric felt a very familiar warmth as Uncle Patrick manifested beside him—just as he had done 20 years earlier as his niece's Spirit Guide. Eric felt tears fill his eyes when he looked at his granduncle. "Hey, Eric, today's pretty special. It's Little One's Feast Day and your 20th anniversary as King. She told me to tell you how much she loves you and what an amazing man you are."

Eric nodded, hugged his granduncle, and cleared his throat. "Thank you. Today is very special. We're all attending the special mass for Mommy this morning. It doesn't feel like it's been 20 years. I remember every minute of that day so clearly. I always will. My sons turned 13 that day. Mommy marveled at how they were teenagers," Eric recalled with a smile. "It was such a happy day, and there was no hint of what would happen. Nothing. But I knew something was wrong as soon as she went upstairs. I felt it. Don't ask me how or what. I can't explain it. But I felt it in my heart."

"I know, Eric. You and your mother always had this connection. So did Angilia and Eric. It was just always there. I saw it in them, and then in you two. The three of you are tightly connected. Of course you feel like part of you is missing without them here. But you'll be whole again when you reunite with them, you know," Patrick gently said.

"I know. That's all that keeps me going. Hey, why don't you come with us to the church today?"

"Really? I'd love to. I'll hang out 'til it's time to go. I'll wear Little One's favorite suit. It still fits, you know," Patrick winked. Eric laughed and hugged his eternally youthful granduncle again. Patrick had been born nearly 132 years earlier and had died over 112 years earlier. He was frozen at the age of 19, however, an immortal teenager. "I love you, Uncle Patrick. I'm so glad you're an envoy angel."

§§§§

At 9:00 that morning, Eric, Prince Patrick, Prince Eric, Giselle, Prince Stefan, and Uncle Patrick, with Leigh and Yvonne, left the palace. The mass began at 10:00, and they spent the hour prior meeting and talking with people on the mall and outside the church. Someone offered Giselle a huge bouquet of flowers, so Prince Eric took Stefan and held him. People were delighted to see the young father talking to his son as they greeted people. Stefan smiled, grabbed Prince Eric's jacket lapel, and unexpectedly stunned everyone.

"Daddy."

Giselle quickly turned to look at her husband and her son. "Oh, your first word! Oh, Eric, Stefan called you Daddy!"

Practically everyone clapped or gushed, while many took pictures of the moment. "The little prince spoke!" someone exclaimed.

"Daddy, Daddy, Daddy," Stefan repeated as he kicked his left foot in excitement.

"Yes, Stefan. I'm Daddy, and I love you, son," Prince Eric replied with a huge smile. He kissed his son, only to receive another surprise when Stefan kissed him. "I love you," Prince Eric restated through his tears.

Giselle did cry—happy tears—while Eric and Prince Patrick watched with smiles. So did Uncle Patrick, who knew that his niece and his brother were watching from Heaven. They had seen and heard little Stefan's first words to his father on this very special day: Angilia's Feast Day and the anniversary of her death; the 135th anniversary of Eric's birth; King Eric's 68th birthday and his 20th Jubilee; the twins' 33rd birthday; and Stefan's first words—so many milestones on this one day. How perfect, Uncle Patrick thought, as he gently squeezed Stefan's hand.

§§§§

Finally, the Royal party entered Saint Angilia Church for the special mass. Reverend Emerson greeted the Royal Family, talking with them for several moments before the mass began. He stepped to the pulpit and welcomed everyone who filled the church to standing room capacity. "Greetings on this unseasonably gentle November 17. We gather here today, in the church named for her, to commemorate the life and the work of Saint Angilia. Not only is she Valdavia's Patron Saint, but the Patron Saint of cancer patients, musicians, writers, teachers, students, and horses. However, as many of you can testify, we can pray to Saint Angilia for whatever troubles or ails us, and she will take our prayers before God.

"While she lived among us on this earth, people approached her countless times for her intercession. They asked her to pray for their loved ones or themselves, usually requesting a cure for a serious illness or disease. Saint Angilia always prayed to God, asking him to do what was best in each case. She knew that God had a purpose behind everything, even something tragic. She understood that something much larger was at work, and she had faith that God would always do the right thing in each case. He did. Many people, and even animals, were cured as a result of her intercession.

"We come together on this, her Feast Day, to pray to Saint Angilia for her continued payers and benevolence. We pray that she continue to watch over us, and that she pray to God for our safe-keeping and well-being, both personally and nationally. She always cared about us, the citizens of Valdavia, but she also cared about the nation of Valdavia. She prayed for our continued peace, stability, and strength, so that Valdavia would exist for many hundreds of years.

"To Saint Angilia, we offer our prayers and our gratitude. Through her life, we see the great wisdom and glory of God at work, and we rejoice. We thank Saint Angilia for her service to us and to God. We thank God for the life of Saint Angilia." Reverend

Emerson bowed his head in silent prayer for three minutes, and then nodded to Prince Patrick.

Prince Patrick walked to the pulpit, bowed his head, and silently prayed. When he finished, he looked at the people crowded together in the church. They were all there because of his grandmother, because she touched their hearts and their souls. He thought of all that had happened in the 20 years since her death, and he knew that he would not have accomplished what he had were it not for her influence. She, more than anyone, gave him the arsenal necessary to persevere, to keep going when his heart threatened to crumble under the weight of it all. She did.

Prince Patrick smiled from the immense joy of that truth. He prayed that all who suffered felt that relief from their burdens. "Psalms Chapter 16, one of my grandmother's favorites. She read this to me often while I was growing up, even over the phone if we were not together. *'(Michtam of David.) Preserve me, O God: for in thee do I put my trust. O my soul, thou hast said unto the LORD, Thou art my Lord: my goodness extendeth not to thee; But to the saints that are in the earth, and to the excellent, in whom is all my delight. Their sorrows shall be multiplied that hasten after another god: their drink offerings of blood will I not offer, nor take up their names into my lips. The LORD is the portion of mine inheritance and of my cup: thou maintainest my lot. The lines are fallen unto me in pleasant places; yea, I have a goodly heritage. I will bless the LORD, who hath given me counsel: my reins also instruct me in the night seasons. I have set the LORD always before me: because he is at my right hand, I shall not be moved. Therefore my heart is glad, and my glory rejoiceth: my flesh also shall rest in hope. For thou wilt not leave my soul in hell; neither wilt thou suffer thine Holy One to see corruption. Thou wilt shew me the path of life: in thy presence is fulness of joy; at thy right hand there are pleasures for evermore.'*

"May God bless you and keep you in the warmth of his love forever. God loves you, my grandmother Saint Angilia loves you, and I love you."

§§§§

After the mass, Patrick changed back into his jeans, t-shirt, and red hoodie, the outfit he had worn almost constantly since he had died wearing it. He returned to Heaven and found his family gathered at his parents' home. "Hey, Father, Mother," Patrick greeted them, kissed their cheeks, and smiled broadly.

"Patrick, my little renegade," Matilda said and pulled him down for a kiss. "You haven't been little since you were 12 years old. You sprouted like a vine, I swear. So tall."

"Well, at least you didn't call me a weed," Patrick giggled. "Today was awesome, it really was. I know you all saw it, and I'm glad you did. Little Stefan stole the show, you know. He's just super, he really is."

"Oh, he is. To see my son and grandson together today, and to hear Stefan call Eric '*Daddy*' was so beautiful," Julianne said as she looked at her family.

"Yeah, today was pretty magical. It could have been a sad day, you know, but it wasn't. They'll never forget what happened 20 years ago, and they shouldn't, but they don't let it bring them down. They miss you, Little One, they do. They always will. But they know they'll be with you again. Their faith is strong," Patrick told them.

"I know it is. I love them so very much. I also know how much this has all gotten to Patrick over the years. He is extraordinarily sensitive and emotional. He's doing well, though, and I'm so elated for him. His lifelong dream is a reality, and he has worked so hard to make this happen," Angilia shared. "I remember when he shared this dream with me when he was a child. I knew he would make it come true, because it means so much to him. He told me then that this is his life's purpose, his reason for living. He told me that this is what he's meant to do. I'm so happy."

"Yeah, it's going to be official very soon. He told me today that he's hired the faculty and staff, everything is in place and ready, and they already have over 5,000 students enrolled. He's so focused on making this work, on making it right. It is. It will be. We'll see this thing explode and grow for quite a long time," Patrick said about his great-grandnephew's university.

"I can't say I'm surprised by any of this, but I am amazed by how quickly Patrick has managed to get this off the ground. He's still so young, and yet he's accomplished so very much. Just like his grandmother," Eric said and kissed the top of his daughter's head.

§§§§

"Hello, and welcome to our sunrise news on this Tuesday, January 3, 2090. I am Bennett Francis, and I am coming to you from the campus of Valdavia's first university. Saint Angilia University officially opens today, on the 94th anniversary of Saint Angilia's birth, with the first classes beginning at 8:00 this morning. We have watched the construction of the buildings and the progress for the past few years, and now the day for which His Royal Highness Prince Patrick, Doctor of Education, has worked toward is a reality.

"Prince Patrick has told us that there will be more construction and additions to the campus as the University grows. This first term sees an enrollment of 5,795 students according to the Registrar, Dr. Margery Simon. Many of those students have moved into the residence halls, where they will live during this academic term. One of those students has agreed to speak with us on this very exciting morning. Thank you for joining us, Miss Bethany Brooks. Tell us why you decided to enroll at Saint Angilia University in its inaugural term. What brought you here?"

"Thank you for having me. I graduated from high school in May of last year and started looking at colleges and universities before that. My grandfather actually told me I should get more information about Prince Patrick's university. I want to become a nurse, and he had read that Saint Angilia University would have a nursing program. So I contacted them.

"The faculty that Prince Patrick had hired were highly respected and professional, so that was a major point for me. But my grandfather told me that any university of Prince Patrick's would be excellent, and he said I should apply."

"What made your grandfather so certain? The university hadn't yet opened, after all, and there was so little known about it."

"Well, my grandfather went to Oxford in the early 2000s, and his literature professor was Saint Angilia. She was Princess

Angilia then, and she was this teenaged genius wunderkind. He said she knew so much about so many things, and she was always so kind and helpful. He said her grandson had to be the same way to want to do this so much. I met Prince Patrick at a walkabout once, and he is very kind and nice. So this is where I applied, and they accepted me. I'm very excited for my first day of classes," Bethany enthused.

"Saint Angilia was your grandfather's professor, and now Prince Patrick is the founder and President of your university. How very perfect," Bennett smiled.

"Yes, it's all very copacetic. My grandfather taught me that word when I was young. He learned it from Saint Angilia when they studied <u>Hamlet</u>," Bethany explained, an anecdote that made Prince Patrick smile as he watched the news from his university office. Yes, everything was indeed very satisfactory, he thought as he looked out of the window at his university's campus.

"This is due to you and God, Grandmother. Both of you gave me what I needed in order to make my dream come true. You gave me the inspiration, and God gave me the strength. Thank you, both of you."

§§§§

Eric answered a call in his office as he and Leigh prepared for an energy council meeting for the following day. Leigh noticed his friend's expression when he finished the call and asked what was wrong. "That was Scott's nurse. He's dying, and he asked for me to come. Would you mind handling things here for a while? Yvonne and I will stay with Scott." Leigh nodded, and soon Eric and Yvonne arrived at Scott's home and entered his bedroom. They had last been in that room the day Darlene had died.

Yvonne kissed Scott's cheek, fighting back her tears, and told her lifelong friend how much she loved him.

"I love you. I watched you grow into a lovely lady, Yvonne. Your parents were two of my best friends," Scott weakly said.

"I know. You, Darlene, Shannon, Mom, and Dad were always the COC friends. I've known you my whole life, Scott."

"So have I," Eric added with a sad smile. "You are a wonderful man and a great friend."

"That's easy when you love people," Scott said. "I was just wondering who my Spirit Guide will be. It will be wonderful to see my parents and grandparents again. It's been a long time, a very long time."

"I know, but that will all disappear when you get to Heaven. There is no time there, just eternity. That's so hard to really understand for us. We live by the clock. We're ruled by time. But that doesn't mean a thing in Heaven. Imagine what that must really be like. No time. No night." Eric sighed as he recalled all that his mother and his granduncle had taught him about Heaven.

"I know. I was also thinking about the first time I'll see Darlene again. I hope whoever is my Spirit Guide can tell me where your grandfather is. Where King Eric is is where Darlene is, that's for sure. I'm sure I'll have to pry her away from him just to give her a hug," Scott said as he gasped for breath.

"I doubt that, Scott. Darlene loves you dearly. We all know that," Eric said and patted Scott's arm.

"She sure does. You two were adorable together," Yvonne smiled.

"We were happy. I'm ready to be with her again. We'll be happy forever, won't we?"

"Yes, you will, Scott," Eric agreed.

Eric and Yvonne sat with Scott for over two hours while he went in and out of consciousness. Finally, he barely opened his eyes and smiled. "Mom's here. I love you both."

"We love you, Scott," Eric replied as Yvonne cried. The nurse confirmed Scott's death at 2:24 on the afternoon of March 10, 2090. Eric said a prayer, and then smiled at Yvonne. "I hope Uncle Patrick tells us all about Scott's reunion with Darlene. It's bound to be exciting." Yvonne could not help but laugh at the image that Scott had painted for them—him having to force Darlene away from King Eric just so he could greet her.

"It's a good thing Scott likes your family. He's going to be around them an awful lot, you know," Yvonne said with a tearful giggle as she and Eric hugged.

§§§§

"Go on, son. Darlene spends most of her time with Angilia's family," Mrs. Ransdale told her son and hugged him.

"I expected as much. Thanks, Mom. I'll come see you and the family," Scott promised, kissed her cheek, and walked toward Eric's and Marisol's house. He saw many of the DeBruce Martineau family gathered there, listening to Eric's father Gerard tell stories of his young sons' childhood antics. Scott smiled at the laughter he heard, and shook his head as he got nearer and heard a very familiar voice.

"Oh, I can just see it. King Eric was the most perfect little boy who ever lived. I bet he never once got in trouble."

"Well, no one is perfect, Darlene, but no, Eric never got in trouble. He was never punished or grounded, no," Gerard confirmed.

"No. That was my territory. Compared to me, Eric was perfect," Patrick giggled.

"Oh, Uncle Patrick, stop the bad boy antics already. You were never as naughty as you'd like people to believe you were," Angilia said and ruffled his hair.

"Compared to him I sure was. I disobeyed Mom and Dad a lot, and they grounded me once or twice a week."

"True, but only to teach you respect for rules and discipline," Matilda added. "And then I felt guilty for keeping you in your rooms, so I always ended up in tears over you."

216

"I wanted to be more like Eric, I did, but that was next to impossible for me. I did try," Patrick said and wrinkled his nose. "I did. But I just couldn't be so studious and serious all the time."

"You're fine the way you are, Uncle Patrick. I'm glad you're the way you are. In your own way, you are practically perfect, too. You're right, though. No one can compare to Daddy," Angilia said, stood on her toes, and kissed his cheek.

"No one," Darlene dreamily said, and leaned on Eric's arm.

"Darlene." She seemed not to hear, although everyone else did.

"Scott!" Angilia exclaimed and ran to him in a hug. "Oh, it's so nice to see you. Welcome to Heaven!" She led him to everyone, and Matthew hugged his friend as well.

"Darlene," Scott said again as he stood before her. "I'm here."

Eric nudged Darlene, and she suddenly looked up and saw her husband. "Scott! When did you get here?"

"Not too long ago. Mom brought me. Of course, I had to come find you. I've missed you, Darlene."

"Oh, that's sweet, Scott. I have missed you, too. You're the only person who really understood me, you know. Oh, come here," Darlene said and held her arms open for him.

Scott pulled Darlene into an embrace that made everyone smile. Marisol put her arms around Eric and softly said, "Darlene's husband is here now. Maybe she won't cling to you so much, mi marido."

"Don't count on it," Patrick whispered. "Scott's presence did little to curb Darlene's enthusiasm on earth. I can't imagine it will be any different here."

Eric closed his eyes, hung his head, and groaned. Angilia sometimes felt they did relive that slumber party over and over ad nauseam. She had long understood her father's appeal and charm, but she also understood how very uncomfortable the attention made him. Angilia put her arm around her father, bowed her head, and silently prayed to God that Darlene cease in her displays of affection for King Eric. *Dear God, you know my father's heart, and you know how this makes him feel. This is intensely uncomfortable for him. He dislikes that this still happens here, of all places, where the worship should be directed toward you. I realize that there are far more serious problems with which you have to contend, but I ask you to help Darlene see that this kind of attention toward my father is inappropriate. Please cure Darlene of her lovesickness. In your loving and holy name, this I pray.*"

§§§§

"Happy birthday, Dad," Prince Patrick said to Eric as they went down to breakfast.

"Thank you. Happy birthday, Patrick. You have been such a blessing to me, son. Both you and your brother have. And now Stefan and his soon-to-be-born little brother or sister. I never thought I would be this happy."

"Aw, you deserve to be happy, Dad. You work so hard, and you spend so much time caring for others that you should be happy. Blessed, actually. That's the word Grandmother would use," Prince Patrick smiled as they entered the dining room, soon joined by Prince Eric, Stefan, and a very pregnant Giselle.

Prince Eric helped his wife into her seat, and then helped almost four-year-old Stefan into his chair. "Happy birthday, Grandfather. Happy birthday, Uncle Patrick. Happy birthday, Daddy," Stefan said to the three men.

Giselle smiled and leaned over to kiss her son. As she did, she gasped. "Oh, my, this little one is active this morning. I guess that's his or her way of telling you all happy birthday, too."

"Thanks," Prince Patrick giggled. "Hey, why didn't you two want to know the sex of your baby?"

"We just want to be surprised, that's all," Prince Eric answered with a smile. "It really doesn't matter, but we just decided we don't want to know before he or she is delivered."

218

"When will the baby be delivered?" Stefan asked.

"In about one month, Stefan," Giselle smiled. "Around Christmas probably."

"Is the baby my Christmas gift?" Everyone laughed.

"The baby is the entire family's Christmas gift," Eric answered with a huge smile.

"That's nice," Stefan said and ate his oatmeal.

"Yes, it's very nice. I have some birthday gifts for my two boys this morning," Eric added. He handed Prince Eric a small jewel box. "Grandfather gave this to me on my 12th birthday in 2033. His father had given it to him on his 15th birthday in 1969. Now I give this to you."

Prince Eric opened the hinged lid to see his Great-grandfather's signet ring. Tears filled his eyes as he removed it from the box and slipped it on his right ring finger. "Thank you, Dad. This is such a special ring, and I will treasure it always. Someday, Stefan, you will get this ring, and it will be passed down to a son in every generation of our family."

"Thank you, Daddy," Stefan said.

"That's so cool," Prince Patrick smiled as he looked across the table at the ring.

"I have something for you, too, Patrick. You are now the second Duc de Valmondois. Grandfather created that title for Dad on his wedding day, and now you bear that title. Like the ring, this title will be passed down to every generation of our family."

"Dad, really? You are giving me Grandfather's title? I don't know what to say. Thank you," Prince Patrick said and hugged his father. "I love you. I love all of you, Dad, Eric, Giselle, and Stefan."

"I love you, Uncle Patrick," Stefan said.

§§§§

The Royal Family, Leigh, and Yvonne returned home after the Christmas Eve church service, and soon they all slept soundly in their beds. Everyone except Giselle, that is. "Eric," she softly said as she shook him awake.

"What is it?" Prince Eric groggily asked.

"It's time," Giselle calmly replied.

"For the baby?" he asked and abruptly sat up.

"Yes. My contractions are close together now, and I think we better get to the hospital soon."

"All right, darling. Let me tell Patrick, so he can listen for Stefan," Prince Eric said and quickly went into his brother's suite. Prince Patrick hugged his brother, promised to watch after Stefan, and alerted security to have the car ready while his brother and sister-in-law prepared.

A few hours later, when Eric awoke, Prince Patrick happily informed his father that Giselle was in labor. Eric smiled, hugged his son, and said, "What a Christmas miracle. Our new baby is born today."

"Yeah. Christmas is a very special day for our family. It was 97 years ago today that Grandmother's soul entered Great-grandfather's heart. Now the baby will be born on Christmas Day. This is a miracle, Dad."

By 2:00 that afternoon, Eric, Prince Patrick, and Charles Potok took Stefan into Giselle's room in the maternity ward of King Gerard Hospital that had been named in honor of King Eric I's father, the baby's third great-grandfather. "The new baby is here?" Stefan asked.

"Yes, Stefan, my son. Your baby sister was born on Christmas Day," Prince Eric knelt and told his son.

"I have a sister? The baby is a girl? She's mine?"

Giselle held her daughter and smiled at her son. Prince Eric hugged his son and said, "Yes, she is. She is ours. We will love her and take care of her forever, won't we?"

Stefan nodded. "Yes. Can I see her now?"

"Yes, Stefan. Come here." Prince Eric lifted his son onto the bed next to Giselle, and Stefan kissed his mother and told her he loved her. Giselle kissed her little boy and then gently pulled the blanket away from the baby so that Stefan could see her better. "Stefan, meet your sister Angilia Erica Patricia," Prince Eric said through his tears.

Eric inhaled sharply, and Prince Patrick felt tears trickle from his eyes. Stefan leaned over and kissed his tiny sister, and Prince Eric smiled at his father and his brother. Giselle cried, too, and pulled Prince Eric close to her for a kiss.

"Do you want to hold her?" Giselle asked Stefan. The boy nodded, so Prince Eric helped him position his arms just right as Giselle carefully placed Angilia in his arms.

"She's nice. Is she named after Great-grandmother?" Stefan asked his father.

"Yes, she is. She is named after Great-grandmother, Great-great-grandfather, and Great-great-granduncle Patrick."

"So she is the future and the history of our family," Stefan stunned everyone by stating.

"Yes, Stefan, she is," Eric said. "Great-grandmother Angilia was born almost 96 years ago. Our little Princess Angilia Erica Patricia DeBruce Martineau Taylor was born on Christmas Day 2091. Almost one century separates their births. But these two very special ladies named Angilia connect us for all time."

Prince Eric beckoned his father, his brother, and his father-in-law to him for a family hug. Eric gently kissed his granddaughter's forehead, and she opened her eyes, looked at him, and placed her tiny hand on his cheek.

CHAPTER 10

“Angilia, come with me,” Michael commanded when he walked upon Angilia and her family. She obediently stood and followed the Archangel. “You have been chosen by God as your son’s Spirit Guide, and you will go to him soon.”

“Eric is joining us! I am so happy!”

“Yes. His earthly life is nearing its end, and he will soon come to Heaven. God will let us know when you should go to earth.”

“Thank you. I am so honored to be my son’s Spirit Guide. I gave him life on earth. Now I get to escort him to his eternal life in Heaven,” Angilia smiled up at Michael.

§§§§

Eric went to his suite, feeling inexplicably peculiar for a Friday afternoon. He tried to tell himself that he had been exceptionally busy that week and was simply exhausted. He knew it was more than that, though, and he called his son to come to him.

Prince Eric knew something was wrong, so he rushed to his father’s suite. His heart jumped when he saw his father sitting sideways in his desk chair, one hand grasping the back of the chair, the other hand clutching the edge of the desk. "Dad! Come on, let's get you in bed," Prince Eric said and supported his father.

Eric was out of breath, so Prince Eric removed his father's tie, unbuttoned his shirt, and reached for his phone. "I'm calling the doctor."

"No. Patrick. Call Patrick. No doctors." Eric insisted.

"But, Dad. . . ." Prince Eric began.

"Patrick."

Prince Eric quickly called his brother at his university office and told him to hurry home. Prince Patrick ran in just over 10 minutes later, and Prince Eric looked at him with tears in his eyes.

"Come here, both of you," Eric requested. Both men went to him and sat beside the bed. "I love you both so very much."

"I love you, Dad," Prince Patrick said as he fought his tears.

"So do I," Prince Eric said.

"I know. I have some things to give you. Patrick, please bring me the wooden box that's on top of my chifforobe."

Prince Patrick walked into his father's dressing room and gasped when he saw his grandfather's wooden memento box. He had only seen the box once, the day after his grandmother's funeral. He regained his senses and quickly took the box to his father.

"Patrick, I'd like you to keep watch over this box now. The contents are far more priceless and miraculous than you realize. All of Mommy's notes, cards, and letters to Dad are in there. All of them." He saw the tears in his son's eyes, and touched Prince Patrick's cheek. "You are the guardian of these now."

Patrick nodded, unable to speak.

Eric removed the pendant from around his neck for the first time since his mother had placed it there the day she died. He watched the scene once more, knowing that he would soon be with his parents and grandparents. He smiled and looked at his sons, understanding what they felt. He had felt the pain of his mother's death deeply.

"I first saw this pendant when Mommy was dying. She'd worn it from her wedding night until Grandfather's 75th birthday, when she gave it to him. He put it around her neck again the day he died."

Both men looked at their father, sadness and questions in their eyes. He handed the necklace to Prince Patrick and said, "Look into the pendant."

Prince Patrick watched his great-grandparents and grandparents together. *How? When? Where?* Suddenly, Prince Patrick knew, and he handed the pendant to his brother, a look of awe on his face.

Prince Eric inhaled sharply. "Is this. . .? Is this Heaven?"

"Yes, Eric. This is what awaits us," Eric softly said. "I want you to wear this for the rest of your life. This will remain in and with our family forever."

"Dad. This is a miracle," Prince Eric said.

"Yes, it is. So is something I want to give to you, Patrick. Inside that wooden box is a note Mommy wrote to Dad on one of his birthdays. Would you get it out?"

Prince Patrick finally found the note and read it aloud at his father's request. He and Prince Eric were stunned. The note was dated September 30, 2071, nearly two years after Angilia's death. Their frantic brains could not process what that meant, until Prince Patrick recalled his graduation gift from his grandmother. "Of course! Uncle Patrick brought this to Grandfather, just like he brought Grandmother's manuscript to me."

"Yes, he did," Eric confirmed. "I didn't know any of this until after Dad's death."

"What did Camillus paint for Grandfather?" Prince Eric asked.

"This," Eric said, picked up the portrait from his bedside table, and handed it to Prince Eric.

Prince Eric stared at the portrait for several moments before he smiled and handed it to Prince Patrick.

"Grandmother!" Prince Patrick exclaimed.

"Sons, you are the guardians of these precious family treasures. Stefan, Angilia, and any other children either of you have will become the next guardians," Eric told his sons and reached for their hands. "I do love you both."

At that instant, Prince Patrick leapt to his feet. "Grandmother!"

Prince Eric felt his father's hand tighten, and he gasped. "You are here!" he said.

Angilia smiled, realizing that her grandsons had been permitted to see her, just as her father had more than 118 years earlier. For that, she was grateful. "Oh, my precious grandsons, how you have grown into such fine, godly men," Angilia said. "Eric, my strong, intelligent Eric, I love you," she said and hugged him. Prince Eric held her tight as he cried. It had been almost 25 years since she had last hugged him. Angilia put her hands on his shoulders and smiled up at him. "You are such a remarkable man, Eric."

Angilia looked at Prince Patrick and said, "So are you, my dear Patrick. Oh, I love you so." She put her arms around him and felt him tremble as he held her close. "You are so courageous and wise, Patrick. I always knew your dream would come true."

"It's all because of you, Grandmother. Oh, Grandmother, I love you. I love you so very much," he said as he pulled her closer to him.

"I know, my dears. I love all of you. Eric, Patrick, Eric, Giselle, Stefan, and Angilia. I love you more than words can ever tell you."

"More than life," Prince Patrick smiled as he cried.

Angilia smiled at the familiar refrain and kissed his and Prince Eric's cheeks. She turned when her son said, "Mommy."

"Oh, my very precious son, how I love you," Angilia said and held his hand.

"You are my Spirit Guide," Eric said as he looked into his mother's turquoise eyes.

"Yes, darling. God selected me for this honor. Michael came and got me. No one else knows you are coming. How joyful they will be," she said, and then turned to face her grandsons. "I know how much pain you and the children will feel. I wish you wouldn't hurt, I do, and my soul aches that you will."

"I remember what we learned when Great-grandfather died. You told us that day that our pain equals our love. It's true," Prince Eric said as tears fell down his cheeks.

"Yes, it is. There is no greater truth," Prince Patrick said as tears fell from his eye.

"Yes, there is, Patrick. I know your pain is deep and very real, but there is a much greater, more powerful truth. Pain is part of life on this earth. Pain is the price of love. But this life is temporary, and the pain ends. It does, believe me. I know that."

Patrick nodded and hugged his grandmother. "I know, but I'm not as strong as you or Great-grandfather. How can I live through so much pain?"

"Oh, Patrick, you are strong, both of you are. You have the same people around you as I did who will help you through the pain—your family, the people of Valdavia, and God. You are both so selfless, and you devote your lives to helping others. That will help you a lot. That's one thing that helped Daddy and me. When we are immersed in the care of and concern for others, we don't have time to let our own pain take over. We are too focused on other people to let that happen.

"Eric, you will be the next King, and you will make our country and our people your focus more than ever. Plus, you have your wife and two young children who need you. They are your priority.

"Patrick, you have your students, faculty, staff, and university in addition to your Royal duties. You will always place your family first, followed by your students, faculty, and staff.

"You both place others' needs over your own, and that selflessness will carry you through anything. So will God. God is your greatest ally and support, you know that. Pray for his help and guidance, as you have always done. As intense as the pain feels, God will never let you endure more than you can bear. He must think you are quite strong if your pain is as great as you say. You are both so incredible. I do love you," Angilia said and hugged them. "Say farewell to your father, boys. It's almost time for me to escort him to Heaven. Just hold onto the truth that you will join him there someday," she softly said and kissed them.

Both men swallowed their tears and nodded. Prince Eric held his father's hand, bent to kiss his cheek, and said, "I love you, Dad. Thank you for everything."

Prince Patrick patted his brother's back, hugged his father, and fought his tears. "Oh, Dad, I love you so much. I'm going to miss you."

Eric nodded, unable to speak, and lay quiet and still for several moments. His sons held his hands, while Angilia stood with her hands on their shoulders. When Eric gasped his last breath, Prince Patrick began crying. Prince Eric held him and also cried, both of them brokenhearted.

"Eric, Patrick, we have to leave now. We love you. Hold onto that," Angilia said, blew them a kiss, and smiled at her son. Eric likewise blew a kiss to his sons as he and Angilia disappeared and went to Heaven.

§§§§

30 September 2095

Our beloved father, King Eric II, died today at 3:32. We were both with him, and as much as our hearts ache, we are grateful that we shared these last hours with our father. Sharing his physical death with our father is the most spiritual experience of our lives.

We love our father, and we will deeply miss his physical presence. However, we know for an indisputable fact that he lives eternally in Heaven. That fact, coupled with the anticipation of reuniting with him—and the rest of our family—brings hope and light to both of our souls.

Our father's state funeral will be Sunday, 2 October 2015 in Saint Angilia Church beginning at 11:00. He will be entombed in the Royal Vault directly following the funeral.

We thank you for the love and support you have shown to our family over the years. You bless our lives tremendously, and for that we are thankful.

King Eric III

Prince Patrick, Duc de Valmondois

§§§§

"Oh, Mommy, Heaven is more beautiful than I could ever imagine. There is no word to describe Heaven, to capture all of this," Eric marveled when he and Angilia entered Heaven.

Angilia smiled up at her son, just as she had done so very long ago in the Unborn Children Sphere, and said, "No, there isn't. Uncle Patrick and I tried, but we just couldn't do Heaven justice. Heaven is far beyond human comprehension, because Heaven is unlike anywhere else in existence. Oh, Eric, my heart is so full of joy, my soul is now complete. You are here!"

"That's the perfect way to describe how I feel. I am whole. I am peaceful. You are here, I am here, and Grandfather is here. The emptiness inside is gone. It's just gone," Eric smiled.

Angilia nodded. "I know, my darling. When I came here and reunited with Daddy, my pain instantly disappeared. That's such a splendid feeling."

"Speaking of Grandfather, where is he? I want to see him."

"Everyone is at Uncle Patrick's house. Come on."

"Uncle Patrick has a house?" Eric asked with a giggle. "Somehow I just imagined him as some nomad angel, wandering through Heaven and getting into mischief."

Angilia giggled. "Well, he doesn't stay there a whole lot, no, but he does have a home. Everyone does. His is up ahead," Angilia gestured as she and Eric neared.

Eric suddenly stopped walking, gasped, and softly said, "My family. They are all here. Oh, Mommy this is the moment I've dreamed about for so long."

Angilia smiled as they approached and her father saw Eric. Everyone stopped talking, stood motionless, and watched as the two men embraced. It had been more than 30 years since they had seen one another.

"Grandfather. Grandfather, I love you so."

"I love you, Eric. How glorious that you are here. We are together again. We are complete once more," Eric told his grandson with a smile. The two men pulled Angilia into the embrace. "We are complete forever."

Archangel Michael put his hands on Patrick's and Marisol's shoulders. "They are complete. The soul is complete once more."

§§§§

The Royal Family—Eric, Prince Patrick, Giselle, Stefan, Angilia, and Uncle Patrick—traveled through Valmondois in a horse-drawn carriage, accompanied by lifelong family friends Leigh and Yvonne. Eric was attired in the regalia last worn by his father, the 764-year-old coronation uniform and robe. The Royal party garnered cheers of support on their journey to Saint Angilia Church for King Eric III's official coronation as the 22nd Monarch de Valdavia. There had been but one hereditary Queen, his grandmother Saint Angilia.

Four-year-old Princess Angilia pointed to a large sign that bore her great-grandmother's picture and the words *HAPPY 100TH BIRTHDAY SAINT ANGILIA*. Uncle Patrick lifted her onto his lap, smiled, and said, "Your Great-grandmother Saint Angilia was born 100 years ago today, on January 3, 1996, Angilia and Stefan. We are so blessed to have her in our family."

"She's an angel in Heaven," Princess Angilia said.

"A real angel, like Michael and Gabriel," eight-year-old Stefan added.

"Yes, she is, Stefan and Angilia. Your great-grandmother is one of God's Supreme Angels. He created her as such, and he destined her for a wondrous life on earth and in Heaven. She loves you so very much, Stefan and Angilia, Patrick and Eric, and Giselle. She loves you more than I can tell you," Uncle Patrick said.

"More than life," Stefan said.

CHAPTER 11

31 *December 2099*

I spent all last night and today in Grandmother's sitting room engrossed in her diaries. I read them all in chronological order, beginning with the ones she wrote when she was five, the ones chronicling her time in the Unborn Children Sphere and the Angels Choir. What an exceptional life she has lived, both in Heaven and on earth! She stuns me every day. As well as I've known her my entire life, I have come to know her so much more intimately through her diaries. All of her thoughts, feelings, perceptions, and experiences are recorded there. What a truly priceless treasure they are.

I love her so very much. I love each of my family members. Each one. Grandmother, my precious, angelic grandmother! Grandfather, such a compassionate man. Great-grandfather—what can I say that will do him justice? A more godly man never lived, of that I am sure. How I revere him. Dad. My father. So wise, so kind and caring, and so much like Great-grandfather. I am so very blessed to have had them in this life!

Mom. I never met her, but I love her so. She is so bright, kind, and happy—who couldn't love her? Great-grandpa and Great-grandma Taylor, Grandfather's parents. They must be fantastic to be his parents. Dad told me and Eric how much fun they were when he was a child, and how much they loved people. Great-grandmother, the woman who gave life to Grandmother but never lived to even see her baby. The love of Great-grandfather's life, the woman to whom he was devoted for 70 years! How amazing! My great-great-

grandparents. Great-great-great-grandfather Stefan, for whom my nephew is named. The man who was Great-grandmother's teacher in the Angels Choir! He manifested only once—the day Dad was brought home from the hospital. The photographs of that visit still hang here on Great-grandmother's sitting room wall, where I sit at her desk. I look up at those pictures and am amazed by my family. There also hangs the portrait of King Stefan that Great-grandmother found in that antique store two months after the assassination attempt. 2012. In a dozen years, that will be 100 years ago! Incredible.

How very much has happened since then. Such history. More than that, though, are the people who have influenced this world and its people. My family foremost among them. They are part of me. They are in my blood, in my heart, in my soul. They live in me. They live in Eric, Stefan, and Angilia. They are the reasons we are here now. God chose them as our ancestors. God predestined us from the beginning of time. We are all meant to exist. We are all part of God's plan, something much larger than any one of us individually.

I am meant to live the life I am living, meant to do all of the things I have done and will do. When I first told Great-grandmother about my dream of opening Valdavia's first university, she told me that the idea was no mere coincidence. She told me that God had gifted me the dream, the ambition to make it a reality, and the stamina to make it succeed. It has succeeded. Saint Angilia University has thrived and grown since it opened nine years ago— almost 10 years, one decade! Its 10th anniversary is in three days, the anniversary of Great-grandmother's birth. Stefan has told me that he will become part of the university, and that he will help to carry it forward into this 22nd century that begins in a few short hours.

Speaking of Stefan, he turns 12 years old tomorrow. 12. How he is maturing into a fine young man. He will be a fabulous, godly King Stefan II when he ascends the throne. What a comforting thought. Our future, the family's future, is secure in these two children—Stefan and Angilia—who are named after such remarkable people! Valdavia is blessed to have them, more than it knows. History has recorded the Monarchs de Valdavia—the 21 Kings and one Queen—as history's most godly monarchs since Kings David and Solomon. What an exceptionally appropriate analogy!

We are more blessed than we know to be members of this family. We have learned from them, and we will pass those lessons to all future generations. Our lives are enriched by the legacy we have inherited, a legacy of faith, hope, compassion, and selflessness. As Paul so beautifully writes in one of my favorite verses, 1 Corinthians 13:13—"And now abideth faith, hope, charity, these three; but the greatest of these is charity." Charity is Grandmother's third name. Love! Charity in this context is love! Love surrounds our family, and will guide us for all time. Thank you, God!

CHAPTER 12

"Welcome to a very special and historic ceremony. Today we mark the 100th anniversary of the Eric DeBruce Martineau Scholarship for Musical Excellence at the University of Oxford. What a glorious moment.

"I truly am delighted to welcome everyone. I am the host, Thomas Arden, Dean of Christ Church College, and it is my supreme honor to introduce His Majesty King Eric III de Valdavia."

Eric received a lengthy standing ovation from the capacity crowd. "Thank you so much. I am so blessed to be here today for this 100th degree ceremony. This scholarship meant so much to my grandmother and to my great-grandfather, and I truly enjoy coming here every March."

"All of us at the University of Oxford are grateful to you and to your family for the perpetual support you have provided. The story of how this scholarship came to bear your great-grandfather's name has by now become legend. Suffice it to say that the naming of the scholarship stemmed from Saint Angilia's deep, abiding love for her father," Thomas said.

"Yes, it did. My grandmother often said that her father was the greatest love of her life. That was always evident, I think," Eric said with a smile.

"Indeed, it was, never more so than 100 years ago today. On March 7, 2012, Princess Angilia saved her father's life, but nearly died from wounds she received during an assassination attempt. She selflessly placed her father's safety above her own. She was prepared to die, if necessary, in order to protect him. She was willing to make the greatest sacrifice one human being can make for another."

"Yes, Dean Arden, she was. She also had faith that God would not allow his destiny for her or for her father to be destroyed. She had faith that she would survive so that she could give life to my father. I, my brother, and my two children are here today, a testament to her unwavering faith."

Eric received another enthusiastic standing ovation. When it subsided, Thomas announced a treat for the audience. "What better way to commemorate this 100th scholarship ceremony than with a look back at the very first scholarship ceremony. In its entirety, we will show that ceremony from Monday, March 5, 2012, which was hosted by my predecessor, Dean Kevin Lawrence."

For the next two hours, everyone in the theatre watched as Kevin hosted Eric and Angilia throughout the question-and-answer session and then the short concert. Eric performed publicly for the first time that day, and everyone smiled to watch him look into his daughter's eyes as he sang. They also noticed the love for her father shining in Angilia's eyes as she looked at him. King Eric III, Prince Patrick, Prince Stefan, Princess Angilia, and Giselle wiped tears from their eyes as they watched. What history indeed.

So it was that King Eric III awarded the 100th Eric DeBruce Martineau Scholarship for Musical Excellence to a young classical pianist from Dublin, Ireland, Casey Raymond. The scholarship was but one more way in which his beloved Grandmother and Great-grandfather continued to help people.

§§§§§

"Good morning, and welcome to the sunrise news on this glorious Saturday, August 20, 2112. Today is the historic opening of the time capsule that was sealed and placed in the base of the statue of His Majesty King Eric I 100 years ago. August 20, 2012 was a Monday, and the second day of His Majesty's week-long 20th Jubilee.

"The citizens of Valdavia organized the Jubilee to publicly honor and thank their beloved King Eric. Yes, 2012 marked his 20th year as King de Valdavia, and there more than likely would have been a jubilee to mark that milestone. However, Valdavians were prompted to show their love, respect, and appreciation for King Eric after the assassination attempt of March 7, 2012. As many people said at the time, the realization that His Majesty could have been murdered made them want to show him what he meant to them.

"So it was that several thousand people gathered in what was then called Central Park for a day of festivities. The Royal Family spent the day meeting people from across Valdavia and the world, and many of those people brought items that were placed in the time capsule. That night, after the festivities, the titanium time capsule was sealed in what became the base of King Eric's statue.

"That statue has stood here for 99 years, and people still leave flowers and gifts at the statue. Yesterday, the statue was carefully removed from its base long enough for the time capsule to be removed. Today, the statue stands once more alongside the statue of his daughter, Saint Angilia.

"The time capsule is under the protection of two soldiers until its opening ceremony at 10:00 this morning. After that, the contents of the time capsule will be housed in a permanent gallery at the Musée National de Valdavia. We will return for our live coverage of the time capsule opening ceremony in a few hours. Until then, thank you for joining us."

§§§§§

"Hey, guys, guess what's happening on earth today."

"Hi, Uncle Patrick," Angilia giggled and kissed his cheek. "What's happening?" she asked, looking curious.

"It's been a hundred years, and it's being opened today," Patrick replied.

"Whatever are you talking about, son? One hundred years since what? What is being opened?" Gerard asked.

"It's August 20, 2112 today," Patrick answered, which meant nothing in particular to most of his family and friends.

Angilia, however, did remember. "The time capsule!"

"Time capsule? What time capsule?" Gerard asked.

"It's from Daddy's 20th Jubilee. On August 20, 2012, a day of events took place in Central Park, and a large time capsule was filled with artifacts from Daddy's life," Angilia explained.

"Yeah, they removed it from the statue base, and it's being opened today," Patrick added.

"It's been 100 years since that?" Eric asked.

"Yeah. Eric, Patrick, Stefan, Angilia, and Giselle will be there at the opening. It's all the rage, you know. It's what everyone's talking about," Patrick told his family and friends.

"I seriously doubt that, Patrick. You and Angilia have a tendency to exaggerate these things," Eric responded.

"No, they don't, King Eric. You're the most popular king who ever lived, you know. Well, everyone else knows that. You're kind, compassionate, benevolent, talented, and extraordinarily handsome," Darlene stated matter-of-factly as she stood with her arm around Scott.

Eric shook his head in disagreement, though everyone else mumbled their agreement. "Darlene is right, Sir. I saw it the first time when you visited Eric in Paris. When I became Eric's personal assistant, I saw it every day for the rest of my life. The love people have for you is massive," Leigh said.

"It sure is, Eric," Yvonne added. "Your popularity sure did keep the Press Office on its toes. We were always busy."

"Sure, Grandfather, you never saw it, but everyone else did. You are so loved and respected. People love you," Eric II said.

"Of course they do, Daddy. They always will. You are unique in all of history. Everyone loves you. I love you. You are the greatest love of my life," Angilia declared, stood on her toes, and kissed his cheek.

"That's so beautiful," Darlene sobbed. "This family has always been surrounded by love. I am so lucky, I mean blessed, to know all of you." Scott patted her back and echoed his wife.

"We are equally blessed to know you, Darlene. You are an amazing friend," Angilia smiled, her arms linked through her father's left arm.

"Indeed. We are blessed by one another," Stefan said as he stood between Angilia and Patrick. "And we are blessed by your prayers, my great-granddaughter," he said and kissed the top of her head.

"Yes, especially for Darlene's condition," Matthew quietly said.

Patrick giggled and whispered, "I always said your prayers are powerful, Little One. Your prayer is the only thing that cured Darlene."

"For that I truly am grateful, Angel," Eric whispered, kissed her head, and thanked God as Marisol hugged him with a smile.

§§§§

"Eric, Patrick, Stefan, and Angilia asked me to attend the time capsule opening with them. Michael said I could. Is there anything you want me to say or do?" Patrick asked his brother and his niece.

"Tell them how much I love them, and that I am so gratified by them. At the ceremony, would you tell the people how blessed they continue to make my life, and that I am incredibly humbled and honored that they remember me," Eric said.

Angilia smiled up at her father as he spoke, her love for him, as always, glowing from within her. She kissed his cheek, and then said, "Tell Eric, Patrick, Stefan, and Angilia, and Giselle how very much I love them, and that my heart rejoices every time I look down from Heaven and witness their compassion, devotion, and dedication. They are each so astonishing, and they fill my soul with such joy. Thank everyone for loving Daddy and for honoring him today. That fills my soul with such warmth."

"Sure thing. I'll see you all later," Patrick said and went to earth, to Valmondois.

§§§§

"My brother, wife, children, and I are so delighted to be here today for this once-in-history event. We are also honored and grateful to have our Uncle Patrick join us today, for he is our family's representative from Heaven," King Eric III said with a smile. "My brother and I were eight years old when our great-grandfather died, but we both remember him so vividly, and we love him tremendously. I am named after him, which is an immense honor.

"He is such an awe-inspiring, splendid man, and he fulfilled his various roles with the utmost love, dedication, grace, and faith that any one person can possess. He was a devoted husband, maintaining his marriage vows decades after his cherished wife's death. He was the absolute most loving and devoted father to his daughter, Patrick's and my grandmother, Saint Angilia. He was such an affectionate, compassionate grandfather and great-grandfather.

"My brother and I learned so many essential lessons from him in eight years. From his example, we learned how to become caring, concerned, responsible, courageous, faithful, and godly men. Patrick and I have taught those qualities to Stefan and Angilia. We have done so, we know that, for we see these qualities in this young man and this young lady every day. They are the living legacy of King Eric I."

The thousands of people gathered in King Eric Celebratory Park cheered and applauded. King Eric III stood next to his great-granduncle Patrick, while his brother Prince Patrick stepped to the podium. "It's been more than 47 years since our great-grandfather died. Nearly half a century. Like my niece and nephew, some of you who are here today were not yet born. Many of you were children, as my brother and I were. Some of you remember that day vividly, and Eric and I remember speaking with some of you on the mall that day with our father and our grandmother. We are all present today because of King Eric I.

"We all love and respect him, and we treasure his legacy. His work, his influence, shines forth across Valdavia, the country he loved and worked to maintain as a safe, peaceful nation. You were his major concern after his family. You. The people of Valdavia, his neighbors, friends, and fellow Valdavians. Even if your birth was but a far-distant event during his lifetime, he cared about you. He always considered the effect upon future generations of every law, program, and decision he made.

"No monarch ever cared more for or worked so tirelessly for his fellow citizens as King Eric I. None. History has already recorded him as such, but we don't need to read history books to know this. All we have to do is look around us. Valdavia is such an oddity in the 22nd century, with virtually no crime, no taxes, no poverty, no homelessness, and a 781-year history of no wars or uprisings.

"We live in the best nation on earth, in large part due to King Eric I. He is an eternal blessing to me, my family, all who live in this nation, and to Valdavia. How incredible to look back at his life and his reign in this historic way today. Thank you all for sharing this with us."

After the applause ended, Prince Stefan went to the podium. "I thank you, too, for being here today to honor and to remember this great man. King Eric I is Angilia's and my great-great-grandfather, a man we never had the chance to meet, but a man we love deeply. Our grandfather, our father, our uncle, and yes, our great-great-granduncle have told us so very much about him. We have read the history books and watched films of his speeches and public appearances. We are constantly amazed by his accomplishments and life.

"But we also know him more intimately than that. We have come to know his soul, his heart, his core. We know many of you know or sense his godliness, for it shone through in all that he did. I am here because of him, because of his daughter, our great-grandmother Saint Angilia. Who we are is, in many ways, due to them and their influence.

"The fact that Queen Angilia was canonized is no coincidence. Oh, I know that God destined her for this life, but I also know that she herself credited her two fathers, as she called them, for making her the woman she was. God and King Eric I. Part of her destiny was as King Eric I's daughter, and that is crucial to her development. When she was born as a human on earth, she learned godliness and faith from her earthly father, Eric Richard Constantin DeBruce Martineau. God selected Eric as Angilia's father in the same way he selected Mary as Jesus' mother.

"God recognized Eric as a godly and righteous human being, and destined him for the life we come here today to honor. King Eric I truly is unique. He is one of a kind, even though his spirit lives in my father, my uncle, my sister, and me. We, you, and Valdavia are the beneficiaries of his life and his legacy."

King Eric III hugged his son when Stefan stepped away from the podium. The applause was exuberant for the 24-year-old Prince, and Uncle Patrick radiated joy. He also felt something he had not felt in a very long time when 19-year-old Princess Angilia stood at the podium. He felt his body tremble with intense emotion. How incredible to listen first to the young man named for his grandfather, and now to this girl named after Little One—his niece Saint Angilia. Patrick smiled up at the statue of his angelic niece and winked as Princess Angilia spoke.

"This is such a fantastic day for me, I have to say. I love Great-great-grandfather more than I can tell you. Like Stefan said, we know him so very well. Our great-grandmother often said that her father was so easy to love. He is. She also said he was as close to perfect as a human being could be. He is.

"I use the present tense intentionally when I speak of or write about him, because he still lives. He lives eternally in Heaven. We know that. We believe that. Even without Uncle Patrick's stories about and messages from Great-great-grandfather, we would know and believe that as an absolute truth. How? Why? After all, it's not something we can prove beyond reasonable doubt.

"We don't need to. The greatest lesson my brother and I have learned from Great-great-grandfather is faith. Faith does not require proof. Faith exists in the soul. Faith means trusting and believing in God regardless of what happens. Faith means believing God. Believe what he promises us, including the gift of eternal life.

"Great-great-grandfather's love for and devotion to his wife Marisol is legendary, a love story for the ages. That love story was Saint Angilia's favorite. Eric wore his wedding band every moment of his life from the second Marisol placed it on his finger. He never even considered another romantic relationship. He lived 70 years after Marisol's death as a widower. While that at first seems like a tragic, sad story, it is not.

"It was neither tragic nor sad to Eric. Yes, he admitted that he missed Marisol every second. She was, after all, the one true love of his life, the only woman to own his heart. But he also believed that he would reunite with her when his body died and his soul entered Heaven. That truth carried him through 70 long years separated from his wife. His faith was the lifeboat that kept him afloat when it would have been so easy to drown in sorrow. He could never do that. He could never jeopardize his reunion with Marisol. He knew they would be together for eternity, so 70 years was nothing when compared to that.

"Great-great-grandfather's faith is the greatest lesson I will ever learn. I know that someday, when my body dies, I will meet him, and I will be able to tell him, face to face, how grateful I am and how very much I love him."

By that point, most people were in tears, overcome with the emotion, truth, and beauty in Angilia's unscripted, unrehearsed speech. Like her namesake, she spoke from her heart, and in doing so she touched people deeply. Her family embraced her as Uncle Patrick prepared to speak.

"Wow, thank you for being here today. My brother Eric really is the most awesome man I've ever known. We are all so incredibly blessed by him, we really are. He asked me to tell you how blessed you make him, and how much he loves you. He really does. I see it. His daughter, my niece Saint Angilia, asked me to thank you for loving her father and for remembering and honoring him today. She said that fills her soul with warmth. I know it does. Her emotions always show in her eyes.

"My family. What can I say? I love them, I treasure them, I am blessed by them. Hey, let's open this time capsule and look at the history of my brother's life."

Everyone screamed their agreement, so the museum staff began opening and removing the cover of the titanium box. As they did, people sang the ballad Angilia had written and that Valdavian schoolchildren had performed at King Eric I's 20th Jubilee Tribute Concert. The song embodied how people felt about King Eric I. His daughter had known the legacy he would leave behind.

We give undying devotion,

You we ever applaud.

You live with grace and piety,

Touched by the hand of God.

In this world of sin you remain

Unequaled and unflawed,

Pious, angelic, and saintly,

Touched by the hand of God.

By you we are forever blessed,

By you forever awed.

For the depth of your sanctity,

Touched by the hand of God.

Gracious, kind, wise, and loving,

You receive all the laud

That we can give to our King

Touched by the hand of God.

Soon, King Eric III, Prince Patrick, Prince Stefan, and Princess Angilia put on museum gloves and removed some of the artifacts. King Eric III held up a newspaper from his great-grandfather's coronation. Prince Patrick held up the wedding dolls of Eric and Marisol. "Great-grandmother has these! They're on the shelf in her sitting room," Princess Angilia excitedly exclaimed. What a beautiful moment.

Stefan held up the copy of the Mother's Day/Father's Day Proclamation that Princess Angilia had written and that King Eric I had made legal with his signature. The sight of the proclamation brought more tears, for everyone knew that the love between Eric and Angilia was unlike any other. The original was still framed on the wall in the office now used by King Eric III.

Angilia held up the first picture of Eric and Marisol that Alejandro, Marisol's father, had placed in the time capsule. "How perfect! My great-great-grandparents, Eric and his Marisol!" she squealed, much to everyone's delight.

People continued to look at the hundreds of items: newspapers, magazines, posters, stamps, dollars, coins, books, copies of King Eric I's speeches, photographs, letters, cards, and souvenirs. Finally, Prince Patrick picked up a small book, and smiled when he saw what it was. "My grandmother made this book for the time capsule. She made the paper, she hand lettered it, she illustrated it, and she placed this in here 100 years ago today.

"This small book contains the lyrics of her song "The Gift of You," the song written for her father. She recorded that song on March 6, 2012, the day before she nearly died while saving his life. She made another copy of the book for Great-grandfather, and it is still in his sitting room. This is priceless," Prince Patrick said as he began to cry. King Eric III hugged his brother.

"Yes, this is such an incredible experience," Stefan said. "King Eric I is incredible. I am so glad he is my great-great-grandfather," he said before his tears took control.

Angilia put her arm around her brother, and, through her tears, said, "Great-great-grandfather is one of the greatest men who ever lived. I love him."

The people gathered in the park cried, applauded, and even kissed the statue of King Eric I. Uncle Patrick smiled as he embraced his family. The love people felt for Eric was more intense than ever, even if seeing the ceremony made Eric uncomfortable. Uncle Patrick was certain that, as Eric watched the ceremony from Heaven, he was as flabbergasted by it as always. He was the only one ever astonished by the love and respect people felt for him.

Sure enough, Eric responded as Patrick knew he would. "Hasn't that gone on long enough? I'm flattered, but really."

"Eric, you acted the same way that day in the park," Katherine reminded him. "People love you, that's a fact, so just accept it. It's not going to stop, you do realize that."

"Mom is right, Eric. Your legend keeps growing, until someday you will have mythical status, like King Arthur. You, my father-in-law, are deeply loved," Matthew said and put an arm around Eric's shoulder, while Angilia beamed.

"Am I the only one who remembers the prophecy that came true today?" Daniel suddenly asked.

"What prophecy?" Mitchell asked.

"The one Angilia made that day," Daniel said.

"Oh, that," Angilia said with a smile. "Remember, Daddy? As we walked away from the time capsule that morning, I said, *'In 100 years, your great-great grandchildren will open this time capsule and marvel at you all over again, Daddy.'*"

"They have indeed," Gerard proclaimed and embraced his son, the most revered King de Valdavia in history.

Sheilah R. Craft is an English professor, writer, blogger, poet, artist, ardent genealogist, and book lover. Born and raised in the Midwestern United States, Sheilah was born surrounded by a close family—including several educators—books, and animals. She began reading and writing very early, and has published short stories, articles, and poems. She was literally born a writer. Her series of novels centered on the lives of one family dynasty and spanning more than two centuries began in the fall of 2012 with the first volume, <u>Heart-Glow</u>. The second volume, <u>First Love Never Dies</u>, was published in the spring of 2013. <u>Heart Eternal</u>, the third volume in the series, was published in the spring of 2014. <u>Life Eternal</u> is the fourth volume. Two more volumes are planned.

Web Site and Exclusive Content

Please visit the companion web site, which contains additional information, pictures, and exclusive features. Those who purchase this book have access to specific password protected content on the web site. To access the exclusive content, please visit *Heart-Glow: A Novel* at **http://www.heartglownovel.org**

On the password protected pages, when prompted for the password, please enter **heartglowcraft16***

BOOKS BY SHEILAH R CRAFT

Published by <u>STARLIGHT Books:</u>

•HEART-GLOW: A NOVEL

•FIRST LOVE NEVER DIES: HEART-GLOW
VOLUME II

•HEART ETERNAL: HEART-GLOW VOLUME III

•LIFE ETERNAL: HEART-GLOW VOLUME IV

•MARY MAGDALENE: A MYSTERY PLAY

Published by <u>Little Butterfly:</u>

•THE QUEST FOR PERFECTION: SHELLEY AND
THE POET-HERO

•A DAY WITH TEDDY BEAR